The Hookmen

Also by Antoni Gronowicz

AN ORANGE FULL OF DREAMS

The
Hookmen

ANTONI GRONOWICZ

DODD, MEAD & COMPANY · NEW YORK

ISBN: 0-396-06748-4
Library of Congress Catalog Card Number: 72-12017
Printed in the United States of America
by Vail-Ballou Press, Inc., Binghamton, N. Y.

To my wife

The Hookmen

✠ Chapter 1

It was an evil dream that started many years ago around four o'clock in the afternoon.

The August sunlight played into the open window and crept over the carpet toward the grand piano. Franklin Don Kapistrot let his fingers run easily over the keys. The Chopin mazurka was bringing back memories. . . . But here, in America, he was building a new life.

Suddenly Don Kapistrot stopped playing. A strange awareness broke into his dream, cutting him like a knife. He sprang from the piano stool to the open window, unaware of the last dissonant notes fading from the room, and stopped, motionless, a brooding darkness against the window light. He was a tall, handsome figure, in his late twenties, with a shock of dark hair which he pulled at excitedly, as if his hands moved of their own will.

Turning, he rushed for the door, and in the corridor punched blindly at the elevator button. Unable to stay still for a moment, he hurried desperately back and forth between the corridor window and the elevator doors.

When the doors slid back, a pale and expressionless pair of eyes blinked at him from behind glasses. Don Kapistrot passed nervous fingers through his hair. "Who lives in the penthouse?"

"Mr. and Mrs. De Jager." The bald-headed man spoke with a ponderous, maddening deliberation.

"Don't you notice something?"

The man stared. His face was empty. But he straightened as Don Kapistrot scowled at him and quickly said, "No, sir! No I don't, sir!"

Don Kapistrot had rushed by him into the elevator and was staring upward with gleaming eyes. "Take me up," he repeated. "Take me up."

The little man was distinctly nervous, and started the elevator quickly downward. The result was more violent than he could have imagined. Don Kapistrot's long arm shot out, and his fist slammed into the wall inches behind the little man's neck. "Take me up, or I promise you . . ." The elevator jolted to a sudden stop between the eighth and ninth floors and began to ascend.

Don Kapistrot moved toward the doors. They slid back.

"Penthouse," said the little man weakly.

Don Kapistrot leaped out. The trembling, white-gloved hand of the little man rubbed at his neck as the elevator sped downward again.

The De Jager apartment was disturbed by an impatient bell. The gilt doors silently opened and a tall, listless butler looked out.

"Flowers, burning roses . . . do you smell them?" Don Kapistrot's head strained forward intently, while his bright blue eyes searched beyond the butler's shoulder.

The eyebrows lifted slightly. "What did you say, sir?"

"Roses, roses!" Don Kapistrot rushed into the spacious room. The butler recovered from his surprise and started after him. "If you please, sir! Your name."

Don Kapistrot had no ears for him; then the appearance of

a young woman in a blue sunbacked dress made him pause.

"Madame . . ." the butler began, but she turned to the stranger unperturbed. "What is it you want here?"

Don Kapistrot smoothed back his hair and straightened up, as if waking from a nightmare. His voice shook a little, but it had quieted. "There is someone here burning roses."

The woman smiled as she eyed him steadily. "That is my daughter." She was a shapely, self-possessed woman with auburn hair.

"No, no," said Don Kapistrot abruptly. "It cannot be your daughter."

Mrs. De Jager laughed. "But it is. My daughter is burning dried roses."

"It must be my wife."

Mrs. De Jager glanced at the butler and became solemn. "My daughter Tessa is a child. . . . I'm afraid it most certainly is not your wife."

Don Kapistrot sank down on the large sofa, and pressed his white face into his hands. Mrs. De Jager signaled to the butler to leave them alone. After a moment Don Kapistrot slowly lifted his head and gazed at her. She sat down opposite him and spoke quietly.

"Are you Spanish?"

He stared at her, unhearing, and began to apologize. "The last time I saw my wife, some withered roses burned accidentally. I was to leave that night for the front. My wife cried and said it was a bad omen. I never saw her again after that."

Mrs. De Jager remained sympathetically silent.

"But the roses burned in my mind. They have followed me from Europe to America. Then I thought I had forgotten all. But that burning today . . . I suddenly thought of Silucia—of my wife again."

At the sound of the name, Mrs. De Jager stirred suddenly

3

in her chair and her expression froze. At first she could barely make her words audible. "Are you Franklin Don Kapistrot?" She made an effort to smile. "Yes, I believe I've seen your picture in the papers."

"I am," he answered mechanically, staring around the room. "I live just below you here."

As she got up, Mrs. De Jager's eyes were lowered. She walked to the table, took a cigarette from a long box, and lit it very carefully. After a moment she sat down again and spoke flatly. "Our maid worked with your wife as a slave laborer. It was on a farm in Germany."

Don Kapistrot looked at her with wide eyes and made a weak effort to get to his feet. "Is that true?"

"Yes, it is true. But your wife did not escape. She died from exhaustion."

There was a numb silence in the room. He did not look at her. His eyes had wandered to the floor. Gradually, faint strains of piano music drifted into his consciousness. Someone was playing in another room. He became drained of all thought. The melody took possession of him and soothed.

Then it stopped abruptly. Mrs. De Jager began to speak again. "During the war, my husband was a railroad specialist in the American army, with the rank of general. He met Mrs. Bacun, our maid, in Germany after the liberation. It was in the same village where your wife and Mrs. Bacun worked together."

"But the roses?" His voice was hollow.

"Before your wife died, she made Mrs. Bacun promise that once a year, on the thirty-first of August, she would burn some dried roses."

Don Kapistrot absorbed every painful detail, yet seemed afraid to make a sound.

"Mrs. Bacun promised to do this. But she failed to keep her word until she came to America as our servant. Then

4

she related the whole story to my husband and me. My daughter overheard us; and now, since Mrs. Bacun's death, every time there are roses in the house she insists on burning them. I am worried about it."

Don Kapistrot's response was halfhearted. "Naturally."

"Shall I bring her in to meet you? Perhaps you can talk to her a little. Perhaps you can make her see."

Again his mind had wandered to the last days spent with his wife and how they planned to bring up their children. He did not answer.

Mrs. De Jager went to fetch her daughter. She had scarcely been gone a moment when the front door opened abruptly. A tall, thickset, well-dressed man entered. Behind him was a policeman. They stood in the doorway as if expecting something to leap at them. Edging around them came the cautious small figure of the elevator man.

"That's the man, Mr. Higginbottom." He pointed his finger at the man slumped on the sofa.

Before they could reach him, Mrs. De Jager reappeared, holding her daughter by the hand. "Fred!" she exclaimed. "Whatever is the matter?" Quickly she explained the whole situation to the tall man, her brother, whose manner immediately changed from belligerence to extreme suavity. The policeman was ushered back into the elevator, the ruffled feelings of the little operator were most expertly soothed, and Frederick Higginbottom returned.

He was clearly a successful man. While he was in the army working with his brother-in-law, Willie De Jager, he was considered extremely capable, and now as a railroad man on Wall Street he was a man to emulate. Quick in observing people, he came to the snap decision that this stranger with his overworked imagination could be cured by friendliness and alcohol. But upon the arrival of a battalion of bottles and glasses Don Kapistrot gave him a polite refusal. Instead he

5

turned to the blue-eyed Tessa, and followed her into the next room to hear her play a Chopin rondo for him.

Leaning over her, Don Kapistrot watched her hands moving like pale butterflies over the keyboard. The little girl was playing from memory. She had started on a ballad, but she became confused and stopped. Don Kapistrot bent over her, his cheek nearly touching the blonde hair of the child. With his right hand, he played the phrase over for her. Tessa looked up at him with a quick smile and continued playing with new confidence. Don Kapistrot sank into a chair, his eyes still on the small figure playing with such deep concentration. She played unusually well for her age, but her blonde hair and blue eyes began to remind him of Silucia.

After a moment Mrs. De Jager and Frederick Higginbottom entered with their cocktails. Just behind them, the butler made a sudden noiseless appearance. He announced that Mrs. Lloyd Abdoller had called, asking for Don Kapistrot. She was on her way up.

Frederick Higginbottom straightened up at once and looked with interest at his guest. "Mrs. Abdoller! Huppa Abdoller? You know her?"

Don Kapistrot nodded.

"Mrs. Lloyd D. Abdoller?"

"Yes, it is she—International Oil." Don Kapistrot smiled. He was amused; but his smile also expressed gratitude. "To her I owe everything," he explained. "My concert tour following my appearance at Grand Hall would not be possible without the support and encouragement the Abdoller family has given me."

"I presume she must be very anxious about you," Mrs. De Jager remarked with studied casualness.

Don Kapistrot stood up. "Please forgive me for this intrusion, Mrs. De Jager. Now I must leave."

Frederick Higginbottom was loud in his protest. "Please

6

stay with us a while. Just the other day I saw Huppa at the Wall Street Art meeting, and she invited my sister, Mr. De Jager and myself to Beekman Place for a Saturday. But if she calls on us first, that'll be fine, won't it, Gusty Mary?"

"Of course," Mrs. De Jager answered quickly. "Please stay for dinner, Mr. Kapistrot." Then seeing that his eyes were on Tessa, who was watching from the piano bench, she added, "Tessa will be very unhappy if you don't stay for a while longer." She leaned over to him and said in an undertone, "Even the doctors don't know what to do with her."

He looked across at the girl and beckoned to her. Tessa started toward him but, suddenly pausing, she turned to her mother. "Please, Mama, ask Mr. Kapistrot to give me piano lessons instead of Madame Sklarov."

The request seemed to startle her mother and uncle, who glanced at each other. Don Kapistrot was quick to notice this, but he turned to the girl. "Your playing is certainly remarkable."

"But Madame is not good . . ." Before Tessa could finish the entrance bell rang. Gusty Mary went quickly to her daughter's side. "Please, Tessa, go and change your dress, and you may have dinner with us."

The girl ran off delightedly. The next minute the butler made an appearance, and the charming voice of Huppa Ab-doller, with the poise of her rank in international society, rang out. "Franklin, I see you have lost your way!" She had heard a strange story from the elevator man.

Franklin rose and walked rapidly to meet her. "Sometimes it happens," he said with a smile.

Higginbottom laughed heartily. "It has turned out to be a very pleasant mistake. You see, my sister and Franklin had a kind of mutual friend in Europe."

Mrs. Abdoller glanced at Franklin sympathetically. "But it is thought that your wife is no longer living."

7

"She died before the liberation," murmured Gusty Mary as she took Mrs. Abdoller's hand. "Now, Huppa, come and sit down. Tell me how you are."

Don Kapistrot found his thoughts drifting back to Tessa, and he was hardly aware of what they were saying. Huppa Abdoller, however, was a woman of exceptional understanding, and for his sake she directed the conversation to the affairs of society. Don Kapistrot remained unaware of this— just as he was still unaware of the significance of Huppa's family oil and her constant praise of his talent in the most exclusive circles. He was thinking of how flame withered in an instant the curled petals and long broken stems, and he was soon lost in his own reverie.

The conversation that kept up incessantly during dinner at the De Jagers' had nothing in it to interest Don Kapistrot. He was anxiously waiting for the arrival of Tessa, but the time passed, and the child remained absent.

The news that came to him on the following day shocked him more than he cared to admit. He learned that Mrs. De Jager, on her husband's return from his business trip, had abruptly left for their summer home in Short Isle. It seemed most strange to him that, after spending some time with her the day before, she had made no mention of such a move. In fact, she and her brother had promised to attend a party Huppa was giving the following Saturday.

The day of the party came. Mr. and Mrs. De Jager did not appear. Don Kapistrot drove all speculations from his mind and concentrated with desperate energy on his coming concert.

On the day of his concert he was in his apartment, preparing to leave. He was feeling completely relaxed, and thinking that success in New York would mean success throughout the States. The Latin American countries could be conquered easily.

There was a faint knock on the door. He called out, but there was no response. He was about to investigate when, through the mirror, he saw the door opening slowly. He watched in curious anticipation. The next moment, he was standing transfixed at the reflection of Tessa De Jager.

Tessa was smiling timidly. She spoke in a whisper. "I am here."

He turned sharply and strode to her side. "How did you come here?" His voice was harsh with violent emotion; but Tessa could not understand and began to cry unashamedly, letting the tears fall without covering her face. Don Kapistrot put his arm around her comfortingly, as he led her to the sofa. His voice had changed. As he repeated his question he was like a father speaking to his one and only child.

Tessa became relaxed. Her tears soon stopped. She leaned against him and began to speak, a little unsure and faltering at first. She began with her remembrances. The story was not completely clear, since it was made up of scattered, confused impressions and feelings of very early childhood.

Tessa remembered the farm where her mother and Mrs. Bacun worked as slave laborers, the cold and the big fence. She remembered Mrs. Bacun's coming to her early one morning and telling her that she would never see her mother again. Tessa had never known her real name. The De Jagers had spoken as if she had always been their own child. She could not forget, though. When she saw Don Kapistrot and heard his name, it suddenly came back to her that Kapistrot was her mother's name. But then something had happened to the De Jagers. They had locked her up in her room the night when he came to dinner, and the following day they had hastily moved to Short Isle, where they kept her under constant watch.

Don Kapistrot kissed Tessa with tears in his eyes, and then reached for the phone—Huppa would arrange everything.

When she arrived soon after, she had with her a lawyer

from Rollon, Casevant, Small & Abdoller, Counselors at Law. The lawyer was not encouraging, and he emphasized the very real difficulties of establishing parenthood in such a case. Don Kapistrot insisted that Tessa looked exactly like her mother, Silucia, but this was of little importance to the lawyer.

The conversation was interrupted by the telephone. He left it to Huppa to answer. After a few seconds, she called out, "Don, Mr. Honback from the World Concert Bureau wants you to hurry so as not to be late. The hall is packed to capacity and everyone is waiting. He is very anxious."

Don Kapistrot nodded his head apathetically. The ten months' work by a leading New York psychoanalyst was rapidly being undone in these moments of agonized remembrance. The past had risen again and the present was lost. He started for the library.

"But, Don, where are you going?" Huppa's voice was filled with concern.

"My daughter is still in the library. I am taking her with me."

Huppa Abdoller glanced at the lawyer. The man was quick to explain that Tessa must be returned to her parents without delay. Otherwise Don Kapistrot could be arrested on kidnapping charges if he tried to keep her before the courts had established his right. Huppa sensed what Don wanted and undertook to call the De Jagers. Tessa was safe with her, she explained, and would be returned home to Short Isle.

Franklin Don Kapistrot took Tessa gently by the hand and led her out of the apartment with him. His face was afire with happiness.

✠ Chapter 2

No more music for Franklin Don Kapistrot; no more kid-napping; but—after some years—Katie, and again a very different life.

Katie's fondest dream and her one great ambition, next to being married to Franklin and raising a family, was to own a home, and if possible, to be in Tackahoe near her parents. She had been born and had spent her entire life within the borders of one state, and yet deeply rooted within her were the feelings and yearnings of the Polish peasant stock from which her parents had descended. For them, owning a home was as great a necessity as Sunday prayers. It was the symbol of a good and peaceful life, God's own blessing, and therefore something to be regarded as a sacred heritage.

How often and how joyfully had Katie thought of attaining this dream, Frank's promise to her. Her own home, near her parents, raising her children in this tranquil little town, everything clean and country-fresh. It was here in Tackahoe that she had known a happy childhood, close friends, and the security of a small world that was familiar and good to be alive in. This one pledge, of all those Frank had made, was always uppermost in her mind.

Then shortly after John was born, Katie's father died, and soon after, as though unable to endure the separation, Mama Michalski joined her husband. The friendly house on Oakland Avenue, the scene of so much family happiness, was sold to cover debts. The rest of the small inheritance was spent on funeral and burial expenses. Frank had told her then how sorry he was not to be able to save the house from being sold to strangers, but he gave Katie a solemn promise that he would someday build a more substantial home for them, a home she would be very proud of. Another dream, another promise, was added to the list of his vows to her. Now it had vanished, the bubble of fancy gradually deflated into nothingness.

Katie was a good wife, adept at keeping their apartment clean and bright and at managing the weekly allowance Frank gave her. She delighted in preparing the Polish recipes she had learned under her mother's tutelage and then watching Frank as he devoured the *lazanki*, the *barszcz*, the *kielbasa*, and *kapusta*. When Frank pushed himself away from the table, obviously satisfied, Katie would tease, "I'm sure that you only married me because of Mama's recipes."

"I think you're right, Mrs. Kapistrot," he'd say sternly, and then kiss her and pull her hair, pretending to be a cave man.

But now it was all so different. Once or twice she had broached the subject of his long absences from home and he had given her the same reply. "Conference at the office, can't help it." It made her furious.

"How long have they been working a night shift in your office?"

"We're putting out a big new brochure, Katie, a rush job. And I'm writing most of it." He spoke without looking at her and both of them knew how unconvincing he sounded.

And so it went, day after day, their tenth anniversary drawing ever closer as they drew further apart. On Sunday Frank had offered her a little affection, a strained tenderness. But the thought of sharing his life with another woman sent shivers through her and she was unable to return his affection.

Katie finished her dusting, cleaned the kitchen, and went out to do her marketing for the day. She hurried as quickly as she could, knowing she must be at the lawyer's office promptly. Returning from the stores package-laden, she fumbled for her key to the downstairs door, when suddenly it was opened from inside. Richard Marchand and his sister, Eleanor, greeted her cheerfully.

"May I help you with those?" Richard offered, taking two large bundles from her arms.

"Thank you, Rich. I . . . I just couldn't find my key."

She was not very happy to have met her friends just now, the brother and sister who looked nothing like one another. Rich was tall, slim, a good-looking man just a year older than Katie's thirty-one. His sister was short, heavily built, and her face reflected none of the fineness of her younger brother's.

"Say, you're going to the lawyer's today, aren't you?" Richard asked, and without waiting for a reply he quickly added, "Let me drive you there, Katie. I'm absolutely free today, all day."

"I don't want . . ." Katie started to say, but Eleanor cut her short.

"Don't be silly, Katie dear. Why ride those awful subways when you can go in a new car? I've got to do some errands downtown and I don't want to drag Richard along. Besides, you know he'd love to take you."

There seemed no way for her to avoid the offer and it would be more pleasant than taking the subway.

"Well, all right. I am late as it is. I just have to change my dress and I'll be right down."

"Wonderful!" Richard said joyfully. "My limousine and I are deeply honored. Let me carry these packages upstairs for you."

"Good-bye, you two," Eleanor said. "And remember, Rich, dinner is at seven."

Katie opened the apartment door and showed Richard where to put the packages.

13

"Please sit down, I'll only be a minute," she said, going into the bedroom and closing the door. Taking a dress from the closet she felt a twinge of guilt at the thought of being alone with Rich in the apartment. Of course it's silly, she told herself, you've known him years longer than you've known Frank. It was Rich who had first proposed marriage to her, and when she turned him down he had introduced her to Frank. Earlier, in her teens, she had often thought of marrying Rich; it was Eleanor's domineering influence over him that had decided against it. Marrying Rich would be like taking a child from its mother's breast. Yet she had always felt that Rich still cared a great deal for her, and her discomfort at the thought spurred her to leave the apartment as quickly as possible.

Since the day Katie had confessed to Rich and Eleanor her plans for a divorce, Eleanor had made constant insinuations, describing in glowing detail Richard's merits as a brother, and as a prospective husband and father. She had said almost everything to Katie except perhaps, "You must marry Rich as soon as you're divorced from Frank." Eleanor's aggressiveness made Katie feel an almost physical disgust, but she could find no way to escape her friend's onslaughts.

When they were in the car, heading toward the bridge, Katie asked Richard why he wasn't working.

"Day off," he said happily. "I just got myself a nice raise and a promotion. Something to celebrate, eh?"

"Yes, I guess it really is," Katie said, dreading now the moment of facing the lawyer and answering all the difficult questions he was certain to ask. She remembered that she must stress how important, how necessary it was for her to have custody of John. Could there be any question about it? Would a judge give custody of a child to a man who had deserted his wife for another woman? She was on the point of asking Richard's opinion but quickly changed her mind.

As they crossed the bridge, Katie looked down at the peaceful river, the sun brightly reflected upon its surface. For a moment her attention was diverted by a tugboat pulling a coal barge upriver.

"Of course, you know divorces are only granted in our state when adultery can be proved," Richard said, interrupting her thoughts.

"Yes, I know," she answered softly.

"Can you prove it?"

"I don't think it will be too hard. If Frank wants his freedom, I guess he'll help the lawyer prove it."

"Perhaps, if he really wants it," Richard said.

They were silent until he turned off the bridge on the city side and headed uptown.

"Katie, when this is over, do you think . . . ?"

She knew immediately what he was thinking of and abruptly, almost angrily, cried, "Rich please! I can't think of anything right now, except that I want to get it all over with as quickly as possible."

"I'm sorry, Katie," he apologized. "I think you've always known how I felt about you." He patted her hand to show he was sorry.

Richard waited for her in the lawyer's reception room until the consultation was over. Then Katie emerged looking as though the earth had split wide open and she were about to fall into a crevasse.

"What did he say?" Richard asked her finally, when they were once again in the car going downtown toward the bridge.

"He said the case was hopeful," she replied, and then began to cry, softly, as someone who awakens to the full realization of a great tragedy.

Dinner in the Kapistrot apartment that evening was unusually quiet. When Franklin had finished, he went into the bedroom to put on a clean shirt and his good blue suit. Katie left the dishes on the table and John sitting on the floor in front of the television set, and followed Franklin into his room, closing the door behind her.

She stood facing him but her eyes were on the floor.

"I went to the lawyer today," she blurted out, before the words could stick in her throat. "He said he was sure I could get the divorce."

Then she looked up at him to see if he had heard her. For the first time in many weeks she saw how terribly tired he was. And her words had stunned him, she could see that plainly, although she could not understand why. Without a word, he opened the door, walked through the living room and into the kitchen, where he sat down, his shirt still unbuttoned and hanging loose around his waist.

That feeling of emptiness rose up once more to overwhelm Katie, as it had after she had left the lawyer's office. His questions, necessary questions that had to be asked, had drained her of all feeling and emotion. She sat down on the edge of the bed, but now she could not even cry. She just sat, feeling empty and completely helpless. Was Frank stunned because he thought she hadn't the courage to go through with it? He hadn't said a word. No explanation, no apology. And he hadn't made the slightest effort to try to convince her that it was all a misunderstanding, a terrible mistake.

When she went back to the living room John was still in front of the television.

"It's time for bed, John," she said wearily.

"Gee, Mom, what's the matter with Pop? He's just sitting there in the kitchen with the lights off."

"It's nothing. He's just tired. Please go to bed."

The boy kissed her good night, peered into the kitchen to say good night to his father, and then closed his bedroom door behind him.

Slowly, mechanically, Katie snapped on the light, cleared

the dishes from the table, and carried them to the sink; she washed and dried them, and put them away. Franklin was still sitting motionless, one hand covering his eyes, his shirt still unfastened.

"I'm going to bed," Katie said. "Shall I turn off the light?" He made no answer. She left the light on and went to her bedroom, thinking that if he didn't go out he would follow her. She lay awake for a long time, waiting in the darkness for him to enter the room. Finally she fell asleep.

The next few days were intolerable for Katie. They lived together as strangers. On two evenings Franklin failed to come home for dinner although he did return to sleep for a few hours. Katie could stand it no longer. She kept John home from school and telephoned Sue Edwards in Tackahoe to ask if she and John could spend a few days there. Sue told her to come immediately and stay indefinitely. She was an old friend of the Michalski family, and, since she was alone, she welcomed the chance to entertain Katie and John, who were like her own family.

When she had learned the reason for the sudden visit, Sue Edwards did her best to ease Katie's mind. But nothing she could do or say made Katie feel less worried. Katie had left a brief note for Franklin telling him where she had taken John. Now it was up to him, if he intended to do anything at all to effect a reconciliation. Waiting, hoping, expecting him to call or write plunged her deeper and deeper into the abyss of loneliness. This was their first real separation in ten years of married life.

Katie had turned it over and over in her mind since coming to Sue's quiet, old-fashioned house in the little town she loved so dearly. Being away from Frank had given her a chance to see her decision in a slightly different light. If Frank would only call her back, she'd go, she knew it now, for John's sake if for no other reason. She had seen and read about what happened to children when their homes were broken up and their parents separated. Her own happiness was no longer important; it was John's welfare that counted most.

It was a bright, sunny morning, just like the morning in Brooklyn when Katie had sat in her own living room, knowing she was to see the lawyer about a divorce. Ten years ago to the day—also on a beautiful morning—Katie Michalski was married to Franklin Don Kapistrot with the tearful and joyous blessings of family and friends. They had been married right there in Tackahoe by the same old priest who had christened Katie. How well she remembered their wedding feast in her parents' home, with Franklin gaily playing Chopin on the piano, the Polish food, the laughter, the wine, and best of all the great hopes for the future she and Franklin shared. All day long Katie could think of nothing else but that on their tenth anniversary she was here and Franklin was somewhere else, she scarcely knew where.

Now the old railroad clock in the hallway chimed six and Katie sat, as she had all day, on the window seat, looking out at the occasional traffic on Oakland Avenue. John had been invited to dinner at a neighbor's house and though Sue tried to persuade Katie to go with him, she had refused.

Suddenly a car pulled up in front of the house. She recognized Richard Marchand as he came up the walk, and opened the door for him.

"Hello, Katie," he greeted her in his usual cheerful manner. "It's good to see you."

"Hello, Richard."

It was a weak welcome she gave him. Of course she had hoped that Frank might be with him. There was little chance that she would hear from him now.

Sue came to greet the visitor.

"Well, Richard, you look very prosperous."

They shook hands.

18

"No complaints, Miss Edwards," he said, laughing and pinching her cheek teasingly.

"Well, what are we standing in the hallway for?" Sue asked crisply. "Come inside, children, come inside."

"Katie," Richard said when they were seated in the living room, "I'll bet you can't guess why I've come."

She shook her head, waiting for him to continue.

"Your parents' house. It's for sale. I just found out the owners are moving to Chicago. Eleanor and I are thinking of buying it. What do you think, Katie?"

She felt it was not good news he had brought. "I don't know what to say, Richard."

"We thought you'd be pleased with the idea."

"Yes . . . yes," she stammered, "of course I am. I'd rather you and Eleanor had the house than . . . some strangers." She felt confused and utterly lost.

"I'm going over to look at the place now. Will you come with me?"

"I don't know . . . it's been so long. . . ."

"Of course she'll go," Sue answered for her. "Do you good to see the place again."

"All right," Katie replied reluctantly.

"And I'll go too," Sue laughed. "I have to admit I'm fond of the old place myself."

As the trio walked toward the old Michalski house, all the memories of her happy childhood came crowding back into Katie's mind. There were no real problems then, no terrible decisions to make. Those were wonderful carefree days.

"That's funny," Sue said as they approached the gate, "the flowers look freshly watered. Richard Marchand, I thought you said the owners had moved!"

"They have," he replied.

"Look," Katie cried, "the old brass door knocker has been

polished."

"There's no one here," Richard insisted. "Come on, let's go in." He opened the door and ushered them inside.

"We'd better leave," Katie said. "We can't break into someone else's property." Standing there, in the hallway, she felt that old familiar sense of security, of being where she belonged.

Richard took them both and led them into the large room just off the hallway. The table was set for dinner, with silver and flowers and a large candelabra holding freshly lit red candles. Katie could almost see her family around the large table just as they used to sit, eating and laughing, and having a wonderful time.

"Hey!" Richard shouted, "don't we get any service?"

The kitchen door opened and in walked Franklin, carrying a silver tray with four glasses and a bottle of champagne.

Katie began to cry. Franklin set the tray on the table and took her in his arms.

Later the same night, while they were driving happily back to Brooklyn, the old house—due cither to faulty rewiring or some other cause—burned to the ground.

▣ Chapter 3

The beginning of American big business was quiet and innocent. The beginning of a tragedy usually is quiet and innocent; and this book is no exception.

But since this is the real introductory chapter, let me introduce myself. Franklin Don Kapistrot, age forty-eight; six feet, one hundred and seventy-six pounds; graying brown hair, pale complexion, blue eyes; married, two children and plenty of troubles. I live in Rose Hill, in a house with a heavy mortgage. And my occupation? I must have a pursuit, or calling, or vocation, naturally. I am assistant professor of American civilization, currently on leave of absence from N.P.U.; also a writer, a renegade pianist, a defender of many causes. My hobby? Definitely I must have a hobby. Trains, all kinds of trains.

Trains have fascinated me ever since I was a youngster. I grew up on a farm in Europe, and I had no toys and no playmates. Even at that time I loved my enemies and hated my friends. The wooden cattle cars, passenger trains, and locomotives that rattled along the old tracks bordering the field where I pastured cows were my playmates and my favorite game. The trains chugged by four times a day and each time one appeared I would run after it, barefoot and panting, waving an excited greeting to the engineer in the cab. Slow as a train was in those days, it was far faster than I, and when it had outdistanced me I would return exhausted to my chores, content to watch over the grazing cattle until the cars came by again. The hours were speeded by my daydreams. When I grew up I was going to ride on those trains—all the way to Paris or Madrid and maybe even farther. And in the meantime I could imagine all the activity behind the windows: the engineer at the throttle, guiding his machine with experienced calm; the conductor resplendent in his uniform, taking tickets and giving information to the fashionably dressed ladies and gentlemen who were his special charges; the cattle, resting peacefully on the straw-strewn floor of the cattle car. I knew every car and locomotive by heart, and could recognize each train as soon as it appeared. And of course, I had never been inside a railroad car in my life.

That childhood love has remained with me to this day. I travel by automobile, boat, or plane when necessary; the trips I really enjoy are those I take by train. And the longer the ride, the more I like it. The short hop between New York and Philadelphia is a pleasant break in the day; the long trip between New York and Chicago is a major event.

One evening, not too long ago, I was sitting alone at a table for two in the dining car of the Coast to Coast Railroad Company's C-C Limited, speeding smoothly on its way from Chicago to New York. The C-C Limited (the name by the way, is used for two identical trains: eastbound, no. 27 and westbound, no. 25) consists of fifteen metal-clad cars, powered by a General Motors diesel and electric engine. All the cars are air-conditioned. The kitchen shines in stainless American Steel, and the twin-unit dining car is equipped to serve sixty-eight people at a sitting. There is telephone service; any city in the country is as near the passengers as the black-faced dial. The train includes a luxurious lounge with a glistening bar, and a spacious, glassy observation car. There are six types of sleeping accommodations, ranging from roomettes to master rooms, each furnished with a comfortable foam-rubber mattress. The train rides easily on its insulated roller-bearing trucks, its safety insured by tight-lock couplers. China and silver stay where they are put; glasses do not slither precariously on the tables.

As I sat waiting for my Cudahy's steak, I chewed on a stalk of A&P celery and meditated. If I did not see the scenery speeding by through the Libby-Owens-Ford windows, I would hardly have known that the train was moving.

Harry Smutters, the steward of the diner, whom I knew from my previous trips on the C-C Limited, came over to greet me. Harry is a tall, thin man with gray hair and gold-rimmed glasses, who looks more like a college professor than I do. But his dignified bearing is not out of place in the dining car of a luxury train. The C-C Limited is, after all— like its companions, the Soul of San Francisco, the Senator, and the Yellow Arrow—a palace on wheels, and one of the

22

fastest trains in the world. And Harry's job is an important one; he is responsible for satisfying the demands of hundreds of stomachs daily. In this task he acquits himself nobly. The food on the C-C Limited is excellent.

When I commented to Harry how much I always enjoyed my trips, he told me the history of the train. The first C-C Limited, he recounted, then called the American Special, left Jersey City for Chicago at five minutes before two, on the warm afternoon of June 15, 1902. Its departure was a gala event, and a crush of well-wishers stood by to cheer it off. The American Special was the most luxurious and up-to-date train in operation. It had four wooden cars. First was a diner, "elegant, all mahogany"—and here Harry's eyes were shining with the pride of the maitre d'—"and it served a banquet of roast prime ribs of beef, broiled leg of mutton, or roast duck, topped off with bread pudding and cognac sauce, ice cream, crackers with cheese." After the dining car, "The Chile," came a Pullman, "The Tyrone," where the distinguished passengers would sleep; then a lounge car, "The Utopia," the last word in comfort, equipped with chairs and couches upholstered in soft, rich leather, a handsome writing desk, a barber shop, a bath and a library. The four cars were preceded by a D Sixteen, an American Standard Engine which belched forth great clouds of black smoke as the train pulled out of the shed.

I nodded my interest and Harry talked on.

"When it arrived at the old Canal Street Station in Chicago at eight fifty-two the next morning, it had broken all speed records. The fifty-odd passengers and the engineer, Jerry McCarthy, were greeted by a crowd of over a thousand people. There was even a delegation of Chicago's city fathers!"

According to Harry, the old-timers who were on hand that day say that Jerry's dark eyes shone out of his coal-grimed face like two gleaming lamps, and that his wide grin almost split his face from ear to ear as he was carried triumphantly on the shoulders of the crowd out of his locomotive and into the ornate waiting room, where an official reception for the American Special was held. This was a great event in the history of American railroading—a trip of over nine hundred miles had been completed in less than twenty hours, breaking the previous record by more than eight hours, and even arriving three minutes ahead of schedule! Jerry McCarthy and the American Special broke still another record on this trip by covering the three-mile stretch between Lima and Elida, Ohio, in only eighty-five seconds—a speed of 127.1 miles per hour.

"But," Harry observed, "it's a far cry from the old American Special to the C-C Limited. We've cut over four hours from the traveling time. We've got facilities they never dreamt of. The passengers certainly wouldn't recognize the train, and the crew wouldn't either. I bet Jerry McCarthy could have broken any record there is if he'd had a rest in the crew dormitory." Harry's pride was understandable. The two C-C Limiteds together cost over five million dollars—which makes them twenty times as expensive as their wooden grandfathers.

The C-C Limited is not the only evidence of the company's development. Today the Coast to Coast Railroad Company is the largest and most efficient railroad in the country, serving nine of our ten biggest cities. Its twenty thousand miles of line and its fifty thousand miles of track crisscross thirty states, from the Ohio River north to the Great Lakes, from New York south to Norfolk, and west across the Mississippi and on to San Francisco—from the Atlantic coast to the Pacific coast. And by arrangement with other railroads, the CCRR runs trains even beyond that area.

The figures are staggering. The CCRR's track region covers nearly seventy-five per cent of the total population of the country. The railroad serves nearly 20,000 industries and 12,000 communities, with 7,800 freight trains and 2,500 passenger trains. It employs over 200,000 people and its 10,000 stockholders—controlled by the Rollon, Abdoller, and Meynemar families—have always received a dividend, even during the Depression years.

Harry left me to attend to some other diners. I was just resigning myself to eating in solitary splendor when a rather tall, handsome man stepped up to the vacant chair at my table, and speaking in a well-modulated voice said, "May I take this seat?"

"Please do."

A closer inspection showed my companion to be in his middle fifties. His eyes were blue and penetrating, his hair iron-gray, his forehead almost completely unlined, and his nose straight and high-bridged. His gray suit was almost the color of his hair. Well-cut and beautifully tailored, it was probably made to order in London. His dark blue tie had a small white pattern. He looked like a thoroughly pleasant, highly prosperous businessman from Boston or a senior agent with the FBI. I noticed that the Negro waiter treated him with a special deference, and it occurred to me that he might be someone important. I thought back, but I did not remember ever having seen his face.

We chatted for a moment about the food, the weather, and the trip. He apparently believed in my cordial recommendation of the steak and ordered one for himself. My enthusiasm for the railroad must have been quite obvious, for when we had exhausted the usual introductory trivia, he smiled at me and said, "You seem to be a real railroad fan."

"I am," I replied. "The only thing that's missing on a train like this is a good small band and dancing, a bit of entertainment."

"Dancing?" My companion lit a cigarette. "Would that be practical?"

"I don't know why not. They've done just about everything

25

else. And think what an attraction it would be for the young people."

Our steaks arrived and both of us turned our attention to the food. My mind was still on the railroad, however; and while we were waiting for our coffee I told my neighbor a true story I had heard from Harry Smutters, who during World War Two had worked on the Moonray Special from New York to Fort Worth.

"One night," I said, "when Harry was working the Fort Worth run, he was passing through the sleeper on his way to see the conductor. He noticed a passenger who had obviously had a drop too much making his wobbly way to one of the lower berths. Harry helped him to his berth while the passenger thanked him profusely in a rich Irish brogue. Later, when Harry was on his way back to the diner he came through the car again. The inebriate was snoring gently behind his curtains. A young clergyman was trying to get into the berth above. For some reason, the man of God did not bother to use the ladder, and in trying to hoist himself up, stepped heavily on the Irishman's face. That poor fellow woke up with a howl and started to curse out the intruder in a juicy, imaginative prose. He tore the curtains apart and thrust a brilliant red face between them roaring every profanity. But when he saw the offender, his voice changed abruptly. He hastily pulled the curtains around him—and with a muttered 'Oh, it's you, Father. God bless you!' he retired."

My companion chuckled heartily. "I suppose railroad people get to see a lot of funny things," he said.

"And they have to put up with a lot, too," I answered. "They must run across some pretty peculiar passengers once in a while. It's just lucky that the little people who work for the Coast to Coast Railroad have a sense of humor. And that the well-paid people who run it have done such a tremendous job."

"Yes, you're probably right there, too," he said almost thoughtfully. "A railroad is quite a big project."

"It certainly is." My enthusiasm for my subject kept me going at full speed. "And the odd kinds of problems the workers come up against!" I shook my head. "They have to be experts in a million different ways."

"Well, I suppose they're all experts on railroading, if that's what you mean." My tablemate stubbed out his cigarette.

"That, of course," I said. "But experts in other things too. For instance, Harry told me another story about the Moonray Special. As I said, he was on that run during the war, and a lot of his passengers were war brides and their babies, on their way to or from visits to different army posts. All those babies had to have their formulas, of course, and their bottles had to be sterilized, and Harry was perfectly willing to put some men in the kitchen on this job. As a matter of fact, that's just what he did. But mothers are mothers, and apparently they felt that the cooks and waiters couldn't prepare a formula as well as they could. They didn't say much, but Harry could see that they weren't very happy."

"But what else could he do?"

"I don't know whether you or I would have been able to figure out anything else," I continued, "but Harry did. After about three trips, he worked out a solution. He had the chef, Slocum Maxwell, boil lots of water, and after dinner was over he had the water brought into the dining car in large pots. Then he called all the mothers in, and they hopped to it, fixing the formula in their own special motherly ways. They were happier, and Harry and Chef Maxwell were glad to do what they could."

By this time, we had finished our coffee, and at my suggestion we retired to my roomette to continue our chat. When he left to turn in, my new friend said, "I've enjoyed myself." He gave me his hand. "I'm a railroad fan, too. My name is William De Jager. When you next come to Philadelphia I hope that you'll come to see me. My office is in the Washington Building, and we have a home just outside the city. You must come to dinner and meet my wife and daughter, and we can talk some more about trains. I hope you'll have some more amusing stories to tell me."

"Thanks," I said. "I'd be glad to come."

I got up rather early the next morning, got dressed and went into the diner for breakfast. The sun was just coming out, and through the dining-car windows I could see the fields changing from gray to misty yellow.

"I wonder what kind of a day it will be," I said to the waiter as I shook out my napkin. "Yesterday it was a hundred degrees in Chicago—unbearable."

"You'd never know it on the train." The waiter smiled. "It's always a comfortable seventy degrees. They ought to put that in the ads."

As I was starting on my fruit cup I felt a hand on my shoulder. I looked up. Mr. De Jager was standing next to me.

"Good morning. Won't you join me for breakfast?" I asked.

"Thanks, but I've already eaten. I just came by to remind you to come and visit us."

"Don't worry. I won't forget. I intend to take you up on your invitation."

We shook hands and he left. As the waiter was bringing me my eggs, my friend Harry Smutters appeared. "Do you know that gentleman who just left?" I asked. "I met him last night. He seems a very pleasant person."

Harry looked at me in astonishment. Then he began to laugh aloud. "Know him? I've never played poker with him, if that's what you mean. But I know him, all right. That's William 'Willie the Whistle' S. De Jager—the president of the Coast to Coast Railroad Company!"

My mouth dropped open. De Jager! I should have recognized the name. And I've been telling him railroad stories and giving him suggestions about how he should run his business.

That episode was the real beginning of this book. For as I sat over my eggs and coffee, I began to think more about the CCRR and its president, and the more I thought, the more eager I became to really investigate them.

The railroad is in many respects a symbol of America's swelling growth, its so-called economic greatness, I thought to myself, of the fantastic speed with which the country has developed, always pushing ahead by sweat and labor. I don't know if its president, too, isn't something of a symbol, representing as he does his company and all it stands for. Then I thought that perhaps De Jager was more than merely a symbol of the railroad. I had heard enough about him to know that Willie the Whistle was a man who made it the hard way, who worked himself up from the traditional humble beginning to the top of the heap. And so he personified the American success saga. Beyond that, I knew only that he was said to have a very beautiful wife.

Finally, I had an even more compelling reason to be interested in Mr. De Jager; he seemed to me to be an attractive personality. I said as much to Harry.

"Yes, yes," Harry observed in somewhat bitter tones. "As you say, he's the symbol of a vitally important industry and he's the personification of the Horatio Alger legend. He's a colorful individual in his own right. But I guess I know what you'll find underneath." Then he looked at me quickly. "Did he tell you about his daughter? She isn't married."

"But I am!" It was too much for me and I jumped to my defense. I explained to Harry that I wanted to find out more about Willie the Whistle and more about the railroad. I wanted to discover what made them both tick. And I had the feeling, too, that if I knew more about this man and more about the company he headed, I would be able to both understand and completely indulge my lifelong interest in railroads. Perhaps I had my private reasons too.

Harry didn't give up. "You would find out about the CCRR and Willie the Whistle," he said, "but now, I've been in this business a long time. I can tell you, men like that don't care to listen to train whistles. They don't care about people. The only thing they love is the money they make."

I only said that Mr. De Jager certainly would be seeing me, and probably sooner than he expected.

That was our last meeting. A month or so later, Harry Smutters, starting home on the wrong side of the track, was killed by the C-C Limited. He went straight to the local funeral home. A few friends helped his wife to piece out her small pension.

▣ Chapter 4

One early morning about six weeks after my chance meeting with William S. De Jager on the C-C Limited, I received a special delivery letter:

Confirming our telephone conversation of this afternoon, Mrs. De Jager and I will be glad to discuss with you the writing of our biography at dinner on the evening of Friday, September 8. This is also in accordance with our conversation on the train some time ago.

If you will come to my office at five P.M. on the eighth, we can go together to my home where we shall spend a comfortable evening around the dinner table.

With warm personal regards,

Very truly yours,
W. S. De Jager

Almost simultaneously a telegram arrived from his vice-president in charge of public relations, Bartholomew Alphonso Leach: UNFORTUNATELY I WILL BE AWAY IN CHICAGO ON THURSDAY, SEPTEMBER SEVENTH, BUT I SINCERELY HOPE YOU CAN JOIN ME FOR LUNCHEON ON FRIDAY THE EIGHTH. I AM EAGER TO MEET YOU AND TO GIVE YOU ALL THE HELP I CAN.

The morning of the eighth I entered the great Romanesque building that houses the CCRR Station in New York. The old familiar landmark would soon be a thing of the past, I recalled, as I walked down the concourse to the escalator. According to an agreement between De Jager and the realty firm of Srul & Bull, the building was soon to be torn down and a new ultramodern one erected in its place. The enormous sprawling structure aboveground purchased for the sum of fifty million dollars would be transformed into the new American Steel skyscraper, named the Palace of Free Enterprise. A five-hundred-foot structure with over seven million square feet of floor space, it would be the home of thousands of businesses. Showrooms for hundreds of industries would make it a permanent World's Fair, with exhibitions of handicrafts and manufactured items from all over America and from foreign lands as well. Karam Kermin, the famous theatrical entrepreneur, had been appointed president of the Palace.

However, the CCRR had retained title to the property below street level—the two levels with the vast waiting rooms, the tracks, the platforms, and the operating offices. Its seven hundred regularly scheduled trips to and from the city would still arrive and leave from the same spot, although the station, too, would be completely remodeled.

A wave of nostalgia swept over me as I entered the building, which resembles the Roman Baths of Caracalla; but it soon faded. The old station is, after all, lagging behind the spirit of the times. It was built around the turn of the century when it was the height of modernity; today it is decidedly old-fashioned.

31

The new Palace of Free Enterprise will superbly reflect both the present, and with luck, the future.

I boarded my train and settled myself comfortably in my seat. I was on my way to Philadelphia, first to meet Bartholomew Leach and some of the other CCRR officers in their headquarters, and later to visit De Jager. He had been very much in my mind since our last encounter, and I had already begun my researches into his life and character.

As the train pulled out of the station I lit my pipe and started to mull over what I had learned about De Jager thus far. I had spoken to a long list of people—none of them employees of the CCRR—ranging from train conductors and porters to railroad presidents. Such experts as Simon A. Clutz, president of the Old Mexico Railway System, Max Burlley, president of the Main, Tampa and Santiago Railroad, and Rolph R. Older, chairman of the board of the Old City Central, had been cordial and most willing to give me their time. My conversations had convinced me that Willie the Whistle, as all of them called him, was enormously respected in his profession.

Perhaps the most interesting interview was the one I had with Baptist Black, the former president of the Old City Central, who is now president of the Meynemar and Hudson Company. The two men are friends of twenty years' standing. They are the same age; Black is De Jager's senior by only a few weeks. Their careers also bear a startling resemblance to one another. Both men started out as simple clerks on the railroad and both rose through the ranks to their present eminence. If any single person, other than Willie the Whistle himself, could get, as it were, inside the man, that person was Bap Black.

Black, a long-legged, pleasant-looking fellow, was enthusiastic about his colleague. He had nothing even mildly critical to say about Willie the Whistle; he was, as he said, completely sold on the man.

Puffing contemplatively on his big cigar, Black compared De Jager with his predecessors on the CCRR—the two previous presidents of the company, both of whom he had known: John Victor Casevant and Thomas S. Roach. Casevant, Black pointed out, was a highly competent, personally charming man, but an autocrat in his business methods; Casevant made millions for himself. Roach was brilliant, possessing a fine mathematical mind, and ran the railroad as if it were impersonal and inanimate, like an algebraic equation. To Roach people were less interesting than machines. He also made millions.

"Willie the Whistle is different from both of them," Black said. "Willie is an operating man by background and a traffic man by instinct." He fell silent for a moment, fingering his glasses, and then looked up at me. "Willie the Whistle is the number one railroad-operating man in America, and I'm certain, the rest of the world." His firm, quiet voice carried conviction. "He loves his job and his good living, and he has respect for the men who work for him."

It was from Black that I learned something else that both interested and embarrassed me—the fact that the CCRR had recently tried to include entertainment for its passengers in its working schedule, but had abandoned the idea at the planning stage when it proved highly impractical. I felt quite foolish, remembering how cavalierly I had offered the suggestion to De Jager. Well, my ignorance would have to serve as my excuse.

It was after eleven when I arrived at the twenty-one story office building on Nassau Street, Philadelphia, where the CCRR has its general office. The ambitious plans for New York's CCRR station are matched by the equally ambitious plans the CCRR has in its native city. A new development, to be called CCRR Center, is being built, which will be more than a mile long, running from Town Hall Place to Eighteenth

33

Street, between Old Market Square and Roosevelt Boulevard. The CCRR Center complex will contain several modern office buildings, a thousand-room hotel, a thirty-story luxury apartment house, and a shopping concourse. There will be a new Transportation Plaza containing two spectacular office buildings with five hundred thousand square feet of floor space, a bus terminal, an airlines office, and garages that will hold a thousand cars. In the middle will be a long mall with trees, flowers, and fountains. The main station and the Twenty-ninth Street station will tunnel commuters to this collection of buildings and walks. Some of the CCRR Center is already completed; other buildings are still under construction. But everything was born in the brain of Willie the Whistle with the practical help of Abner Bluefield, who came to this town from Poland sixty years ago with one pair of pants, and today is the biggest real estate operator in the country.

While my main intention was, of course, to see De Jager, I wanted first to talk with some of the men who worked closely with him. I wanted to know something about their personalities, something about their relationships with one another and with their boss, something about what they thought of him. I had therefore wanted to meet Bartholomew Alphonso Leach.

Leach, a big man with a fleshy mouth and sensitive hands, greeted me cordially. He looked like a combination of a heavyweight boxer and a philosopher. He had thick, graying hair, a high forehead, large brown eyes, a sharply crooked nose, and a firm, rather heavy jaw. His voice was gentle, yet as strong as his manner. This blend of man of action, man of corruption, and man of thought that I noticed in his appearance was evident in his behavior too. In his work he displayed a thoroughly realistic, even brutal intelligence. But in his private life I discovered he was something of a romantic. An accomplished amateur painter and a lover of popular music, he lived with his hazel-eyed, sex-hygienist wife, Amelia, in a manner more

34

suited to a college instructor than a grasping business executive.

By the time we had introduced ourselves to one another and he had shown me around his office bustling with shapely girls, it was a little after noon and Leach invited me to join him and some of the other two dozen vice-presidents for luncheon in the executive dining room.

The food, a seven-course feast cooked by CCRR chefs, was excellent indeed; there was fifty-year-old whiskey (by appointment to her Majesty Queen Victoria) and lively conversation. These men obviously knew how to live and relax, and realized that they would be much more efficient in their jobs, much better able to project priorities and cope with problems, if they were able to get their minds off their work during such social interludes as lunch.

Walter M. Colegrove, the young-looking, articulate millionaire's son who was vice-president in charge of finance, started the conversation off with some amusing anecdotes about Willie the Whistle's Negro valet Maxwell, who had been assigned by Willie to work in the private car used by the President of the country for his railroad trips. Once, according to Colegrove, some Secret Service men came to inspect the car before permitting President Roosevelt to board it. They looked in every nook and cranny, and even gave the kitchen a thorough goingover. Maxwell had stood by patiently during most of their inspection, but when they intruded upon his kitchen he simply could not submit.

"If I wanted to poison the President who did so much for poor people," he raged, "I could have done it a million times over. And I wouldn't use any stupid trick that you could find out. Do you think this is the first time I've taken care of a President? Now you just get out of my car before I get really angry! You may be paid for watching the President, but I love him!"

This was, of course, only one of many run-ins Maxwell had with the Secret Service. Their investigations never failed to infuriate and enrage him and his opinion of them was unprintable. He let them know how he felt on every possible occasion.

When Maxwell took suddenly ill, President Roosevelt, who appreciated such dedicated service, took a personal interest in his situation. The President arranged for Maxwell to be admitted to the best hospital and had a talk with the surgeon who was scheduled to operate on him. All the services were so eager to be of help that three ambulances—one each from the Army, the Navy, and the Air Force—pulled up in front of Maxwell's modest house in the Negro section of the city to take him to the hospital. Ill as that worthy was, he was delighted with the attention he was getting. And even then he could not forget his dislike of Secret Service men. As he was being bundled onto the Navy stretcher, the attendants heard him mutter, "I know how to take care of President Roosevelt, every Negro know. I don't need no police messin' my business."

After lunch Colegrove approached me directly. "I know you've been commissioned to write a book about Willie the Whistle by that ambitious wife of his. And I understand, I must say, why you want to get information and opinions from as many people as you can."

I looked at him inquiringly.

"I understand because I once felt the same way. I've never wanted to write about the railroad, but when I was first appointed vice-president in charge of finance, my father and I decided to do a little checking. After all, we figured, I would be working pretty closely with De Jager, and I wanted to find out what I could about him."

"Well?" I asked eagerly.

"I finally decided, after all the things I'd heard, that one of two things must be true: either Willie the Whistle was the greatest guy in the world, or else he had the best damn press agent I'd ever come across."

"Which was it?"

"Why, don't you know?" Colegrove looked at me. "Why, years ago, Mr. William Simon De Jager contracted a press agent for life."

"So you don't think much of Mr. De Jager?" I grinned.

"And I'm not the only one who feels that way. I'm only the most outspoken."

Just then Bart Leach came over to join us. "I see Walter's been telling you some things. Why don't you and I," and he nodded in my direction, "talk some more in my office? Maybe I'll be able to add to Walter's information."

I was glad to follow his suggestion and when we were comfortably settled I came straight to the point.

"Since I've been here I've learned a good deal about you executives, and I've enjoyed myself. But what about the ordinary people who work on the railroad, the ones who have nothing to do with the big-business side of it? The brakeman and the conductors and oilers, what kind of lives do they have?"

Leach looked at me pensively. "I guess the best way to answer that is to tell you a story; I would like it to be in the book, too. I hope you don't mind if it's a little long."

"Go on."

"Well, you know, I come from a railroad family myself. And when I was a boy of about ten I learned my first lesson about railroad people. My mother taught it to me, and I'll never forget it.

"She was a pretty grand person: a fine housekeeper, a good wife, and a wonderful mother. She was also a superlative cook, and took great pleasure in making good things for us to eat. Christmas was an especially marvelous time for us. Not only because of the presents, although like all children we looked forward to them; we particularly loved a Christmas because

37

mother really did herself proud as a cook on Christmas Day. Christmas dinner was the biggest event of the year, with all of us sitting around the table and stuffing ourselves full of good things to eat.

"In the South, where I come from, goose or suckling pig is traditionally the main course on Christmas Day, and every year my seven brothers and sisters and I would try to figure out for weeks in advance which one of those delicious treats we were going to have on December twenty-fifth. This particular year, I recollect, it was goose. I remember it so well because that year my father was not at his accustomed place at the head of the table, and mother was struggling to carve the big bird."

I puffed on my pipe and listened.

"And while my poor mother was working over that goose— I must admit, she wasn't very good at carving—we children were bombarding her with questions. 'Where is Daddy?' 'Why isn't our daddy home?' 'All the other daddies are home.'

"Mother finally completed her carving. Then, as she was serving us delectable pieces of goose—as I remember it, I had a wing—she spoke.

" 'There are many people who have to work on Christmas Day. We've been very lucky so far; this is the first holiday we haven't all been together. You know, children, that your daddy works for the railroad, and you know there are people who have to go long distances by train to get to their families in time for Christmas. Your daddy is helping them to get to their homes. He'll come back in the evening. I've saved the fruit-cake and we'll have our dessert together later.'

"But somehow mother's answer didn't satisfy me. 'But why does it have to be my daddy?' I asked. 'Why does he have to help other people get home? Who's helping him?'

"Mother looked at me thoughtfully for a moment, and then she said, 'Your daddy is a railroad man, just as I said before.

But he certainly isn't the only one. There are thousands of others. They all work together to see that the railroad runs properly, that all the passengers are taken care of, and that all the freight is delivered on time so that we can have our goose for dinner. The trains run all the time—day and night, ordinary days and holidays. And the railroad people have to work just as long as the railroad itself. They're the ones who have to see that everyone is helped, that everyone gets where he wants to go. The railroad men don't mind that at all; they like their job, because it makes them feel good to know that they are helping others and helping themselves to get the goose and the fruitcake!"

Leach noticed that I had discovered his pitchman's intelligence; he smiled at me helplessly.

"Well," he said, "nothing has really changed since then, except that now I make plenty of money, and I understand even better what mother meant."

Clever fellow, I said to myself.

"Working for the railroad is still a twenty-four-hour-a-day job, because the railroad always operates around the clock. It doesn't matter what job a man has, whether he's a yardmaster or the president of the CCRR, he's still very conscious that other people's lives and happiness depend on him. He takes his work very seriously, and he's proud of what he does.

"Another thing"—Leach thumbed through some papers on his neatly arranged desk—"all railroad people on CCRR today, thanks to me, feel very close to one another and to the board of directors. The yardmaster and our director, Roger Rollon from Pittsburgh, head of the banking and oil empire, know that they have a lot in common. The people who work for the CCRR are real people. The railroad isn't just a berth and a salary, it's a way of life for all its employees."

As I took my leave, I pondered over the story that Bartholomew Alphonso Leach had told me. He was right. Railroad people and their directors were real people, but totally unlike, and the difference between them was many millions of dollars.

▣ Chapter 5

It was a wet evening both outside and inside the big colonial house at 333 Rich Acres Road when I arrived with William S. De Jager in his custom-built Cadillac. Outside a light rain had started, while inside guests were swimming in alcohol and a cacophony of loud voices and dance music.

On the steps leading down into the foyer my coat was removed by two servants and I was greeted by Mrs. De Jager in a pink dress flanked by a tall old gentleman with a well-shaped gray head and a young girl who wore a long red gown.

"Those were lovely chrysanthemums you sent, and Mr. De Jager joins me in thanking you very much."

"Are you one of those fellows . . ." began the tall gentleman.

"Pardon me," interrupted Mrs. De Jager with a broad smile that showed the ridge of her gums. "This is Mr. John Victor Casevant, the former president of the CCRR and our great friend; and this is my daughter, Tessa."

Mr. Casevant shook my hand. "Are you one of those fellows who keep a record book on everyone's birthday, telling how old they are?"

"A record book?" I asked.

"I hope you only do it to your men friends, not to your girl friends. They might be inclined to resent it."

Mrs. De Jager, still smiling, intervened. "This, you will realize, is an appreciation of your birthday greetings."

"I didn't know that it was your birthday, Madame," I said. "I sent flowers to you and the book to your daughter hoping to be gallant—also, to be honest, on the advice of Mr. Leach." Mrs. De Jager laughed loudly while Mr. Casevant looked solemn. Tessa, who had not been listening, broke in and pulled me out of my embarrassment.

"Such a wonderful surprise, Mr. Kapistrot, to receive a pre-publication copy of your latest book!"

"Miss De Jager, I have to confess that it is not my book."

But she was looking at my grayish temples and continued. "It was awfully kind of you to autograph it. I must . . ."

"Miss De Jager, that isn't my writing."

". . . I must admit it is the first book I have ever received from the author himself; now my ambition will be to have a book dedicated to me." She smiled. "I feel very honored. Thank you so much."

Then Mrs. De Jager took me by the arm and led me inside. "My daughter, Mr. Kapistrot, is sold on a certain young economist named Bill Wattson. Frankly, I'm worried about it. My husband has given him a fine job, but meanwhile he is writing a novel about Russia and I think he may be some kind of socialist in disguise. I'm going to ask you to read his book for me and tell me if it is so." She stopped. "You understand that you will be rich," she said in a low voice, "if you write me a good book on my husband and our railroad family."

At this moment Mr. De Jager took me in tow and started introducing me to some of the most important guests. Among them was tall, dignified Lloyd D. Abdoller, whose family not only exercises control over CCRR but also owns the largest bank in the country, together with huge steel and oil companies. I had known his wife previously as a patroness of the arts; her newest protégé, the young Austrian violinist Pierre Schon, was having a brilliant success. I had met Lloyd much later, one summer when I was working on the staff of the

Abdoller Family Advisers for his younger brother Russell's nomination to the American Presidency.

When I recalled this, Lloyd observed in his quiet, assured manner, "Next year Russell will be nominated and elected President."

"I hope so."

Mr. De Jager broke in. "I'm glad you're up and around again, Lloyd."

Abdoller turned to me. "I should explain that I was taken very ill about two months ago, and was rushed to the hospital by ambulance."

"I am sorry to hear that."

"I was in the hospital for a whole month, and then I was permitted to come home, but I had to stay upstairs on Beekman Place for three more weeks. Now I am permitted to come downstairs, to go anywhere, provided I only go upstairs twice a day. I'm getting a man to design a baroque elevator for me, to go with the room."

"What was the matter with you?" I asked politely.

"It wasn't a repetition of my coronary trouble, but was due to too much thick red blood. Too many corpuscles."

"Your hemoglobin?"

"My hemoglobin was as high as seventeen point three. But at that, I guess I was fortunate that it was too much red blood, rather than too many white corpuscles."

At this moment Jack Small, chief executive of the Allen-Bevan-Cornell Glass Company, half drunk on his beloved martinis, approached me. "Bless me, Franklin, nice to see you!" And taking me aside, he reached into his pocket. "You said the other day that you would like to see real evidence of my good work as a dollar-a-year man for the unemployed."

"I don't recall, Jack . . ."

"Oh yes, you asked me that in my own office. Don't you

42

remember?" Saying that, he pushed a letter in front of my face. It was on White House stationery, dated September 27, 1938, and addressed to the Honorable J. V. Small, Administrator, Census of Partial Employment, Unemployment and Occupations, Department of Commerce Building, Washington.

Dear Jack:

Your final report in four volumes is now before me and I hasten to extend hearty congratulations upon the successful completion of a fine piece of work. Since you will have completed the miscellaneous duties in connection with the work by October thirty-first next, I accept, effective as of that date, your resignation as Administrator of the Census of Partial Employment, Unemployment and Occupations.

When I appointed you as Administrator of the Census of the Unemployed I realized that I was giving you a formidable task. It was necessary for you to blaze new trails for there was nothing in our national experience to serve as a guide or model. With a real genius for organization you marshaled your forces in a surprisingly short time and carried out the actual work of the count with equal dispatch. The results of this work in their final form will be a gold mine of information to all who desire to go to the bottom of the pressing question of unemployment in all of its diverse and complex phases. It is also noteworthy that as a result of your efficient organization and wise disbursement of funds, this gigantic task was completed at a total cost of less than half of the sum made available to you for the work.

To you and to all who have worked in cooperation I return hearty thanks and an assurance of sincere apprecation.

Very sincerely yours,
Franklin D. Roosevelt

When I had finished reading the former President's letter, Jack commented, "It was difficult for us industrialists to work with Roosevelt, but today we have organized and are successfully operating the Union of Unemployed, for the benefit of American workers all over the country. Doug Seymour is in charge. He is our real genius and philosopher. You should meet him and get acquainted with his U. of U."

"I will, Jack. If I understand rightly, Mr. De Jager is connected with this organization too."

"Yes. Practically everybody in this crowd is connected; practically everybody who is important in business is supporting the U. of U. We have true feeling for the working people, I'm happy to say, a deep spiritual concern; we genuinely want to help them."

"Excuse me, Jack. Right now I'd like to get acquainted with some food. I'm hungry."

As I started edging my way through the crowd in the direction of the dining room I noticed many faces of powerful and famous men. It was like flipping through *Time* magazine covers for the last five years. Many of the faces, I saw, were flushed with liquor, and all were turned toward one another, while unnoticed on the walls of every room hung masterful Bonnards, Matisses, Utrillos, Signacs, Vlamincks, Van Dongens, Derains, Puys, Picassos, and even one El Greco and one Rubens.

But I was not thinking about paintings. Instead, Jack was in my mind, and I recalled what his assistant, George Voltaire, had once said to me as we walked through the plants of the Allen-Bevan-Cornell Glass Company. Looking around him, George recalled, "When I first came here in nineteen forty-three, the manufacture of automobiles and private building operations had ceased on account of war and the great glass machines which you saw were lying idle. It was essential, therefore, to convert our plants to war work, and Mr. Small, with his Washington connections, took a very profitable lead in this."

One of Jack Small's outstanding characteristics, as George had observed through the years, was his ability to work effectively behind the scenes in whatever enterprise he was engaged in, whether in the company itself or as a director of CCRR and Bede Aviation; or as leader of the Constructive Catholicism movement, in which he is particularly interested; or as president of the Museum of Art, chairman of the Hospital Building Committee, important organizer for the Union of Unemployed, and acting mediator in industrial disagreements. George had found that Jack Small always had a very boldly conceived yet highly practical solution to problems, and inevitably it seemed to be his solution that was adopted. He was also very diplomatic. At the time when George first came to work for Jack Small, the then executive vice-president who died soon after, had an intense jealousy of Jack and tried to thwart him at every turn. The reason was that the man had been head of the Edward Allen Plate Glass Company at the time of the merger, had very close relationships with all the members of the Allen family, and naturally thought that he should be made president of the Allen-Bevan-Cornell Glass Company. Jack Small handled the situation with great finesse. He rarely did anything without consulting the executive vice-president; he always spoke to him respectfully and deferred to him, and in fact treated him as if he were his most valued friend.

Another characteristic of Small was his intense devotion to his family and to his first and second wives. Not only do Jack and his second wife, Pampinella, together have eight children and numerous grandchildren, but there are also all the nieces and nephews of his first wife; and he never forgets a name or a christening. The children's families stay successively each spring in his enormous home in Washington Hills, while he and Pampinella take their annual trip to Europe.

Jack Small had told George a story about himself which probably should not have been repeated. He said that at the outbreak of the Korean War, Louis Johnson, then Secretary of Defense, called him up and said that the Cabinet was going to decide the next day what to do about the North Korean invasion of South Korea and that he, Johnson, wanted to get Jack Small's private opinion on what to do, because he had great respect for his thinking.

"In my opinion," Jack answered, "the right thing and the Christian thing to do would be to tell the North Koreans that if they do not withdraw in forty-eight hours we will drop atomic bombs on them."

Johnson replied that their military commander had said this was impracticable because of the nature of the terrain. It consisted of sharp ravines, so atomic bombs could not be used effectively. Small said, "Oh, I did not mean to drop atomic bombs on their troops—I meant to drop them on all their chief cities."

The refined little fox, Voltaire, was always scabbing on his own soul, thinking only to remain in his well-paying job. Nonetheless, one day I heard that he had been ousted when Mrs. Small decided to look for a new young assistant to the Chief Executive—" someone more dynamic," as she put it. George then joined the Union of Unemployed.

Using my nose as a compass and navigating toward the dining area, I spotted a great railroad man, Monroe Bootman, with a pipe as his companion, standing in the corner and meditating—presumably about the future of transportation and his consanguinity with the bosses. It was Monroe who some years ago introduced me to good living and excellent pipe tobacco.

As I was going to greet Monroe, my other friend Lewis Gottlov rushed up to me and grabbing me by the arm said, "I will be out of Baton Rouge most of this week, but I'll be in Baton Rouge all of next week and in New York the latter part of next month. I'm giving you all this information because your letter didn't indicate whether you wanted to see me in Baton Rouge or in New York."

"Thank you, Lewis," I said, pleased to see him. Lewis Gottlov had been honored in New York last year with the coveted Justice Louis D. Brandeis Gold Medal Award for service to humanity given by the Jewish Forum Association. According to the Baton Rouge *State Times,* "he has done much for humanity, much to advance many worthy causes. He would not even have been considered for the Brandeis Award if this were not the case. Everyone who has ever been involved in planning civic projects in Baton Rouge knows of Mr. Gottlov's readiness to support worthy programs, of the value of his efforts on behalf of our community. He has given generously of his time and means to make many a project a success. Congratulations are in order to Mr. Gottlov for the Brandeis Award."

At this moment Mrs. De Jager appeared and said, "You must be hungry."

"Yes."

"Then come and we'll sit down."

As we started toward the other end of the house she smiled at me. "You are a lucky man. If I understand correctly, you have already produced a few good chapters of a book that Bart Leach thinks will be outstanding, about Willie and my family and the railroad. Also, as I have mentioned, I would like you to read this novel of my daughter's fiancé, and if it is socialistic, help me to find a way to break off his contact with Tessa. After that, Mr. Kapistrot, you can retire as a rich man."

▣ Chapter 6

The menu was superb. For starters we had fresh fruit cup, mixed olives, fenouille, salted nuts, and Maryland diamond-back terrapin soup. Roast breast of pheasant perigourdine with wild rice was complemented by Clos des Fèves Beaune 1925, braised celery, sweet potato Benette, Belgian endives with Lorenzo dressing, and slices of Smithfield ham. Then came fifty-year-old Napoleon brandy, bombe glacée with cherries and kumquats, and demitasse of Turkish coffee. A small orchestra accompanied our meal.

My companions at the table for eight were Gusty Mary and William De Jager, John V. Casevant, George Allen of Allen-Bevan-Cornell, CCRR vice-president Sam Brunner and his wife, and a Mr. Hans Schmidt from Buenos Aires. Mrs. De Jager, on my right, was quietly passing me tidbits of information and gossip about George Allen, former confidant to Dwight D. Eisenhower, mixed with digressions on her own father and grandfather. But I was doubly interested in hearing what De Jager at the far end of the table was saying about his powerful friend Seymour, since I knew the man was considered by everybody in business to be a fine managerial philosopher. He was chief executive of the Electric, Gas & Plastic Corporation—the largest of its kind in the country—the conviction of which for conspiracy to price-fix had only recently been upheld in the Supreme Court. Seymour was held responsible, but only privately, for at the same time he headed the federal government Business Advisory Council.

Mr. De Jager continued, "and I learned more than I could

ever acknowledge. He became, you might say, my model. I observed him at work and at home, talked about him with his family, associates and friends. From the very moment I first heard of him, I was intrigued and impressed with him both as a person and as a great business mind, the genius behind the national success of the Union of Unemployed. And I am not the only one.

"In speaking to many people, from our personal friends to E.G.P. workers and scientists, I have discovered many reasons for thinking highly of Doug Seymour. The workers like him for such statements as, 'The future of the country demands less special-interest politics and more politics on behalf of all the people'; because he is, as he told me, 'for fair wages, security and protection, for eliminating the dullness and drudgery of routine jobs and seeing that the worker becomes the master, not the slave of machines.' His associates like him for his comradeship and teamwork, his friends for his loyalty."

Mr. Schmidt was listening with apparent eagerness, the others with mild interest; Gusty Mary and I drank more and more old wine and De Jager continued without interruption. If you have to make a living, you must be speechless before business potentates; I learned that many years ago.

"The officers of E.G.P.—such men as vice-president Bob Call and second vice-presidents Carter Boul and Jack Kroot— are unanimous in their praise, and so are all the people in the Union of Unemployed.

" 'Doug is consistently clear and objective in his thinking, planning and building,' Mr. Call told me.

" 'He is a true manager. He can handle risk; he has energy, vision, and a tremendous amount of creative ability,' Boul added. Kroot agreed wholeheartedly.

"Wiand L. Harold, partner of Steelman, Worek, who met Doug when he served on the War Production Board during World War Two, offered an opinion amazingly similar to my

49

own. 'Seymour is a realist, a profound thinker,' he told me, 'and naturally, therefore, a top manager. He came up the hard way, on sheer ability—and probably because of that, he is a hard worker and has a very human understanding of people and their problems. As a matter of fact, he is more concerned about the ordinary man than about anything else except the future of the company.' "

De Jager seemed to be looking in my direction as he spoke. I wondered briefly if I was expected to be taking notes. I listened hard while he continued his cataloguing, and attempted to disguise with a thoughtful expression my interest in the food.

"General Cornelius C. Colt, Chairman of the Board of the World Can Company, described Doug in the crisp words of a professional soldier. 'He is a very strong and fair-minded man with a remarkable sense of organization.' "

While Mr. De Jager waved away his soup, untouched, his wife leaned toward me. "You should meet Colt." She smiled. "He's so very gallant. I call him my Civil War relic—privately, of course."

"A member of E.G.P.'s Board of Directors, Al Piroth of Mutschmann Guaranty Trust Company offered the verdict that Doug is without exception the ablest manager in American business today, a man with a sense of the future.

"Paul I. Havyhead, President of Frear, Freas National Shirt Company, added his observation: 'Doug is out to win in everything. Never admits defeat. He works fast, and even in the most difficult bottlenecks comes through with excellent results.' "

I myself had heard and read much about Seymour. His approach, I knew, was always broad in perspective, composed, and logical. I admired him for such statements as: "My job in E.G.P. is to talk and listen to people at all levels. The manager of big business who does not keep up with the times, or rather with the future, is going to find himself as obsolete as yesterday's newspaper, and almost as quickly.

"The manager must know that his continuing usefulness and profitability depend on a wide spectrum of relationships, involving not only directors and important stockholders, but employees, other businesses and institutions, and the world of politics as a whole." He would pause and clasp his hands, then continue in even more decisive tones. "There are three challenges to American business today: the challenge of uncertain business conditions in the world, the challenge of Soviet technology, and the challenge of various pressures on the business community. All this is to say that a new dimension has been added to business leadership."

Seymour's understanding of working people and their problems is keen: "As employees, people expect not only a satisfying job with good pay, benefits, and the best working conditions, they also expect full information, dignity, participation, recognition, opportunity to advance in accordance with ability, and a rewarding association with the manager and other top-level staff." As a result of this philosophy, Doug was instrumental in the formation of the Union of Unemployed.

Later I came to know Willie's model personally, and found him most gracious in answering all the questions I put to him. He stands about five feet eight inches tall and is quite slim. He has a large, almost oversized head and gray, thinning hair which he parts on the side. He dresses meticulously, usually in a dark blue or light gray double-breasted suit. His favorite reading is economics, and European and American history—when he has a chance to read. He loves theater: musicals. He dislikes Shakespeare and says so. For relaxation, he golfs and works on his Florida ranch near Tampa where, as Eisenhower did, he raises Aberdeen-Angus cattle, citrus fruits and ponies. He and his wife Leoparda lead a fairly quiet life, and do not care too much for social engagements. They have four daughters, all married to men who hold good executive jobs in the Electric, Gas & Plastic Corporation.

On weekends their twenty-room house on Wanderburg Drive in New Jerusalem, Connecticut, is full of laughter and noise. There are youngsters all over: the Seymours' grandchildren love fishing expeditions with their grandfather in his small private lake. The lake is well stocked with bass and sunfish, but the turtles are the children's favorite catch, and their grandfather enjoys helping them.

During the week the house is quiet. Leoparda Seymour, a vivacious dark-haired woman with beautiful brown eyes, gardens, supervises the housework and the cooking (which is done in her model E.G.P. kitchen), pursues her hobby, photography, reads *Current Society Calendar,* and waits for her husband to come home. "Our life is wonderful and smooth," she will tell anybody, when asked about her marriage to the four-hundred-and-sixty-five-thousand-dollar-a-year man she met during their college days, and married a year after graduation.

The Seymours spend their evenings quietly, reading the *Wall Street Journal* or watching television dramas. Once a week they go into New York to a musical or play. On these days, Leoparda Seymour comes into the city around noon, spends some time at their Paris House apartment, and shops for bric-à-brac. She is especially fond of Chinese porcelain figures and odd jewelry. But if somebody should think she is only an ordinary housewife, married to a rich man, her husband will tell you how mistaken that impression is. Doug Seymour loves to say that Leoparda is the reason for his success.

Born on a five-thousand-acre wheat farm, about thirty miles northwest of Walla Walla, Washington, to Donald D. and Columbina Riley Seymour, Doug Seymour maintains a belief stemming from his own experience that a little fellow can reach the big money if he works hard at it. The countryside where the Snake and Yakima rivers flow into the Columbia is exciting and sensuous, rich in vegetation and wild life. But wheat farming in Seymour's youth was a grueling job for there was only a minimum of farm equipment. Mule, horse, and man were, as the motto of the Order of the Bath states, *tria juncta in uno*. It was a tough union and there was no way of avoiding the work; everyone struggled. When the Seymours had farmed the heart out of a piece of ground, which amounted to approximately twenty-five bushels an acre, they moved to another plot. It was difficult to get the necessary fertilizer for such a large farm; it was either too expensive or the family's domestic animals could not supply enough.

During summers, as wheat-harvesting time approached, Doug helped the workers to clean, oil, and fix the big combine harvester and the grain wagons. He fixed fork handles and minded the horses and mules. With the August heat came the harvest, which for the farm hands meant hard work in the field from early morning until way after sundown. All day long Doug watched the workers get the thirty-three horses to pull the huge combine harvester. As the workers sweated under a blazing sun, Doug dreamed under the shade of a tree about a life where he would use his brain instead of his muscles.

When Doug originally discovered that I would be writing about him, he immediately invited me for cocktails and handed me a long-winded vita.

"If you put this material in your book, I will pay you ten thousand dollars cash, so you won't have any taxes to worry about."

Because I am an unscrupulous man, I accepted his conditions.

While he was still in his early teens, Doug had tried to figure out a means of making things easier for himself. He often discussed with his father the possibility of improving their income by organizing the work in such a manner that they would get the maximum from the labor of farmhands, sharecroppers, and seasonal workers.

Donald D. Seymour was an intelligent man with a philosophical, perhaps even resigned, outlook on life; he did much to deepen his son's creative thinking. Mrs. Seymour believed that even the most intelligent boy needed a formal education if he was to succeed in life, and she encouraged Doug to study. He started in a country schoolhouse about three miles from the family home. Later he stayed in Walla Walla during the winter and went to school there.

In 1917, Doug had just graduated from high school when America entered World War One. Although he begged his parents to permit him to enlist, Mrs. Seymour convinced him instead to enroll in college. The next year, however, he signed up as a seaman in the Navy. But he never got to sea; when the Armistice was declared he was halfway through the Officers Material School at Bremerton, Washington. He had the choice of continuing there or going back to college, where he had planned to major in economics. He worked on the farm all through that summer with the help of his hired hands. The wheat sold for two dollars a bushel, so his profit was excellent. Then in the fall he returned to college.

His life on the farm had taught him responsibility and the value of resourcefulness. It also gave him a lifelong interest in agriculture. He believed that every boy should have the experience of working on a farm, where he could develop a love for the land, creative initiative, and the ability to work hard. As far as farming itself was concerned, Seymour had some very specific ideas derived from his own experience. He believed that American agriculture must be organized and operated like American big business, where almost four thousand dollars' worth of mechanized equipment stands behind every man. The farmer, he believed, could operate on a profitable basis only if he took a proper accounting of his production, time, market, and above all, if he saw to it that his equipment was completely mechanized.

In college the enterprising farmer's son was spotted by the president, Dr. K. Herbert Hyde. Dr. Hyde recalls Doug warmly: "He was a great inspiration to others, a superb leader even then. His attitude did much to create a spirit of dedication among the students. He fired them with a determination to serve in a bigger way."

It was at college that Doug met his future wife, then Leoparda Ewing of Seattle. The young couple studied together, and on weekends picnicked near his fraternity cabin. Like his mother, Leoparda encouraged Doug to set a goal for himself and to work hard to achieve it. He washed dishes in the school cafeteria and tended furnaces. For a time he waited on tables at the Seattle Elks Club, and he also kept books for a garage. While he was working at the Elks Club, he met Hosea Phillips, local manager of E.G.P. Phillips and the father of ten daughters, who was impressed with the young man and helped him to obtain a part-time position with his own company selling wooden paddle washers, the forerunners of today's washing machines.

Doug worked afternoons, weekends, and holidays, while he was still at school, handling not only washing machines but vacuum cleaners, irons, gas ranges, light bulbs, and toasters. In addition, with the help of one of the Phillips daughters, he conducted a training course for clerks of E.G.P. in Seattle, teaching them how to sell the household appliances his company manufactured. He also conducted cooking courses with Miss Phillips, demonstrating through the courses the superiority of his company's kitchen appliances.

Even on a part-time basis, he soon outsold all the other salesmen in Seattle and its vicinity, and when Harry Gabbett, district manager of E.G.P., passed through town looking for a young man to sell new appliances in the district, Hosea

Phillips interceded on the behalf of his protégé and recommended Doug for the job.

"The choice is yours," Phillips said to the young man, after Gabbett had expressed his willingness to hire him. "You can stay here or you can go with Gabbett." Then he smiled and shook his head. "No, I've changed my mind. You have no choice. The opportunity there is much better. If you don't take it, I'll fire you and you'll have to leave."

And so Doug began his connection with E.G.P. Gabbett, watching his new man in the Seattle office, liked what he saw. Doug had an easy way with people; he was diligent and ingenious. But he was young and he had his faults which the older man strove to correct. "You get too enthusiastic sometimes," Gabbett explained. "In every business and especially in selling, a man must not overdo his salesmanship. Truthfulness, dignity, and lots of hard work, those are the things that will make you a success."

Just before Doug's graduation, Harry Gabbett called the young man down to his office. When Doug had comfortably seated himself, his superior said, "I want you to know that next year I'll be leaving here. I'm going to San Francisco to become Pacific Coast district manager of the company."

"Congratulations," Doug said with sincerity.

"But I did not call you in to discuss my future, but the future of the job I'm leaving. I want to talk with you about my successor. I have in mind a good, a very capable man, and I wanted to know if you agree with my choice."

"I have absolute confidence in your selection. You know people."

Gabbett went on. "Let's not waste time. I want you to be my successor as the Northwest representative of E.G.P." He spoke very slowly, as if to impress Doug with his belief in him.

During the years, Doug groomed himself with great thoroughness, making it a point, before dropping Phillips' daugh-

ter, to get to know everything about each man in his district
—his selling methods, his personality, his family—and learning, too, about the customers' complaints. Even at this time
he recognized the necessity of planning, of discipline, and of
responsibility. Seymour was a yes man, but he himself has
never liked that breed. "If you give a man a job," he always
said, "give him all the job."

Later, when I was revising these pages, trying to delete
extraneous material, his wife Leoparda, under some pretext or
other, offered me a second ten thousand dollars if I would
present Doug's story as his very own handwritten account.
To appease my conscience I accepted her offer with her explanation that this extensive biography would amount to a
genuinely important historical document of a great American
businessman.

He and Leoparda had been married on a June day. From
the beginning the marriage was "a success in smoothness," as
his wife always refers to it. As soon as he started to earn a
good salary, Leoparda started to bring healthy girls into the
world.

In 1929, the Seymours left the Northwest for San Francisco.
Mr. Gabbett had been called East and had recommended that
Doug be appointed his successor as Pacific Coast district
manager of E.G.P. He saw to it that this suggestion was
popular with the company's employees. Sixteen salesmen under his jurisdiction in an impromptu "bull session" voted
Doug the most likely, competent, and deserving candidate for
the job, since he had so thoroughly demonstrated his leadership to his own team members in Seattle.

But the Seymours had not been settled in San Francisco
for even a year before Doug was saddled with another important decision: the company offered him the choice of stay-
ing on the West Coast, joining the E.G.P. refrigeration department in Chicago, or going to Bridgeport to work for Big

Boss Wilson.

Leoparda encouraged him to make the important move. "Get near the hub of the wheel," she urged him. "Show them your talents. Let's move to Bridgeport."

"With the children so young?" he thought aloud. "Who knows how long I'll stay there? Then to move again? I've got to consider my family too."

"Don't you worry about the family. That's my job," said his stubborn wife. "Let's be near the big boss. Perhaps you will learn something from him, or maybe he will profit from having you."

"Okay," he said, kissing Leoparda. "We will move."

With the growing responsibility of his job, Seymour's family also grew. His third and fourth daughters were born in rapid succession.

Part of Seymour's business philosophy was shown by an event that occurred shortly after he moved to Bridgeport and became manager of small appliance sales. Most of the other appliance manufacturers were selling portable mixers, but E.G.P. still had only an old-fashioned stationary model. Seymour immediately put his engineers to work to design a modern portable machine, and even before the final testing had been completed he set out for a New York department store carrying the mixer under his arm. He returned to Bridgeport that same evening with an order for five thousand mixers to be delivered within a few weeks.

But the order was never filled. For the tests in the E.G.P. kitchens indicated that the mixers did not measure up to the company's standard of quality, and rather than supply inferior merchandise, he was willing to lose the order.

Seymour always believed in supplying the highest quality and the latest styling to meet changes in the public's taste. Material that is not mechanically perfect, he insisted, should be taken off the market and improved before the public is

58

allowed to use it. When he first put these principles into practice, many of his associates were startled to discover the time and money they cost, for Seymour applied this philosophy to every single item. But this is how the name of Electric, Gas & Plastic, and the name of Seymour, have gained the admiration and respect of all other businesses. He believed wholeheartedly in satisfying the customer first.

"Management," he once said, "must have a public trust. And the public is our customer. If we trap him carefully, he will buy our products forever, and that will keep our important stockholders happy."

During his first two years in Bridgeport, he increased sales by seventy per cent, and from then on rose rapidly to even more important positions. In a year and a half he was appointed assistant manager of the entire E.G.P. Appliance and Merchandise Department, and the next year, when Big Boss Wilson was made executive vice-president by E.G.P.'s old-fashioned, iron-fisted boss Otto Vanderflitt, Doug took Wilson's place.

Then, in September of 1940, Doug Seymour left E.G.P. to become president of the Fischer Company in New York. Although innumerable explanations of why he made this move have been offered by unfriendly outsiders, the reason as Seymour gave it was really quite simple: the offer made him was so attractive financially that it would have been ridiculous to refuse. K. K. Klein, the owner of the Fischer Company, had this to say: "We got to know Doug and his work when our company started negotiations with E.G.P. for them to take us over. What we learned of Doug during the time the discussions were going on made us realize that he was the man we needed."

This new experience was of as much benefit to Seymour as to the company. Up till then, he had been primarily a commercial manager, but now he was in charge of every phase of the business: financing, labor, manufacturing. This training at the Fischer Company has stood him in good stead ever since.

Realizing that the extra twenty thousand dollars was as good as in my pocket, I was determined to get more. I approached Doug's four daughters and their husbands with a similar appeal for money, as they were unaware that Doug and his wife had already promised to pay me. "Otherwise," I told them, "I would be unable to complete the story of this great symbol of American business."

Soon thereafter, the eldest daughter's husband got in touch with me and promised a group of select stocks as payment, if I included everything that his father-in-law had written about himself. I consented, because not only would I profit, but also future generations of American businessmen.

Shortly after America entered World War Two, Fischer converted from peace to war production, and almost at the same time federal officials approached Seymour with the offer of a government job. "I wasn't interested in any dollar-a-year job," he said. "I wanted to be considered on the same terms as any other high civilian employee of the government." He had been in Washington only two months when he was appointed vice-chairman of the War Production Board.

The efficient Seymour was depressed by the Washington atmosphere—the red tape and constant feuds between heads of departments over contracts for their companies. But in spite of his famous quips—"Washington is like a handful of worms" or "The man in the capital must grow or smell"— he was performing miracles to crack the bottlenecks, to get contracts for the E.G.P. and Fischer companies, and to help the country win the war.

Three years later Seymour returned to E.G.P. as assistant to the president, the autocratic Otto Vanderflitt, whom Henry A. Ford had called "the greatest salesman of all times" and the man who had singlehandedly put E.G.P. into the appliance business, the farm markets, and air-conditioning. Seymour's new duties included troubleshooting for Vanderflitt, studying E.G.P.'s future potential and its position in the newly developing field of atomic power, and initiating new ideas for the company's liaison with federal and state governments. The assignment was important and Seymour was the ideal man for it. He had worked for big and small businesses, as well as for the government. He knew all phases of local and federal decision-making, he knew industry, he knew his product, and he used his knowledge to reorganize E.G.P. toward larger and larger profit.

He emphasized the importance of long-range planning. "Too many of us with big money sitting in higher offices tend to behave like those on the least responsible level of supervision," he asserted. "The day-to-day work must get done and it is up to the supervisor to see that it is done; but the man who rises higher in the capitalistic organization must delegate daily tasks of supervision and devote more time to thinking ahead. No state, no powerful industry can exercise leadership and move confidently without the benefit of long-range plans. I have always felt that our planning period should be the business generation—a period of twenty-five years at least."

Since he does so much thinking, planning, and research into profit, when he finally does arrive at an answer Seymour believes one hundred per cent that it is right, and personally takes the salesman's approach in promoting it. He has always made it a practice to visit every major E.G.P. factory at least twice a year, and to speak before groups of important E.G.P. people, so that he can learn what they are thinking about his plans and how he can best put them across without applying too much pressure.

The value of this approach has been emphasized by Big Boss Wilson, who said, "Doug was a great hand at cultivating the little fellow. When he worked in Bridgeport he got to know the workers, the foremen, everyone who had anything to do with the E.G.P. Company, and he sold them on the idea of building, of selling nothing but the best, and at high prices. He wanted to be sure that everyone was headed down the right track, the track that had an E.G.P. monogram stamped on it."

While I was working on Doug's profile his youngest and most beautiful daughter approached me and offered herself and money for a complete biography of her father.

I replied, "Sleeping with you would be sheer pleasure. But I just can't write a whole book about your father."

"I don't want you to write anything more. Just add everything that my father has ever written about himself to what you already have."

Immediately I imagined what would happen if this experience with the youngest daughter could be multiplied by four. I deliberated extensively with myself to see if my appetite for money and sex were that all-consuming. Finally I did all those things that they had asked, for the good of America's businessman and American morality in general.

At the end of World War Two, E.G.P. was doing an annual business of almost three billion dollars. As Seymour expressed it, "We were at the crossroads. We could go back to being the seven-hundred-million-dollar-company we were before the war. Or we could take advantage of our wartime greatness and become not merely a great company but an industrial leader." There was no doubt as to the choice. "We're going to be a leader even if we have to start a new war!"

Two critical problems were tackled by Doug in the study he undertook when he became Big Boss Wilson's assistant: automation and atomic power.

"Too often the automatic factory is spoken of with fear, as if we were planning to make men the slaves of machines and business," Seymour said. "In fact, the opposite is true. One of the greatest opportunities of automation is to make more industrial jobs worthy of human judgment and skills. Another is to make products of a finer quality, in greater quantity than ever before. And a third is to reduce the high cost of investment."

When he became vice-president under Big Boss Wilson, he started to gradually introduce his idea of automation. When Wilson retired, Doug succeeded him as president and chief executive officer of the company. But this was not the end of his climb. While remaining in the chief executive's slot he was also elected chairman of the board of directors.

He continued to follow the question of atomic power over the years; and here his pioneering instinct, his preference for risk and opportunity rather than mediocrity, had impressed Willie De Jager perhaps more than anything else in Seymour's entire career.

"The atom is the power of the future," declared Seymour, "and power, all power, is the business of E.G.P." These are not just empty words. Today the company, on the recommendation of its chief executive, has put forty thousand men and billions of dollars into the building of atomic facilities. At the same time E.G.P. laboratories also study radiation effects on plants, animals, and people. Orders for commercial atomic power reactors and equipment are coming to E.G.P. from all over the world, not only because the firm is so large and its production so diversified, but also because of Seymour's government contacts. Profits are growing like mushrooms after rain.

De Jager made himself even more comfortable, and sipping the strong Turkish coffee, beamed. "What a triumph; what an urgently needed victory for freedom everywhere."

Today, behind this educational, economic, and political philosophy of Douglas Seymour, looms a second new organization—the Union of Unemployed, which has been called the most interesting achievement of the country's powerful and patriotic men, and specifically Doug. Doug is very proud of E.G.P. and of the Union of Unemployed on which he spent many years of thought. He looks forward to the future with confidence. "You can gauge a top executive in big business by how many good people in the company he leaves behind him. And my prescription for young men looking for opportunities in our great country is hard work, a clear vision constantly synchronized with that of the directors, plus good fortune and more hard work."

Somebody I am sure should now ask me, "All right, you were offered money and sex, and you published Doug's original story and his friend's recollections without any alteration. But how about your integrity as a writer?"

My reply: "They promised money. They promised sex. But as I secretly expected, they swindled me out of it."

"So why did you print every little thing about Doug and his friends?"

"Because I would like to leave this document intact to demonstrate how great men in America are made. Let the coming generations draw their own conclusions from Doug Seymour's life and the dozens of other lives portrayed in these pages, since the future should find them extinct."

 **Chapter 7**

Before I could escape the horde of intoxicated but important guests in Mr. and Mrs. De Jager's home, I witnessed a stimulating discussion among the friends of De Jager's only daughter Tessa. I observed this social gathering partly on Mrs. De Jager's account and partly on my own. It was held in the left wing of the house in a very large room, next to a yet larger drawing room that had been temporarily converted into a dance hall. Settled in a chair half turned toward the window, I appeared to be a stray guest dozing off the effects of food and liquor.

Tessa, blonde and blue-eyed, was sitting in a large armchair, staring dreamily into space. Next to her was olive-skinned Margie Maxton, crossing and uncrossing her seemingly unmanageable legs, and smoking a thin, jeweled pipe with an incredibly long shank.

Looking nervously around the room, Margie said, "I beg of you, Tessa, this is getting monotonous. We are waiting much too long. There is a limit, even to self-sacrifice and well, as far as Bill is concerned—" She puffed, looked down at the pipe for a moment, and continued impatiently, "Well, you have nothing to say?"

"What do you think, Margie? You are well read, sexually experienced; do you think there are some special characteristics, some way one can define real love?"

"Real love? Why should you wonder about that? Are you by some chance skeptical about Bill's feelings?"

"No, no, that's not it. I meant generally."

"Hm, real love. Who knows? Every issue of the *National Weekly* explains these things differently, advertises particular methods for consideration. . . ." She shrugged her narrow shoulders and relit her pipe. "Our country creates men who have very complicated feelings. It's difficult, difficult to judge. In fact, I don't know. I have had enough of that nonsense. But what does he think, that good-looking Bill of yours?"

"Really, he is terribly long at that rummy game. He was supposed to take Seymour's place for just a while."

"Let's not wait any longer! I don't want to." Jumping up

from her seat, she took Tessa's arm. "Let's go inside. We should have done that right away. Everybody is having a wonderful time. Come on, you can't stay here forever and wait for a kiss."

"Let's wait just a little while longer, Margie, just a little."

Margie released Tessa's arm and sat down. "Would you like to know what I think right now?"

"What?"

"Well, I think Bill is not in love with you. If he were, he certainly would behave differently."

"You are vicious. I beg your pardon, but . . ."

"Oh, I'm not angry. But look. Bill plays rummy and leaves you here. Well, anything may happen. However, you know, if I were you I would try him out."

"Try him out?"

"Yes. A man can't be trusted anyhow, and a man of radical beliefs should be doubted as a matter of course. What if you exposed him to a real test?"

"What kind of test?"

"Oh, I don't know—none of the usual things." She relit her pipe. "During the Middle Ages, a knight in love would take up the colors and yearnings of his fair lady and ramble about the whole world, demolishing the skulls and properties of those who wouldn't recognize her as the fairest virgin wearing a skirt. . . ."

Tessa grew livelier. "And on rose-fragrant nights, he played nightingale serenades for his beloved, not permitting her to get to sleep. Or he stood on one leg for one complete week to prove his love. . . ."

"Yes," Margie said. "Even the cowboys would fight and risk lives for a woman. Then a girl's life must have been interesting."

"Rather different to try the love of our contemporary men with such methods. I can see you would want Bill to risk

66

life for me in a crusade of some sort, or shoot up the rest of the Indians."

"Something more painful."

"For instance?"

"Let's think about it."

"Let's."

Both girls, each in her own way, sat in an attitude of quiet meditation for a moment. Margie Maxton woke up first.

"I've got it."

"So have I."

Full of curiosity they faced each other like actors in a play.

"What? What is it?"

"You know, that idea to try my Bill's love for me is not bad. It's brilliant."

"What have you got?"

"I'll try him out. Although I don't really think it's necessary because I know Bill—but just the same, I'll try him out."

"How? How?"

Tessa slowly and rhythmically hit the side of her armchair in time to her words. "Bill is going to change his profession. He must do that for me, and that's all. No more discussions."

Margie clapped her hands with excitement. "Bravo, wonderful! This is really a modern way. My dear Tessa, a revolutionary method! A man has to change his occupation for the sake of the woman he loves! I think I'm going to insist on that myself."

"Now, this is what I thought out. He studied some economics at N.P.U., majored in political science, doing his writing on the side. Then, right before graduation, he decided to take my father's job at the Atomic Bank of the U. of U."

"Is he already there?"

"Not yet. He intends to be. Can you imagine my future? Mrs. Bookkeeper, Mrs. Cashier . . ."

"As time goes by, with the help of your father or Mr.

Seymour or Jack Small, you can be Mrs. Director, even Mrs. President of the U. of U. Some day maybe he'll get a high position in the CCRR, or be political adviser to those oily Abdoller brothers. One of them for sure will be elected President."

"Some day? Never. At Bill's age a man can graduate and start studying in a new field—instead of writing a sordid novel about Russian wars."

"But why study? Scholarly background doesn't bring a man better possibilities. The higher his education, the more chance of remaining unemployed for the rest of his days. Naturally it's worse for people without connections. But our forebears and spiritual supervisors detest the intelligent and well-educated person. It's the same with me. I can't get a job. 'Overqualified,' they say." She paused. "What do you want him to be?"

"That's it, I don't know. Suggest something. You're clever."

"Hmm. Wouldn't it sound nice if he were addressed as Mr. Secretary of State, or Mr. Senator, or Mr. Governor? Newspapermen would write about Bill, the brilliant statesman, and his lovely wife. You would be parading in the most stylish little suit, over yesterday from Paris. Pictures would be taken of both of you at every step you made; you'd be known all over the world. The African and European newspapers would certainly write about you as much as the American press. The *Atomic Magazine* would carry you on the cover at least five times a year. . . ."

"A dream."

"Not at all. All Bill has to do is to become a famous writer or orator. The Union of Unemployed would publicize him and glamorize him as the benefactor of the people, the social-minded dignitary. Just get him to be that social-minded dignitary."

"You think so?"

"Certainly. You are opening a new way of life for your-self."

"All right. How do I go about it?"

"Your parents will help. Even I'll help, only . . ."

As she paused, the lindy music in the dance hall stopped suddenly and a party of four burst in noisily, Rebecca Neely arm in arm with Frederick Tribbe, and Celine Layton with Stanley Kieb.

Wiping perspiration from his high forehead, Frederick cried, "Oh, I'm about to collapse!"

Rebecca shook his arm. "Fred, look, Tessa and Margie all by themselves!"

"And we were trying to find you all over the house," Celine put in. "You disappeared at the beginning of the dance."

"Why did you vanish?" asked Rebecca.

"And where is Bill?" added Celine.

But Rebecca continued her inquiry. "You didn't dance?"

Tessa shook her head.

"Well, Tessa and Margie are now in excellent form," said Frederick, in defense of girls. "And you, Stan?"

"I no longer can move my limbs, Fred old chap."

"You shouldn't have repeated the lindy."

They took seats wherever they could. Stanley, looking at Margie, observed, "In our country, everything is overdimensioned, but above all the architecture of pipes, and of course, political stupidity."

Frederick, who was over six feet and very long-limbed, agreeably added, "Yeah, everything is super, and this Weltansicht is weltering simultaneously in disappointment and depair. A quote from *Human Tragedy in the Atomic Age* by Professor Marek Katz."

"Yes," agreed Stanley, the older. "Human tragedy, and all we do is dance and drink and let our fathers plan our futures."

"Some play rummy," said Margie, and brown-eyed Rebecca added, "And some flirt."

"What else do you want, Stanley?"

"I know many more interesting delights . . . social games, for instance."

"I love them," said Tessa. "Especially some of them."

Celine looked through her pocketbook and drew out a lipstick. "Best of all, I like dancing."

"Dancing," quipped Stanley, "and sleeping with vitamins. Both bring identical results."

Everyone laughed.

"In my opinion," Tessa continued, "one should try for a variety of amusements."

"I think so too," replied Stanley, with his eyes on Tessa. "Italian sausage and Polish sausage, which one is longer?"

At that moment several couples entered the room and Frederick confronted them. "What do you think about it?"

"What's better, ladies and gentlemen?" Stanley addressed them. "To dance like an exhausted poor gigolo all night long without intermission, or from time to time diversify the evening by playing Chinese checkers, Monopoly, British socialism, kissing games, and other madnesses?"

"*Varietas delectat,*" observed one of the newcomers.

After him different voices added, "British socialism? What kind of idea is that?" "Let's play Chinese games." ". . . American Monopoly for me." "Let's simply relax from all kinds of fair deals, that's all!"

Amid all the noise Frederick Tribbe like a good horseman mounted a coffee table and the others surrounded him. "Who is with us, raise a hand!"

"As soon as the voting is over, shall we dance?" Celine asked him.

"Just an hour intermission."

Most of the party raised their hands, and Frederick said,

70

"My propostion has been accepted."

"I beg your pardon, I didn't take part in your voting. You promised me a dance."

"Celine, let's not indulge in trickeries. This is not voting for President."

At that moment Bill Wattson entered the room and all eyes turned toward him. Tessa went to him. "Ah, here he is! Come here, Bill. Frederick wanted to arrange some kind of national fun."

Frederick went on. "Ladies and gentlemen, I'll now show you a very interesting game. It's new. You don't know it."

Celine tried to be helpful. "Attention! A new fair deal, fresh horizons! What is it, Frederick? What are we to do?"

"Not much and no sacrifices. I'll show you if you want me to."

"Yes, please. If it's interesting."

"It is atomic?"

"All right, then. Let's all sit down in a circle."

Many seized chairs and began to place them in a circle.

"No, not this way. We have to sit on the floor."

Tessa objected. "What's the matter with you, Fred? In gowns, on the floor?"

"Never. Nonsense," agreed Rebecca.

"You don't sit on the floor, you sit on your charming little backsides."

Over the commotion Frederick Tribbe gave an order. "Sorry, that's the game. It's a Greek game."

William Wattson came forward. "As long as it's Greek, the girls can have our hankies. That's correct? The archaic Greek way, men. Out with handkerchiefs."

The boys spread them on the floor as Wattson noddingly approved. "That's excellent. In place of something more substantial, this will always do."

When all were seated, Frederick settled himself nearest

the door and asked, "Do you know what the game is about?"

"No," Celine said, "I don't know."

He asked the same question of everyone sitting in the circle. Then he announced, "The President doesn't know it either. As a matter of fact, Mr. De Jager doesn't know it. And—neither do I!" He jumped up and ran out of the room. Everyone laughed; some ran after him.

Bill Wattson turned to Tessa and Margie. "I have to apologize. It took me so long."

"It simply was mean of you to leave Tessa, Bill."

"It really wasn't," said Tessa. "I've had a long conversation with Margie about life and other matters."

"You have to understand, Tessa. I give you my word it wasn't my fault."

The rest of the conversation was engulfed in noise. In the dance hall the melody of a samba started up. Celine Layton was meditating, "What now? British socialism? What are we going to do now? Play Monopoly? What do we do, Rebecca?"

"Let's go and have something to eat."

"Kissing games? Mexican jumping beans? Monopoly? Somebody give us a suggestion, please."

Rebecca Neely thought a moment and raised her hands for silence. "I'll show you a very interesting game."

"Another far-fetched joke?"

"No joke; fortune-telling. Would you like that?"

"Good. Who's the fortune-teller?" asked Bill. Rebecca took a pack of cards from the table and placed herself in the big Victorian armchair. "Oh, fortune-telling from cards," Bill exclaimed. "Do you know how to do that, Beca? All right everyone, make way for Cassandra! Long live Pythia!"

At that moment Frederick appeared at the open door. "May I come in?"

"Come in," said Rebecca. "We forgive you." She began to sort the cards in her lap.

"What will this be? Four kings and four jacks with identical Persian faces. The Abdoller brothers should be here, they love Persian oil."

"Cabal. I'll foretell all life's misfortunes for you. Career disappointments. Love. How each lady should think of eight gentlemen and each gentleman of eight ladies."

"Shall we select the gentlemen from those present?" asked Tessa.

"Not necessarily, but you may."

The young people in the room looked around and counted on their fingers, whispering to each other and laughing. Rebecca, shuffling queens and aces, turned to Tessa, who was looking over her shoulder. "I'm starting. Do you have eight men?"

"Yes, almost."

"I'm starting with Tessa. Name yours in order."

"Should I say who they are?"

"Of course. Talk openly. No secrets; we're playing open cards. Let's believe once in sincerity, and down with the diplomatic concealment of under-the-table deals."

"All right, I'll name the men I'm thinking about."

"And the cards will reveal what you are thinking of them."

"Oh well, my conscience is clean."

"If you please. We are listening."

"Well, the first will be Frederick Tribbe."

"Thank you, Tessa, I'm in it?"

"He will be the king of hearts," said Rebecca.

"Second—Stanley Kieb."

"King of diamonds."

"Third—Franklin Kapistrot."

"He is not here—who is he? But let him be king of clubs."

"Fourth—Douglas Seymour."

"Not present either. Okay, king of spades."

"Fifth?"

73

"William Wattson?" asked Celine. "Bill has to be in your collection."

"All right."

"Bill is jack of hearts. Who is next?"

"May I mention the same person twice?"

"You may."

After reflection she said, "Bill is on twice. Just because he was fifth in line. But, well, the seventh is one unknown, handsome, winning . . ."

"What?" asked Wattson, irritated. Tessa wanted to say something, but Rebecca decided. "The mysterious unknown will be jack of spades."

"The last, the eighth . . . Jack Small, Junior."

"Jack of clubs. That's all. And now," she gave Tessa the shuffled cards, queens and aces, "with your left hand cut three times in the direction of your heart." Then, taking the cards from Tessa, she put the queens on jacks of the same suit, and aces on kings. "This one tries very much and asks . . ."

"Who? Who tries very hard? Who asks what?"

"The king of hearts."

Tessa searched her memory while the others giggled. "King of hearts? That's Frederick."

"This one you will forget."

"Who? Who will I forget?"

"The king of spades."

"That is terrible. An old friend of my father's—he will be angry."

Rebecca continued. "This one's family would like you. . . ."

Tessa looked. "Jack of clubs? Oh . . ."

"This one is tempting you."

"King of diamonds? That's Stanley. Are you tempting me? Let me look at you. . . ." She turned her round face with its small nose and bright, desirous eyes toward him. "Well,"

74

she remarked to everybody, "we have been friends for years and I learn only now that Stan is the tempting kind."

"It isn't I who am the tempter!" he retorted, with loud laughter. "It's Tessa. It is I who am being lured. . . ."

Rebecca interrupted his clowning. "This one you think about very often."

"Unavoidable."

"This one confuses your heart, Tessa."

"Oh."

"And this one you love very much."

"Ohhh, Beca, not so fast—jack of hearts? Who's jack of spades? Again the mysterious unknown. . . ."

"And this one you will marry, and be rich and happy."

Celine Layton, who was whispering to Frederick, came back to the game. "Jack of diamonds? That's Bill. Long live the young couple! Where is the lucky husband of a beautiful, rich girl?" Searching him out she nodded brightly. "My congratulations and my thanks to Rebecca. Very well done."

Margie, as Tessa's best friend, intervened. "Whether it is well done or not remains to be seen. Tessa vowed not to marry a European socialist type, but a real American democrat."

"Yes, I shall marry only a real American, a benefactor of the American farmers and workers and a great orator like President Kennedy."

Bill Wattson was listening silently, seeming neither surprised nor alarmed, while Margie concluded, "In other words, an American gentleman of way-above-average ambitions."

Celine was sarcastic. "Look at the demands—I wouldn't be surprised if Bill dropped everything and lived as a virgin."

"Poor, poor Bill. No hope here for a writer," said Stanley, and Frederick asked, "What do you say, Bill?"

"Well then, I'll become a social worker—and I am American, after all."

At this, Stanley, who liked Tessa and had his own plans, commented, "Really!"

"Yes, out of spite!"

Celine became more interested. "Stanley, what do you think a social worker really amounts to?"

"You, my steady girl, with all the dancing both of us love to do, and you don't know? I'm amazed."

"Explain it to me."

"Certainly. A social worker, who must belong to our President's Social Corps, is a man who generally sacrifices himself for the good of the rest of the world."

"Sacrifices himself generally?" Celine picked up the words and concluded, "Then teachers, physicians, priests—all those are members as well, aren't they?"

"No. The Social Corps, having no interest in their own profit, are working for the good of the people and for the larger American companies with foreign branches. One can't say that the Methodist pastor is such a man. Though sometimes one finds an exception to this type among people in the branches of the intelligence service, in the optical profession, or among Jehovists."

"If you please, Stan, you don't know a thing. Social workers, Miss Layton, are men. . . ."

"And women, I suppose?" Rebecca interrupted.

"Men," said Fred, "I'm speaking of men who belong to the most exclusive clubs, take part in highly secret indoctrination meetings, go to public gatherings where they lecture with endless depth on Eastern and Western culture and on socialism and other dangers to our country. Then those gentlemen relax from their strenuous talking and thinking at a nice club, restricted, naturally; and later they return home directly into bed under a perfumed canopy with a charming, admirable, working spouse."

While the room was shaking with the clamor of laughter

76

Celine shouted, "You are just making fun. I wanted to learn about the real social workers."

Tessa took a part in the discussion. "Let Stanley talk. He knows about that matter. He's the assistant commander of the League of Young Individualists."

"What are you gentlemen doing in that organization?" Bill asked.

"We intend to rebuild the world," he announced, stepping forward into the center of the room, "on the broad base of American justice. We're rooting out fear and ignorance in anticipation of the—no doubt—approaching social and political cataclysm. We annihilate national sentimentality and ideological timidity in Africa. Socialism and its many manifestations have only hampered and spoiled the real principles of universal justice. We tear apart all national exclusiveness, whether white or black. Against nationalism we pit American justice and love!"

All listened in silence as if hypnotized.

"We deny a way of life that consists largely of the development of heart, soul, or cash, as we are convinced that the completeness of life crystallizes by itself. We stand for real life in real American social equality. Every person must have the right and the possibility to grow to the highest social status by virtue of his moral, intellectual, and material qualifications. Those are the principles of the League of Young Individualists."

"Where is democracy?" asked Frederick.

Bill Wattson broke in. "That's what you call American democracy? I would say it's just another political mixture of the most ordinary American beef stew, pompously titled by some perverted PR type. As a matter of fact, I don't even try to understand the whole mess or to explain it to myself or others; although I heard that the membership of your organization, Stan, consists mainly of sons of important manufacturers, bankers, and other merchants."

"All of us in this room are rich. That's nothing to hold against us. We're an organization interested in the good of humanity, and our members are also sons of farmers, nineteenth-century immigrants, all kinds of things. Our manufacturers and merchants have accomplished a great deal, yet recent immigrants always manage to find an occasion to criticize us. While the rich invest great sums in social foundations for the poor and unfortunate Negroes, and so forth, there are others, like you, who talk nonsense."

"Now I'm catching on," said Tessa. "Excellent, it's the truth—nothing but. My father explained it to me. Every clerk in his company, and for that matter in America, lives on illusions, hoping to become a millionaire tomorrow. Today he owns an old Ford, but tomorrow . . . ! As far as my parents and I are concerned, only benevolent monarchies can really save the world from confusion and mass starvation."

"Yes indeed," Bill Wattson said bitterly. "Now how about finishing our social games for today?" He approached Tessa hastily, but Frederick, saying "Let's dance," was first to get her under his arm. Margie was claimed by Stanley. The music swung into a loud chorus.

As the couples moved to the door Frederick turned toward Bill and observed wryly, "Love and hate are the greatest sicknesses of the human race. By right of being itself, life has to be a row of duties. That is the program of all the literature of tomorrow."

"Evidently the author of this literature of tomorrow never loved," said Margie.

Fred looked at Tessa and whispered, "Even if one loves sincerely, one can discipline one's feelings."

Tessa spoke loudly over the music. "However, as soon as a man is supposed to make a choice between the woman he loves and his social duty of writing a novel on the Russo-

German War, he will take the beautiful Tania, his own fictional creation."

⌷ Chapter 8

"What better things have you to offer, that my wife hasn't offered me?" From my bed I asked Gusty Mary De Jager, as she stood in a pink nightgown at the door to my room. "Do you know the time?"

"Yes," she said innocently, threading her silver hair with her long fingers. "It is two A.M. As to the first question, experience and tenderness." She walked into the room and sat on the edge of my bed. Chanel Number Five reached my nostrils.

"I'm your husband's guest, and right now I'm reading a history of the De Jager family. As you know he is paying me for writing a book, but not for extras."

"Yes, we will make you rich. But tonight your bonus will be pleasure, pure pleasure, and I will do the work."

"What have you under your arm?" I tried to change the subject as delicately as possible.

"Wattson's novel, what he has finished so far—or actually a photostatic copy of it. My chauffeur sneaked into his house and borrowed it."

"Your chauffeur is a handsome man, I noticed."

"He is a good lovebird, but sometimes very brutal."

"May I see the novel?"

"Here it is. Read, and let me know if it is socialistic. If it is—well, my daughter is not going to marry a socialist. To me the title *Brothers in Stalingrad* is communistic. Otherwise,

79

what I've looked at seems neither here nor there. But the people are queer. I don't see why he should try to make them seem so heroic for fighting against the Germans."

"Let me read it first."

"The night is exciting and peaceful, you and I . . ."

I tried not to listen and flipped through the first pages of Wattson's story, wondering nervously what Gusty Mary would do. I felt her staring. Then she stood up and laughed lightly.

"I want you to know," she said, "that most of the women I know would arrange to have you let go for refusing them. But I have other men, and so I don't really need you." She waited until I looked up. "I know what I have to give a man. Now we will forget this meeting. It never took place."

She turned and left, closing the door quietly.

I looked down at my page, relieved; and my embarrassment drained as I took up the thread of Wattson's story.

. . . The black silence of the Russian night was suddenly torn by a thunderous, reverberating roar. Peal followed upon peal, shrill and piercing, like a sharp knife cutting metal. Ugly like a mad beast champing. Seconds between breaths became shivering gasps.

Deep in the startled night a man raged like a beast. His orders were the knife. The man was a general, General Herman von Hoth; and at his command, division after division plunged into the night. Tanks rolled forward. Airplanes leaped into the sky. Guns beat out a rapid and incessant stream of wrath. Bombs fell and soon sprang into geysers of flames. This was the destruction of a great city.

Seconds passed. Minutes. The machines kept up their greedy howls. The people of the city cringed like animals in a trap. Their city was being pulverized like stone fed into a crusher. The inhabitants caught the pungent odor of the sickening nazi cocktail: smoke, fresh blood and dead bodies.

Yet strength grew in their hearts, and became armor to their minds.

"Reach the Volga at any price!" That was the order the Führer had sent into the night to his general, and the general had straightened up to answer this command.

But the tanks had ceased to be certain weapons of destruction. They faltered and crawled and their gunfire had the thin sound of nutcrackers. Even the Messerschmitts were frightened, helplessly flapping their wings in this storm. Their frustration flared in the sky for a few minutes, and then they sank to the earth, wounded partridges caught by huntsmen's bullets. The soldiers became as useless as their implements of war. They could not withstand the invisible force that welled from behind every building wall. The tanks beat a retreat; the Messerschmitts searched aimlessly for safety. And the soldiers, fainting, gasping, and half dead, followed their weapons. They could not endure the seething power, the fire from other guns, the fire from men and women defending their own.

The general's blood nearly burst its veins. His eyes flamed; the foam at his mouth frothed blood. More orders. "Forward. Forward!" But his soldiers could not go on. The more audacious sang *"Deutschland, Deutschland über alles . . . ,"* but this song quickly became a groan and the lips that shaped the words were twisted into agonized grins. The echo returning from the night was not *"Deutschland über alles";* but Volga River laughter.

And so Germans retreated. Night remained mournful, brightened only by flames that scarred her thick black cloak, feeding on the northwest corner of this city, that now became smoldering embers. Von Hoth silenced his guns. His rage subsided. He took a long, lusty drink, removed his clothes, drank once more. And now quite drunk, his shame vanished and he went to sleep.

This hour before dawn was filled with pale, misty calm. Such stillness was not ominous or oppressive, but soothing, like solitude. The ancient who saw in each dawn the birth of a new world was both philosopher and seer. But on this morning, the chill in the gray hour clashed with the vigorous pulse of life—a new and valiant life.

Brigades of trucks rumbled through the streets. Ambulances sped steadily. Motorcycles assumed straight courses among shrapnel-riddled buildings. Their riders dismounted to hunt among the debris for human wisps. The light chill breeze carried no chirping melody of birds; it bore a burden of muffled sobs and agonized moans. The night was not quite gone; it lingered as if defying the day to overcome its devastation. It was a ravenous wolf lurking near a pillaged sheepfold. Its greed for human misery seemed insatiable. And yet, its resolution wilted before the clean-limbed strength of new sun rays.

Something could be seen stirring in the wreck of one building. Silhouetted in black, moving in pantomime against morning's gray curtain, it had no thickness—just some height and slender breadth. It ran. It scurried away like a rat eluding its pursuer. It could have been a wild creature dancing a weird dance, a dance over human bodies. Thin ribbons of smoke rising from the ruins entwined themselves around the figure. Strange scene—this dance of ribbons. The figure faltered, paused, bent down. The silhouette, no longer tall, bent low to the earth. A sound had been heard, not a human sound, but a pleading imperative. A fumbling in the rubble. The source of the plea had been found. A dog was caught in a hole, and at her feet were the mutilated bodies of her puppies. Did she think to call the little creatures back to life through her convulsive howling? The human creature crept close to the writhing animal and murmured something. The dog stirred.

Her plaintive eyes reached those of the person who would have been her rescuer. She had found some small comfort, some sense of kinship. A mother dog and a mother human bound by female tenderness.

The woman knelt beside the dog, and it struggled forward to rest its head on her lap. But the head was soon trembling, and eyes opened wide. Pain departed. The dog was dead. Warm blood still ran from a deep gash in her side. At last she fell back into the hole, into the bloody mass of her puppies.

Dawn was nearer, near enough to let the crouching woman see the red piece of flesh dripping with blood and pus that was the dog's body. The woman shivered and regained her footing.

Rain and snow were now falling, captured by a breeze that occasionally mounted to a whipping wind. The woman wrapped a scarf tightly round her head, and with great effort, dragged herself forward. With every other painful step she paused to look back, and around. Her ears caught the sound of cannon roaring; and guns sputtering far away. Or was it really that far? She could no longer tell. She only knew that she must drive herself forward. She heard sounds—regular, rhythmic ones. It was the clangorous music of tanks. The same tanks that had lacerated the pups and driven them into the hole. The puppies had become steak, German steak. The woman shuddered. She stumbled, fell. Yet once more, recovered enough strength to go forward.

The mother dog had lost her babies. She was now dead. And so would this woman die, as the dog had done.

Factories and schools and homes had been shattered. The acrid, rancid smell of burning flesh, wood, rubber, and even molten metal filled her nostrils and sickened her.

She was not going to die. She must not. She was going to live. She would escape. She must keep ahead of the tanks.

"Tanks! Tanks! Oh, Father! God! Tanks! Father . . . !"

and with this cry on her lips she crumpled. She could go no further. A few feet forward, perhaps it was even a mile distant, was a house that had been pierced many times by automatic guns. She had seen those gun holes, and strangely enough, when she had seen them, they had reminded her of old yellowed pictures of majestic ruins in ancient Rome. These gun holes formed a wreath with their slender openings for firing. The entire structure played on her imagination.

She laughed wildly, but with weakness. But with pride also. For she was a Russian, a living Russian woman, not a Roman woman dead for century upon century. She was a Russian reared on the banks of the Volga, descended from Slav barbarians. Her barbarian ancestors had saved the Volga from thousands and thousands of marauders. She and her countrymen must once more save the great river and its city from the newest marauder, the German superman. Tania, yes, Tania, descendant of Slav barbarians, would help to save the city.

"Tania, Tania!" She called her own name feebly, so feebly. She wept. She slept. She wakened to another cry from her lips: "Jan! Jan! Tanks! Jan!" Why did these two words spring forth? She felt she knew the reason, but was too tired to search in her mind for it. Much too tired. Now she would die with those two words on her lips.

⌗ Chapter 9

Worker Hryc Denczenko crouched on a stool in the cellar room's darkest corner, his shaggy head supported by great, brawny hands. With each breath drawn, his luxurious, abundant mustache waved like an animated mop and cast moving shadows on the dingy wall opposite him. He was no longer a young man, sixty, at least, lean and gaunt-looking. But underneath his strong physical countenance was a crushed spirit. Yet somehow he was managing to hold himself together. His two companions sang, keeping time to the music that one of them, Ivan Skobelev, was drawing from his harmoshka. But not Denczenko. He only breathed, and perhaps thought, perhaps of his native Kiev, a mass of ruins now, or of his family. His wife had died with protest on her lips. His son had died with fists clenched. And his daughter had drifted to death, wearily. All of his family were now dead. He did not know why he was still alive. But as he thought, he realized that he had remained alive so as to satisfy the need for brutal vengeance. Denczenko set his jaw and gnashed his teeth. He was a Ukrainian, and a Ukrainian knows the meaning of vengeance.

The music continued—a perpetual flow of rhythm. Ivan Skobelev sang a feeble tenor. David Rosen bellowed a mighty bass, and as he roared, his feet kept time. If there had been a good light in the deep cellar, it would have shown his beaming face. Such good will. It sparkled in his black eyes. David Rosen neither Party member nor factory worker, neither Jew nor Gentile; was a creature living, throwing his whole being into the song he was singing:

> *But if any foe should try to smash us*
> *Try to desolate our land so dear,*
> *Like the thunder, like the sudden lightning*
> *We will give our answer, sharp and clear.*

These resolute words, given out in measured beats, rolled past the narrow cellar window, and into the disappearing night. The distant, heavy cannon sent back an echoing jeer of defiance. They had nothing but scorn for the bold Bolshevik song. The singers sang even more loudly. David Rosen lost the rhythm in his rage. Ivan Skobelev's tenor became a shrill, insurgent wail. The cannon thundered back.

Still Hryc Denczenko remained silent and oblivious to song and cannonade. His gaunt body waited in the cellar, which was all that remained of the house that had offered him a haven when he first came to Stalingrad. But his mind, his spirit, and his heart were in Kiev, roving up and down a street called Shevtschenko searching for a house. Now they have found the shambles of one. In it lie the bloody, mutilated body of its mistress and the crumpled, stinking mass that once was a boy.

Denczenko stirred. His mind, heart, and spirit rejoined his body, and all urged this silent resolution: "I will make tanks. Tanks to drive the fascist filth into the earth."

If Hryc Denczenko had not forgotten how to laugh, he would have done so over a recollection that came back to him now. When he had first spoken of his decision to go to Stalingrad, a friend had responded, "To make tanks? It is good. The earth will give an abundant harvest after it has been fertilized by nazi flesh and bone and watered by nazi blood."

He had left the destruction that was Kiev to tramp through the dark night. He had hidden in ditches. He had begged for food. Twice the Germans had caught him, and twice through his Ukrainian cunning he had escaped from them. He had gotten to Stalingrad, and then to the Krasnyi Oktiabr factory. The engineer, Ivan Skobelev, had observed his strong hands and his alert, intelligent eyes. He had given him work to do, and saw that he did it with the skill of a master mechanic. Ukrainian, was he? Well, who cared? He wanted to be the man's friend. So he had brought him to this house, and introduced him to David Rosen, then a secretary of the food concern, but now, since the siege of Stalingrad had begun, a worker, too, in the Krasnyi Oktiabr.

The three were companions in the cellar. Ivan Skobelev and David Rosen would have said, had they been asked, that all were friends. Rosen would even have gone further and called them "blood brothers." But not Denczenko. He felt their kindness. He observed their generous desire for friendship. He appreciated it, but had no will to reciprocate. He lived not for friendship, but for vengeance alone. The most powerful force in him was hatred. He felt no loneliness. No desolation. No void of misery. No uncontrollable sorrow because of his family's martyrdom. He felt and thought hate. It was the pit of his existence.

Suddenly David Rosen stopped his singing and exclaimed anxiously, "Where is our fourth tenant?" As he spoke, he picked up his automatic rifle.

Skobelev put down his instrument and walked about the room. He had been worried by Tania's long absence and had not wished to reveal this to Rosen. It was strange for the girl to stay out so long, especially during the firing. The military police should have finished their questioning long ago. She also knew that the safest place was in the cellar.

Rosen's question served to rouse Denczenko from his ugly reverie, and he, like Skobelev, got to his feet and walked about the room. But he did not speak. Speech was a useless thing. Instead, he went to the water pail and gulped down a great draught of water; then he tore a page from *Pravda* and began to roll a cigarette.

"I'm going out to search for her," Rosen announced and moved toward the door. It was a queer thing, that door. Its wood had been splintered in the first hours of the bombardment and quilted rags now hid the entrance. Tania had made it and it was serving its purpose well.

Engineer Skobelev rushed to the door to block his exit. "Stop!" he shrilled, a little hysterically.

Rosen was so surprised that he dropped his cap. As he

stooped to pick it up, he asked gratingly, "Do you think you are still in the factory and have the right to order me around?" The unpleasant laugh and the sneer in his voice continued. "We are in private now, my friend. I may go if I want to. I have a right to look for Tania, while you . . ."

"So have I," Skobelev interrupted. "I've been thinking of her for some time."

"Yes, for some time," Rosen snarled, "for five years. Well, I've had my thoughts on her for seven years." He motioned for Skobelev to move away from the door, but Skobelev stood firm.

Denczenko returned to his stool and appeared to be giving all his attention to his large cigarette. He sucked in the fragrance in deep, lusty puffs.

"I've more right to her than you have," Rosen declared to Skobelev. "I didn't marry another woman. I've been waiting for her consent."

Engineer Ivan, struggled with a sudden spasm of rage, but failed to bring forth any words.

"But what did you do?" Rosen wheezed. "While you waited, you married a wife. Yes, you did, and now that she's dead, you're ready to begin waiting for Tania again." There was a fine righteous scorn in Rosen's resonant voice.

"Shut up, you bastard," Skobelev stuttered. "You, a member of the Party speaking such damnable nonsense."

"Member of the Party or not, factory worker or not," Rosen became more violent, "these things do not matter. This is a private concern of yours and mine. You want Tania. I want Tania. Tell me now, which of us is more worthy of her?" Rosen shook his fist in Skobelev's face. His eyes were flaming.

"David! David!" the engineer had the tone of a master reproving a recalcitrant child. "Come here, and sit down. Let's talk about this. But first, I must tell you something."

Reluctantly, David Rosen permitted himself to be pressed

onto a bench. Skobelev sat down on one of the steps leading to the door. Denczenko continued to suck on his cigarette, apparently quite oblivious to the swift fire of passion that had flamed in the room. The brief, tense silence was broken by Skobelev.

"David," he said with infinite gentleness, "there is no need to look for Tania."

"What do you mean? Is Tania dead, then?" Rosen asked. "Are you hiding some terrible news from me?"

"No, no." Ivan was dealing with a child. "Tania is alive, but most likely in jail. At this moment, our police are likely questioning her."

"Questioning her! Questioning Tania? Are you crazy? Tania belongs to the Party. She is loyal." Rosen jumped up as he spoke, clutching his rifle in his hand, and made a move to sweep the engineer from the doorway.

"For all your experience as a Party official, David, there are still a number of things you do not know," Skobelev spat, and his action brought Rosen to a boil.

"What?" he roared and raised his automatic to a ready position.

Skobelev did not flinch. He was going to take his time. He enjoyed seeing Rosen in a fit of fear and excitement. When he resumed speaking, at last, Skobelev measured out his words in syllables. He would not be hurried, not by David Rosen anyway.

"Being a Party official, David," he said, "you must know that after we took the city of Lwow in nineteen thirty-nine, we sent a scientist there to work at the Polytechnic with a Polish professor."

"Yes, yes," Rosen exclaimed impatiently, "but what has that got to do with Tania Petrovna?"

It pleased Skobelev to ignore the question and to continue in the same manner as before. "This Polish fellow was named

Dobrowicz, if I remember correctly; and our man was Tarasov, a well-known scientist from Moscow University, you may recall."

Another pause followed, even longer than the first one. Rosen stamped his feet and beat a noisy tattoo on the table with his rifle.

"I know, I know!" he cried, "and the two old birds died, didn't they, in some kind of an explosion? And their formula with them. What was it? Indestructible steel, wasn't it?"

"Their formula did not die," Skobelev stated impressively. "It is in the head of a stubborn Pole called Jan Wolski, and Tania knows him."

This revelation startled Rosen. He glared at Skobelev incredulously. Tania Petrovna knew a Pole, she also knew some Americans. . . . The police had probably taken her to underground headquarters for questioning. What did this mean? That Tania was suspected of harboring an enemy? Ridiculous! Tania was of the Party. Loyalty was as much a passion with her as it was with him.

"Now if you have been as faithful to Tania as you say you have been, you could not have failed to observe that she was absent from Stalingrad during the last months of nineteen hundred and thirty-nine." Skobelev chuckled. "She was in Lwow with Professor Tarasov. His secretary, she was."

"Ah!" Rosen finally seemed to understand.

"And just today, we discovered a fellow in my department at Krasnyi Oktiabr who is probably Jan Wolski. He goes under another name also, Kowalski. He has a beard as long as a Siberian monk's. When you talk to him, he grunts and nods his head and pretends that he is deaf. Yet we think, indeed we are sure, he's this Wolski who disappeared. You see now?" Skobelev clapped his hands in triumph and hummed a bar or two of a Russian song.

"And Headquarters thinks Tania Petrovna has seen him

since he came to Stalingrad?" Rosen asked in miserable perplexity.

"Exactly!" Skobelev was exultant. "Our agents have told us that they were together all the time in Lwow. Do you think he would come to Stalingrad and not find her?"

The triumphant expression suddenly vanished from Skobelev's face. The fear that had been seething in him since the morning could not be restrained any longer. He, Ivan Skobelev, engineer of the great Krasnyi Oktiabr, began to sob. So did Rosen. Even Denczenko, still sucking noisily on his great stub of a cigarette was drawn into this little well of fear.

"I don't believe it," Rosen reacted suddenly, and with force. "Not one cursed word of it, I tell you. Tania would have handed him over to the authorities. She is a Russian girl in spite of her American connections. Her country comes first. She understands. No man, not even a lover . . ." Rosen's voice was smothered by his sobs.

"What a fool you are, David!" Skobelev muttered. "You think because a woman has sworn an oath to her country, she will betray her lover! What an idiot."

David Rosen sank down on the stool nearest the door. He kept his rifle in his hand, as if he would soon leave to search for Tania. Doubts whirled through his mind as furiously as jealousy tugged at his heart. This man Kowalski, if he were Wolski, had within his grasp the power to save thousands, perhaps millions, from the nazi heel. Now Tania, loyal patriot that he knew she was, would be the first to realize this. She would turn him over to the authorities. Of course she would. He, David Rosen, knew that she was a good girl, faithful, yes, a hundred times yes. Inaccessible—ah, yes, he knew that, for every effort he had made to win her had failed. Deep in his heart he believed that there was no man in all of the Soviet Union who had the power to achieve her favor. No man whatsoever. And certainly no slinking, spying Pole. David's thoughts were confused. Sometimes they became so entangled in fear and doubt that he could not have expressed them if either Skobelev or Denczenko had spoken to him, but Denczenko, at least, was not likely to do so, for he was absorbed in his own thoughts and a second *Pravda* cigarette.

"Why wasn't Kowalski arrested?" Rosen asked Skobelev, at last. "It would have been soon enough for Tania to be dragged in."

Instead of answering, Skobelev got up from the steps and picked up his harmoshka. He ran his fingers over it aimlessly for a few seconds, and then began to play in earnest. The quick, plucky sounds announced to Rosen that their conversation was over.

Next came a stream of words, and there was nothing feeble in Ivan Skobelev's voice now. They popped out of his thick-lipped mouth in staccato succession, and quickly conveyed to Rosen that Ivan knew he had gotten the better of him in their discussion. The words and their accompanying gesticulations became louder, more flamboyant. Rosen tried to curb his anger and anxiety, and tensed to do so. He wanted so much to spring up and strangle the song, but could not find the final desire. On it went, as a drill drives its way through rock or an electric hammer set for an hour's beating. A cracked mirror, hanging on a rusty nail, trembled. A thick, ungainly tallow candle, set in a brown earthenware bowl, swayed and sputtered. The incongruous harmony of instrument and human voice assailed the brick walls of the cellar, and were thrust back into the room. The vibrations struck in turn the gray tin washbasin that stood on an upturned crate, David Rosen at the base of his brain, the singer Ivan between his teeth, and Denczenko full in the eardrums, for he put up his large hands to protect them from the reverberation.

In the gray dawn, shrouded by smoke as it struggled out of the night, Ivan's song was absorbed in a whirlpool of noise.

The notorious stormoviks zoomed overhead, at a high and low altitude. Cannon roared and echoed. Bullets buzzed and bounced like hailstones.

Rosen sat still. Denczenko sat still. Skobelev, conscious at last of this rivalry of sound, put down his harmoshka and drowned the song on his lips with a great, gulping swallow of vodka straight from his bottle. Swallow followed swallow. The all-enclosing warmth generated by the alcohol transformed Ivan. In a moment, he had become subdued to a gentler mood. Perhaps his condition could not be called maudlin; certainly it was tearful; and the melody that he brought forth from the harmoshka was clear, simple and soothing. It contained child's laughter as well as the quiet of green fields and swaying trees and the golden warmth of summertime.

Denczenko felt it and raised his head. For a few seconds he could forget his family killed by nazi brutes.

Rosen also heard it and the grief on his face vanished. Jewish tenacity was restored to his expression.

The music persisted. Skobelev had finished his last drop of vodka.

The door creaked on its rusty hinges. The music stopped. Tania Petrovna, the fourth tenant of the cellar room, staggered down the steps and ran to her pallet of straw in a corner. She had used up her last bit of strength. She fell, face downward, onto the straw.

Silence filled the room, a silence mingled with growing anxiety. Then consternation which deepened into petrifying fear. The last state accompanied by a terrible trembling, for bombs were again churning up the very earth that supported the cellar. In these seconds, as the threat of instant oblivion stalked into the room, three pairs of eyes turned to the weary Tania. The terror that had been locked into David Rosen's eyes opened to allow the glow of admiration and passion to enter. He truly loved Tania, and his love illuminated the shadowy room.

Skobelev removed his hungry gaze from her just long enough to see this light and to utter in a resonant voice, "A man called Jan Wolski has come from Poland to work in the factory."

He need not have troubled with such an experiment; no tremor ran through Tania's body. She was as unresponsive to Skobelev's words as she was to the greed that narrowed his eyes. If the weary girl, fatigued by work and fear, could have responded to any eyes, it would have been to those of Hryc Denczenko, for his were deep pools of fatherly affection. He looked at her and saw in her not Tania Petrovna at all, but his daughter Kraska.

There was no area of Tania's body that Rosen's eyes did not caress. If she had seen his face then, her confidence in him would have multiplied. She would have lost her girlish desire to laugh at him and to make light of his extravagant, fluently spoken declarations of undying passion. She would have seen abiding sincerity there and a resolution that stood for loyalty. But if she had turned toward Skobelev her attitude would have been entirely different, for his impassioned face was flushed with the hungry desire to possess. Like a thylacine surveying a feast, he fastened his gaze on her strong, shapely legs and on her firm, rounded buttocks. He wanted her, and if he had had more vodka in him, and there had been fewer witnesses, he would have taken her then and there. He would not have cared a wit that she would be too exhausted either to protest or acquiesce. He would have forced himself upon her, and forever afterward she would have been his beautiful Tania, as desirable in exhaustion as in laughing vigor. Skobelev made a vow to himself: he would have Tania Petrovna. She would be his forever. To hell with a disguised Pole, or an American, called Jan Wolski; to hell with a Jew called David Rosen—though as a real Russian, he pictured hell as a deep cavernous mine in Siberia.

Denczenko stirred. He got to his feet, took his thick Ukrainian woolen coat from its hook, and stooping down, with infinite tenderness put it around Tania's body.

Planes zoomed. Guns roared. Tanks chugged, lurched, crashed. A tempest of bullets and bombs tore through the air. Shrieks. More firing. General Herman von Hoth's offensive was finally beaten back. The blood-soaked earth of the Volga's banks shuddered, trembled, and grew strong, only to be shattered again, and again.

 # Chapter 10

In his huge office sat Lawrence Aldrich Abdoller, honorary director of the Union of Unemployed. Sliding doors on the left led into other offices and a double door on the right to the waiting room. At his back were two great windows. On the other three walls hung several bulletin boards containing statistical figures on unemployment interspersed with portraits of the leading industrialists of the country. Among them were William S. De Jager, Roger Rollon, Jack V. Small, Douglas A. Seymour, John Victor Casevant, General Cornelius C. Colt, the five Abdoller brothers, including Lawrence, whose allergy to oil was treated by Dr. Béla Schick.

Mr. Abdoller, a man of forty-five, blond, with a full face and a balding head, finished reading his mail and called in the direction of the door, "Miss Marah!" He closed his folder and put it aside with the exuberant, confident look of a successful political candidate. She did not appear, and so he pushed a button on his desk.

Miss Marah entered quickly from the left, struggling with a

heavy bundle of papers. "Yes, sir!" Through the half-open door came the noise of typewriters.

"You can have the mail now, Miss Marah. This draft on physical education to the Secretary of the Interior I will hold for a while yet. Don't look for it. Anything new?"

She handed him a letter from her stack of papers. "Yes, a letter from the Cooperatives Union. I didn't have a chance to post it."

Abdoller took the letter. "Very good. After I read it, I'll give it back to you. You may go."

Miss Marah added the mail folder to her stack and walked out.

"Ah!" exclaimed Abdoller to himself, reading the letter. "Very good. The President will be glad." He reached for the telephone. "Stipulations?" He raised the receiver to his ear. "Hallo! Honorary director Abdoller speaking. Oh, it's you. How are you? I received an answer from the Cooperatives Union. No . . . that's the answer to our last year's petition in regard to the subsidy. Yes, yes . . . but successful. Two hundred thousand dollars in quarterly payments. Of course. A referendary of the department can be engaged. Self-evident. A well-known economist. No, I have no one in mind. Very well. Good-bye. Eh, hallo, hallo . . . you come over today, will you? Fine, we'll see you then."

Joseph Col, the Negro usher, entered from the right, and presented him a card. "The lady wishes to see you, sir."

"Ask her in. Oh, Joseph—did she say what she wants?"

"She was here last week, when you were out of the office."

"And?"

"She only said she is chairman of those educated, God-fearing ladies, or whatever they are. Who knows? Strange lady to me, sir."

"All right, have her come in."

Joseph Col bowed low and walked out. In the waiting room

his gentle voice could be heard: "Mr. Abdoller is expecting you, madam."

Gusty Mary De Jager entered smiling in a Paris suit. Although past fifty, she moved with grace. She began talking at once in a cheery voice that betrayed a surprising French accent. "Good morning, good morning, Mr. Abdoller. We know your brother Lloyd very well. Do you remember me?"

"Of course, Mrs. De Jager—in spite of the fact that, at this moment, I am unable to remember where we met. Please have a seat."

"Thank you. My husband, of course, is one of the founders of the Union of Unemployed. And we met for the first time in Lloyd's apartment on Beekman Place. I was admiring his marvelous French impressionists. Then the second time was at the ball of the Capital Charity Organization. . . ."

"Ah yes, yes."

"About three months ago."

"Yes, indeed."

"I took you by surprise then, didn't I? You remember, the offer of our ladies' department to cooperate with you? Well, I have the honor of being their chairman. You first thought we were joking, but I spoke in earnest. I am here today to renew our offer."

"Why yes, of course, I remember well. I've thought deeply about your magnanimous offer. Only, I have to admit, there are certain doubts in my mind."

"What could they be?"

Lawrence Abdoller was slightly embarrassed. "You see, Mrs. De Jager, I'm afraid that you ladies—what I mean to say is, you ladies who are accustomed to the graces of society may not approve of our organizational material. The center of our interest and work is the unemployed." He leaned toward her sympathetically. "The unemployed are a group of people who are neglected in every way. Half-people. An underworld. Poverty

97

has demoralized them not only materially but even physically and psychically."

"That is why, my dear honorary director, we have to work intensively for those poor creatures." She spoke vivaciously. "That is why we have to sacrifice ourselves for them. That is why we want to meet them with open arms and words of encouragement and comfort. Of course, the contact with these unhappy victims of the cycle crisis will demand self-discipline on our part, physical strength, and the investment of our egos. However, this will give each of us great spiritual satisfaction, which is, after all, the meaning of life—that is, self-sacrifice. Your four sisters-in-law and your good friends Mrs. Seymour, Mrs. Small, and Mrs. Rollon will be very, very fulfilled."

"Indeed. Yes, yes, self-understood."

She took out a morocco leather-bound folder from her briefcase. "I'll read you our resolution as it was agreed upon during our last meeting. This is the result of long discussions and hard work on the part of your sisters-in-law and your brother Lloyd."

"I will be glad to hear."

"Here it is." She began to read, but quickly interrupted herself. "Oh, these are the changes." Then after a pause she went on. "Here . . . 'We wish to repair the historical blunder committed by many generations, whereby people were judged politically without any benefit of thought with regard to religion or economy. During the last century, the time of progressive capitalism and democracy, we, the leading class, permitted the religion and economy of the lower classes to remain on that level which satisfies only the most basic desires of being, while any participation in real life, operating on a higher cultural level, was completely out of their grasp. During that time of progressive capitalism and theoretical democracy, innumerable slaughters of the European and African people have taken place on many levels.' "

"Sacred truth," said Mr. Abdoller, wiping his round Baptist eyes.

" 'How are we to remedy a mistake of progressive capitalism and theoretical democracy? Only by acknowledging the principle that every member of the American Commonwealth and all civilized society as well has an equal right to participate in the national wealth, the government of our nation and the Stock Exchange. Therefore our association will undertake all appropriate steps and simultaneously will encourage our members to join us in this great renaissance of humanity.' How do you like it, Mr. Abdoller?"

"Very clear and beautifully presented. Only, I wonder, how do you ladies intend to approach this social problem and all that it involves?"

"Our program is all arranged and ready. I have it here: a plan for a lecture series!"

"Lectures? How interesting."

"Why, yes, of course. We wish to share with the unemployed our education and knowledge. What else are we prepared to offer them?"

"Sacred truth."

"Madame Miller intends to arrange for the youthful unemployed a coeducational course in German conversation."

Mr. Abdoller showed worried surprise and Mrs. De Jager clarified, "We have to take into consideration the special qualifications and hobbies of our members. For example, Madame Miller knows the German language very well. She also will lecture on the German government and national heritage."

"Very good."

"Mrs. Colegrove will probably lecture on sports. That, however, is tentative yet. But Mrs. Leach will teach the unemployed girls rhythmic dancing and plastic expression. Amelia is an accomplished sex hygienist. Do you read her articles?"

"No, unfortunately, though of course I've seen them."

"There will also be a lecture series on healthy and inexpensive nourishment. Mrs. Abner Bluefield, the wife of the real estate man, is a wonderful person with real political feeling." She burrowed again in her folder. "I have here a card, on which I have made a notation—not for myself. Mrs. Bluefield has a wonderful reducing diet. She thought it out herself. A wonderful reducing diet!"

"A reducing diet?"

"Yes, a reducing diet. You'd be surprised how many unemployed women are fat. Sixty-nine per cent! Mrs. Bluefield is a very thrifty woman herself, and I'm sure the unemployed will benefit greatly from her suggestions. For instance, at half past seven in the morning, one apple." She noticed Abdoller's impatience and talked faster. "For breakfast, one or two eggs; one piece of bread, corn or wheat; half a teaspoonful of butter; coffee, regular or Brazilian, unsweetened of course; one or two teaspoons of milk in the coffee. Those," she finished proudly, "are only two hundred and fifty calories."

"I beg your pardon, but now I must . . ."

Mrs. De Jager looked at her wristwatch. "Oh, have I taken too much of your time?"

"Not at all, Madame. I'm very glad you ladies are so anxious to help and I shall certainly bring it up at our next meeting. In fact, I shall make a special note for myself to mention to the President that the Association of Elegant Women . . ."

"It's now the Association of Progressive Ladies."

"I beg your pardon, Association of Progressive Ladies." He rose. "I shall phone you with the results of the meeting, Madame."

"Mr. Abdoller, I can't begin to thank . . ."

"Thank you, Mrs. De Jager. I owe a great deal to you and your husband. He is doing a splendid job for us on our CCRR and of course as a founder of the U. of U."

Joseph Col entered unexpectedly. "Sir, a young man."

Abdoller touched his forehead nervously. "Right away, please."

Mrs. De Jager paused at the door. "Oh, Mr. Abdoller. I almost forgot! Would you mention something about our association in your papers? Could you say that our Progressive Ladies . . ."

"Why, yes, of course."

"I have here with me a story which you can use in your newspapers. It hardly needs editing and will save your editor work and time. It's all ready to be printed." Smiling, she gave him a large piece of paper.

"Thank you very much."

"Good-bye, honorary director. It has been a pleasure."

"Good-bye, madam, the pleasure was all mine."

Returning to his desk, he looked at the story. "Through the efforts of Mrs. William S. De Jager . . ."

"Shall I ask him in now?" Joseph asked.

"What is it in reference to?"

"He said a personal matter."

"Okay, okay."

Joseph walked out. "Mr. Abdoller is expecting you."

Wattson entered shyly. "Do I have the honor?"

"Eh, yes. How do you do?"

"May I introduce myself. I'm William Wattson."

Abdoller shook hands and pointed to an armchair. "What can I do for you?"

"I intend to dedicate myself to social work."

"Professionally?"

"If one can say that. Anyhow, I would like to start with a well-reputed social organization. I thought perhaps you gentlemen would—that perhaps I could work with you, or for you."

"Unfortunately, at this moment, I really don't see any possibilities."

"Oh."

"Why don't you leave your name and address with me? Should something come up, I shall certainly let you know. What have you done so far?"

"I studied economics, and I've done some work with the Cooperative Atomic Corporation."

"Cooperative, eh? Well." He uncapped his pen. "Who could recommend you?"

"The Atomic Corporation, perhaps my professor; also Mr. De Jager, President of the CCRR and honorary President of the Cooperative Union and the Union of Unemployed."

"You gentlemen know each other? Eh, of course." He leaned back in his chair and surveyed the young man. "Well, you may know, then, that we intend to inaugurate a cooperative department right here. Do you think you could manage such a department?"

"I would like to do some social work, sir. Manager—that sounds too big for me. I'd rather do strict social work."

"But that is," Abdoller replied with a smile, "of course. All of us here are social workers. But each of us has to be a specialist of a certain kind, doing his own type of work."

There was a knock on the far door and Jack V. Small entered hurriedly. He was the head of the largest glass company in the country, and a recent convert to the Roman Catholic Church. He loved to be called "Counselor"; the title was embossed on his briefcase.

"Hallelujah, Lawrence, in the name of Our Lord Jesus Christ!"

"Why, Counselor," Abdoller exclaimed joyfully, "of all the pleasant surprises!"

"A good, good day to you, my dear Lawrence!" Then he noticed Wattson. "I hope I don't disturb you gentlemen?"

"Not at all, not at all. Mr. Wattson will be one of our new co-workers, most probably."

"Oh, yes? Splendid. A heartwarming decision."

"Do have a seat, please."

"Thank you, thank you."

"It's long since I saw you last, Counselor. How do you feel?"

"Wonderful in every regard—thanks to Jesus Christ. I haven't come to see you, my dear friend, for I was far away."

"Really?"

"Yes, indeed. Not physically, spiritually. Yes, spiritually I have been farther away than physically."

"Really?"

"I have just now returned from the religious recollections, confession, and Holy Communion."

"Really?"

"That's why I am in such an excellent mood, as you see."

"Indeed."

"And so well-disposed, you know. I really feel emotionally elevated, although our present time is far from cheerful."

"Indeed, indeed, unfortunately."

"Not even encouraging for an optimist. I thought about our social duties during my time of recollections. Social duties, I feel, are compulsory for every citizen of our country, of course in accordance with his position and social status."

"I don't think the Counselor has anything to reproach himself with on that score."

"That's just talk. Thank you for the compliment, Lawrence, but now let's take the matter of unemployment in our country. That's your special field, gentlemen, and I know, I know, you are working real hard in order to solve this problem for the future. The present time, gentlemen, the present time is what worries me. How about and what about the present?"

"The Union of Unemployed founded committees and small organizations to distribute food free of charge."

"Indeed so." Small turned to Wattson. "To take care of physical hunger, to see whether the unemployed have shoes or coats, that's important. I don't deny it for a moment. I've done my part in this work too. You must remind me to show you a letter I received from the White House on that score. Nevertheless, *sub specie aeternitatis,* the soul! The human soul, Mr. Wattson, is the most secret and unrevealed part of those habitual idlers. A hateful attitude is forming toward our democracy. Love has vanished from their hearts. Regardless of what you do for them, they dream of annihilating private property, for they themselves have no property. That is natural, natural indeed, but what happens if out of their ill minds, what happens if . . ."

"If I may say something, Counselor," Wattson began. "I should like to mention that, in my opinion, a poverty-stricken man is entitled to all kinds of thinking. The spirit of our time . . ."

The Counselor did not let him finish. "That's the atomic disease, 'the spirit of our time.' Private property, my dear young man, belongs not to the spirit of our time, but to the principles advocated by God."

Abdoller lowered his eyes. "Indeed. Sacred truth."

Jack Small went on with broad oratorical flourish. "This is the principle which stipulates our placing an attitude as well as our hard work in those countries that are really uncultured and in need. It reaches far into times long past, when our prehistoric fathers fought for this principle with stone weapons, when subsequently it was established as the Sacred Right of Law applying to the whole human race, and was formed for Christians on Mount Sinai into four simple words: 'You must not steal!' "

"Sacred truth, sacred truth," Abdoller intoned.

"That is what the Old Testament says, confirmed by the New Testament. It says this so clearly and explicitly, my dear Mr. Wattson, that all judiciary or economic dialectics dissolve in the mouth before they can reach the air. Therefore one either believes or disbelieves. Should one be distrustful as to

God-given rights and laws, then all discussion on this subject is terminated by itself. All arguments are irrelevant, and the disbeliever may as well dwell on the stormy waves of atheism, radicalism, socialism, or any false doctrines of the type called progressive.

"But later, later, my dear Mr. Wattson, such an individual ends in jail." He made a gesture of locking heavy doors. "If you don't agree with me, then this discussion is unnecessary. However, if you see the truth of my philosophy, then stand by hard with full integrity behind God's commandments, and do not permit compromise of any type in the name of the spirit of our time or so-called progress, which offer nothing less than temptation of the most insidious order to spoil your trust in God."

"Self-understood, Jack."

"However, this was not my original errand."

"The Counselor mentioned before that our unemployed are not being taken care of properly," suggested Abdoller.

"Yes. I think that should presently be brought forward as the most important problem we have to solve. Nothing really has been done so far. . . ."

"Improvement centers are being organized. We are starting a great new project for the benefit of the unemployed."

"Yes, indeed. However, in the name of elevating the human spirit couldn't you gentlemen organize religious recollections in strict confinement for the unemployed? Then indeed you would do something great for them, helping them toward the life of full spiritual satisfaction."

"Your idea is very humane, and we would be more than glad to start a special department with this purpose in mind. However, I'm afraid we would face certain difficulties of a plainly technical nature. I would say . . ."

"It would involve getting in touch with my New Christian Institute. But I can make that very easy for you."

"And the financial question?"

"Well, I'll think about that. Your brother Lloyd will contribute a million or two, I will, and my cousin of the Malton Order will not deny his help. The Rollon Bank International would be with you. I suggest that you work out a draft, a project of expenditures. Going with you on this new social venture I would even be figuring on a maximum basis."

"Very well, the Counselor can have it by tomorrow."

"God bless you." Jack Small grasped Abdoller's hand and then Wattson's in both of his. "God bless you, and so long, boys."

"I hope you won't forget us in the name of Christ, Jack."

"My humble thanks, boys, for your sincere opinions."

In the doorway he whispered to Abdoller, "Isn't he an atheist?"

"Oh no, Jack, no," said Abdoller. "He's Willie's boy." Returning to his desk, he clasped his hands in satisfaction and remarked to Wattson, "There is going to be a new department. Willie the Whistle will be delighted. But you almost killed yourself, young man. Remember, the principles of the social executives in the Union of Unemployed tell us that we must follow the golden and enlightened thoughts of the benefactors of our organization. We don't even admit to ourselves how we really feel about such matters. The Counselor is one of the most influential figures in the Catholic Church and in the business world."

"Yes."

"You see. And most of all, he is a great philanthropist."

"Isn't philanthropy a most noble and generous ideology in your organization?"

"However we have streamlined Saint Francis of Assisi—that is what you wanted to say, wasn't it?"

Wattson suddenly recalled his position. "I suppose so, sir. As long as all this leads toward feeding the hungry, giving proper advice to the thirsty, and leading the confused . . ."

"Very well put—to give advice to the thirsty. Very well put."

"And those who donate a pair of old trousers or gloves to the unemployed must not hear a clamor of dissatisfaction from them."

"To some extent that's true, necessarily."

"With our charities we try to defuse the issue and dim all eyes, rather than reach into the midst of evil with reforms."

"Quite so. The sympathy we have for those who are unhappy will not do. Feelings do not matter, but clever action is needed to fight the evil of our time. That's how we built the program of our organization. Do you feel now that you know a little about our goals?"

"A little, a very little. I suppose it is the solution to unemployment?"

"You see, in order to solve this problem, one, first of all, must realize that our unemployed will never again return to our factories. As you also know, our country has to live for herself, and by herself, and count on herself only."

"And what if our own production improves in volume?"

"The number of hands presently employed will be sufficient. Remember automation. Our solid benefactor, Douglas A. Seymour, is one of its strongest proponents. His three famous points: 'One of the greatest opportunities of automation is to make more industrial jobs worthy of human judgment and skills. Another is to make products of a quality finer than ever before. A third is to reduce the high cost of investment in idle machinery and in slow-moving inventory.' "

Wattson looked melancholy. "Honorary director, your horoscope is hopeless."

"That is putting it mildly. I wish to emphasize that it simply makes no sense to try to keep up the morale of the unemployed by a false hope that they may return to their jobs."

"What then?"

"I myself believe that the only reasonable solution to this problem would be to direct those people to the farms. That is the only way out of this confusion. Return to the soil, the mother of men!"

"Under our present system of sharecroppers, with the excess of farm products?"

"That is all—untrue. The soil of our country could, with the help of present technical advancements, easily feed and employ five hundred million people."

"Five hundred million?"

"The farming as such will be done differently. . . . Just a moment, please. What time is it?" He looked at his watch. "I have an important meeting. The best thing for you, as far as your position with us is concerned, would be to contact Mr. De Jager, our honorary president."

Wattson got up. "When can I see him?"

"If you have the time I suggest that you wait here for him."

"Very good."

"Or I have a better idea. Would you like to see our offices in the meantime?"

"An excellent idea."

Abdoller rang for Miss Marah. "Please ask Mr. Cianfarra to see me."

In a moment Joseph Cianfarra entered. He was a very tall man, about forty, with a brown suit and an ordinary face.

"Our executive secretary, Mr. Cianfarra—Mr. Wattson."

"Well," said Cianfarra, shaking hands. "Sir, I would like to relate to you our position in regard to the petition."

"Very good, but later, please. Mr. Wattson intends to work for us. Please keep him amused and occupied with our facilities until the honorary president arrives."

"Very well, sir." He nodded briefly and then returned to his previous point. "As far as the merit of the matter is concerned,

I just want to say that number six of the rules and regulations of the first department . . ."

"Later, later. Please." Abdoller went to the door.

"Too bad—very well, sir!" Cianfarra remarked as he left.

⊕ Chapter 11

Joseph Cianfarra turned to Wattson and said condescendingly, "You would like to work for us?"

"Yes."

"Then, I will do all I can for you."

"Thanks very much."

"The honorary director, I am sure, informed you that I happen to be the only general secretary here?"

"That means?"

"Later. We'll go over that. But have you met the honorary president of the U. of U.?"

"Mr. De Jager?"

"Yes."

"Some time ago."

"He is a well-known businessman and the soul of various operations, and possesses both a theoretical and a practical viewpoint. He is also a man of experience on the railroad, a great outdoor speaker, and a worker-lover."

"Unbelievable qualifications."

"That is certainly true. The president and the director are my personal friends. The salaries here are all right, though of course one always hopes for more. And there is the pension at the end of the road to look forward to. However, why don't you take a seat? Why should we talk standing up?"

"Where is the U. of U. getting funds to pay good salaries? Do the funds consist merely of the contributions of the unemployed?"

"Surely we would be most fortunate if they could contribute more!"

"Where do the monies come from, then?"

"Like most social institutions in our country, we are maintained by funds from private benefactors, by financial resources supplied by the big companies—steel, oil, rubber, glass, chemicals, automobiles, and so on. But in addition the unemployed subscribe to our newspaper."

"A paper?"

"We have our own newspaper—a weekly, dedicated to ideas on how to stop unemployment in the world, how to improve our social system, et cetera. *The New World*—that's the title—is printed in eight different languages, including Mandarin—an excellent idea of our editor. She insists the paper will become popular and I for one agree with her. I believe that the popularity of *The New World* will grow terrifically if it includes articles from courtrooms, on political matters from Europe, as well as romantic material. The public is under the impression that the weekly is not published by the Union of Unemployed but by the Landing Place Company. As far as the merit of the matter is concerned almost all of the stock of Landing Place is in our hands."

"And what is Landing Place?"

"It's a stockholder association, a business liaison for the U. of U."

"Oh."

"And now. Do you intend to work for us? Do you have a working program for yourself?"

"No, I just . . ."

"Then, you'll work here on our plans and programs until you can accomplish something first-rate."

"First-rate?"

"That's correct. You shouldn't see our offices now." Getting up, he looked around. "Have you ever seen offices of this type?"

"I have."

"You worked at the bank?"

"No, I intended to . . ."

"As a government official?"

"I just graduated, and I have to admit I know very little about social work as such."

"Professionally?"

"Generally. However, I would like to learn." He added determinedly, "I have to."

"Certainly. Everybody has to start some place. Miss Marah!"

"Yes."

"Would you please take Mr. Wattson to the Department of Improvements?"

When Miss Marah and Wattson had gone, Cianfarra closed the doors and looked over the papers on Abdoller's desk. He picked one up. "So that's it." From the waiting room came the sound of other voices. Cianfarra hastily put the paper back and opened the door. Joseph Col looked in.

"Sir, a delegation of unemployed has just arrived. They want to see Director Abdoller."

"The honorary director is out."

"Should I send them away?"

"Wait, I'll take care of them."

"Shall I ask them in?"

"Stupid! I won't receive the unemployed here." Touching his tie and hair, Cianfarra composed his expression and then strutted out into the waiting room.

"Good day, Mr. Director."

"Good day. How are you?"

A man stepped forward uneasily. "We are a delegation from the U. of U. camp. We have to have real work."

A woman broke in. "Our children . . ."

"For weeks and months we haven't had a decent meal," the speaker continued.

The woman half-sobbed. "The children scream—we have to have food, sir."

Listening to the conversation, Joseph turned away muttering to himself. "There are so many rich and childless people. They raise dogs and cats, parrots . . ."

A second man took the woman's arm and spoke up. "Not every unemployed is willing to beg on the street corner. You have to get us work."

Cianfarra spoke softly. "That is correct indeed, my friends, but why don't you approach the town's committee for help? They just received fresh funds and a load of potatoes."

The first man explained. "They said they can't help us any longer."

"They never did help us!" someone else joined in.

"We heard you're serving a free meal here once a day."

"A bowl of soup."

"Quiet, mother!"

The first man continued patiently. "We got some potatoes some time ago, but they're gone. Out of every hundred pounds, forty pounds were frozen, uneatable."

Cianfarra withdrew toward the door. "Yes, I can see your point. Only I don't understand why you came here."

"Because this is a rich organization, the Union of Unemployed. The whole world speaks about this organization."

"However, we can't offer you the type of help you want. We have a higher goal, our purpose is above the everyday need of just getting food for the unemployed. But now don't despair, dear people. You know that there is a crisis on now, a general, democratic crisis. You have to live with hope. We are working on behalf of your future."

A short, burly man strode forward. "What in the devil's name are you doing for us? What kind of bloody hope is it, you son of a bitch! Tell me that!"

Joseph Col hurried back. "Where is your civilization? Where is your gratitude? You can't stay here and talk this way."

Now Cianfarra came a step closer. "Calm down, good people, calm down! You shouldn't forget yourselves. I'm really sorry I can't talk to you any longer, but I'm exceptionally busy today."

The group edged toward the door. "We're very hungry, sir. We apologize, but . . ."

"We regret that deeply. But you must leave us free to go on with our work for you. Good-bye!" Cianfarra closed the door with a bang and leaned against it.

As he turned, Miss Marah approached him. "A gentleman, Mr. Cianfarra."

"In my room?" Cianfarra asked in a shaking voice. "A gentleman?"

"Yes, sir."

He straightened. "Thank you, Miss Marah," he said curtly, and hurried from the room.

De Jager and Abdoller entered calmly, talking.

"Any calls?" asked Abdoller.

"Yes, sir. The Landing Place Company. We should pick up a load of five hundred ducklings."

"Very good. On your way, will you please ask Mr. Wattson to come back in? The gentleman to whom Mr. Cianfarra showed our offices."

De Jager continued their conversation as they crossed over into his office. "I myself am mainly concerned with irrelevant subject matter. The work of the social worker should be progressive as far as methods are concerned."

"I have the feeling he is a refractory type. He seems young, doesn't look too clever."

"I know him rather well, and I am sure he wouldn't be like the referee of the Department for Improvements. My daughter has assured me of this."

"Mr. Wattson."

Wattson entered and De Jager got up to warmly greet him. "Glad to see you, William. It makes me happy to see that one man more has been struck by the social-work bug." He turned to Abdoller. "Don't forget the bookkeeper."

"Right away. Excuse me, please."

De Jager turned back to Wattson. "We are looking for somebody who would take care of the Cooperative Department."

"Yes, sir. I see."

"I would like to see you manage the Cooperative Center at the Union of Unemployed." He smiled genially. "You have already seen our place, I hear."

"Yes, except for the library and the printing shop."

"Good. Now, Bill, our institution has undertaken tasks which are especially difficult in an atomic age. They are most complicated, for they mainly concern finding solutions to the serious problem of unemployment. However, that is not the only goal we have."

"Mr. De Jager, do you think getting work for the unemployed on the farms is an economical way of rebuilding for the atomic age?"

"No, not at all. Momentarily it is necessary, but we must plan for the future."

"How do you accomplish this? How, ultimately, can you help the unemployed?"

"Well, for the time being, all of us, each referee in his own department, works on our future mission. We must cover all phases of contemporary culture and civilization. Well—but you said you didn't see our printing shop?"

"That's right."

"And you haven't seen the library either?"

"No."

Abdoller reentered and De Jager stopped him. "Mr. Wattson didn't see the library and several other departments. He should like to go there right now. Perhaps he could also see the Landing Place."

Abdoller took his seat. "Do you think, Mr. Wattson, you can find your way around and out again? If you need any help, just ask Miss Marah."

"Certainly. And thank you both very much." He rose and went out, followed by the polite smiles of both men.

Abdoller turned to De Jager and grew solemn. "Do you really like him?"

"He makes a good impression on my wife and my daughter. What about the bookkeeper?"

"She will be here any moment."

Eleanor Smith entered, carrying two heavy books.

"Now, Miss Smith."

Abdoller walked to the window and ignored the conversation. "Miss Smith, I would like to give you some advice on how to post the money from our magazine as well as the profits from the farms."

"I remember. All of it is to be distributed between the different departments so that it should entirely disappear."

"Good! You're very sharp." He tweaked her cheek playfully. "And donations?"

Without noticing his gesture, she continued, "Funds to maintain *The New World?*"

"The question is, how will you put it so that it shouldn't be obvious?"

Eleanor opened one book. De Jager looked down at the page and muttered, patting her caressingly at the same time, "Cash, banks, debtors, creditors, fund raising—ah, here. A new column: new funds for the magazine, and here, profit from farms. But let's think about it. We have to do this very neatly."

"A new account, Mr. President?"

"Right you are. There could be a suspicion. You know best what to do. This is your secret, of course. We won't remember this fifty thousand."

"Only . . ."

"What?"

"The department heads reproach me for entering too great an expenditure on their accounts. They say they see very little of the millions that come in. . . ."

"Eh?"

"What is going to happen if new questions come up?"

"The referee will be forbidden to look into the books."

"Well."

"No 'well' to me." He moved closer. "From next month on you are going to collect five thousand dollars for *The New World*. This magazine is in the red from then on . . . all in all, the other departments have to do their share to keep the publication alive. It is a moral obligation. They have to do it."

She evaded his hand. "Mr. President, I heard that the Landing Place Company no longer is in need of support. Quite the contrary, I heard it is most profitable."

De Jager looked up. "Who said so?"

"Miss Jones."

"How dare Miss Jones talk like that! I'll fire both of you!"

"Mr. President, I . . ."

"And who authorized you to ask questions about matters that don't concern you? You're through, through!"

"I thought . . ."

"Who the hell entitled you to think like that?" He drew himself up. "No, Miss Smith. We don't want cheap little trouble-makers here!"

▣ Chapter 12

Forty-nine years before the birth of Willie the Whistle, the Coast to Coast Railroad Company was born. The years that followed its devious but successful start were filled with dramatic moments, many of them directly connected with the history of America.

Until 1825, Philadelphia was one of the most important cities in America. Commerce, banking, trade, and cultural activities flourished. The factors of most importance for this development were the great concentration of population and the extensive freedom in financial and political speculation and profiteering. In that year, however, the Erie Canal was completed, and because of it, domestic and foreign commerce gradually shifted to New York and away from Philadelphia. In addition, the aggressive Baltimore and Ohio Company was using all its influence in the Pennsylvania legislature for permission to build a railroad from Baltimore through Pennsylvania as far as the Ohio River at Pittsburgh. If it could succeed in stretching its tracks across the state, Philadelphia's business prospects would dwindle even more and the city would stand to lose the commerce of the area extending from the Ohio to the Mississippi Valley.

As a consequence, one of Philadelphia's most prominent citizens found himself embroiled in controversy with President Andrew Jackson. This infuriated Philadelphian was Nicholas Biddle, director of the U.S. Bank. The exact words of the argument have been lost to history, but bank records indicate that eight million dollars in government deposits was removed from Biddle's case. Three years later, as a result of this withdrawal, the bank was closed. Hard times set in for those who had labored with their hands, and for the small traders. Business depression reigned in Philadelphia, no longer the financial center of the country. Nicholas Biddle was loathed by almost every laborer and shopkeeper.

"We have to save Philadelphia! We must save our city!" It was Herman von Hoth speaking in his usual forceful tones. He cut quite a figure, this light-haired man with his finely trimmed beard, elegant mustache, and impeccable clothes. His words silenced the guests at a dinner party in his spacious mansion on West Walnut Street.

Von Hoth was born in Germany, but spent most of his early years at the house of his uncle, Wilhelm von Hoth of Philadelphia. At nineteen, Herman went into business with his uncle, building printing machines. From that he turned to the fashioning of fire-fighting equipment. Later, he went into the manufacture of marine machinery, an enterprise that offered many more possibilities for his business talents and which considerably augmented his purse. In a short time, he was exceedingly wealthy and had gained the reputation as a shrewd, unscrupulous man of commerce and a generous host.

On this particular evening, a group of leading businessmen sat at his table. Von Hoth, in the prime of his life, a co-owner of the important Southwork Iron Foundry and other endeavors, was applying his business philosophy to the problem of saving Philadelphia from economic disaster.

"Our city is going down gradually, but surely. Business from the West, which is supposed to come to us, is now going to Baltimore and New York. The people are depressed, and no wonder. There's little cause for gaiety in our fine city."

"But practically speaking, Herman, how will we restore business and the confidence of the people in it?" This question was tendered by Henry Towne, von Hoth's friend and business partner. He, of course, was familiar with Herman's scheme and was helping to introduce it to the rest of the guests.

"Do you know, gentlemen," Herman continued, "that to travel from Philadelphia to Pittsburgh takes five days?"

Expressions of surprise, agreement and doubt came from all corners of the lavish dining room. Von Hoth stroked his mustache and resumed. "Not so long ago, I myself undertook this voyage. I boarded a train right here at Vine Street and traveled the eighty-two miles to the town of Christopher. From there I took a canalboat for one hundred and seventy-two miles to Harrisburg; next the Portage Railroad took me thirty-six miles through the Allegheny Mountains to Johnstown. The final trek consisted of a boat ride one hundred and four miles on the Conemaugh and Allegheny rivers. And in that fashion I reached my destination. Altogether I traveled almost four hundred miles with what seemed like as many changes and inconveniences. And remember, gentlemen, it took the major part of a week to do it!"

As he lit his Cuban cigar, James Magee remarked, "And it would take you a lot more time, Herman, if the water in the canals was low."

"You're absolutely correct," echoed John Wright from across the table as he reached for a brandy decanter.

"In the wintertime"—it was now Stephen Colwell talking with the grim, hard look of experience on his fleshy face—"the water's frozen. And in the summer, the water is all dried up. That makes transportation of my freight almost impossible."

Herman continued. "That's it, gentlemen, that is the situation. Furthermore, the West is becoming more populated and all kinds of trade are resulting . . . even in women. . . . We as individuals can become millionaires and as a community we can become the most prosperous and powerful in the country if we can quickly and cheaply organize the transportation of people and goods in a straight course between Philadelphia and Pittsburgh."

"A railroad! We need a railroad!" A dozen concurring, excited voices rose above the brandy and smoke, and supplied the obvious conclusion.

"Gentlemen, I agree!" He corrected himself, "We agree. But let us consider what happened just seven years ago to the Conrad Railroad. Selfish canal companies and the Main Line group killed Robert Conrad's project. Today those same financial forces, now grown infinitely more powerful, are still working against any attempt to build a railroad where the canal interests are involved. Narrow-minded people fail to think in terms of progress. We need plenty of money to fight, compete, or even argue our points with guns in our hands."

"We can subsidize the officials of the various counties through which the railroad will go." Richard Wood, at Herman's right, joined in. "If we can convince them that a railroad through their county will bring them plenty of money and stimulate business and contribute to the welfare of their people, we shall gain their support."

"Mr. Conrad did precisely that," Herman responded. "One March day, he called together a general convention in Harrisburg. Delegates from twenty-nine counties of the Commonwealth as well as some from Ohio came. And what happened? The combined interest of the canal companies bribed or otherwise persuaded through force all these men, so that the plan of Robert Conrad never even reached the state legislature!"

In spite of such obstacles, some months later Herman T. von Hoth and his group of financiers began to organize a railroad company that would run between Philadelphia and Pittsburgh. But their approach was a bit different from Robert Conrad's. They bribed not only the county officials but also the clergy, the police, the very cream of the politicians, and even the governor's mistress. Then they made a direct appeal to the populace-at-large for moral and financial support, with the promise that the railroad would stimulate new business.

The seventieth session of the commonwealth legislature received pressure from various private interests all over the country. It took three months, but on March 26, the legislature finally passed the charter for the new railroad. Simultaneously the legislature, bribed a second time, gave permission to the Baltimore Railroad Company to build tracks through the state to the city of Pittsburgh. On April 13, Governor Francis R. Shunk signed Herman's railroad bill, and eight days later he signed the Baltimore bill.

The conditions were firm. If Herman von Hoth should during the next twelve months secure a subscription of three million dollars in stocks, ten per cent of which were paid for in cash, and if thirty or more miles of railroad track were under actual construction, Governor Shunk would announce that the rival bill was null and void.

This was just one of a dozen obstacles that were presented to the new railroad. It was a well-known fact that the other railroad company had plenty of money and more than enough influence in the capital. It was known, also, that the canal companies and the New York banks were supporting the Baltimore Railroad, because von Hoth had been trying to build up an independent base centered in Philadelphia and had therefore not made any deal with them.

In the meantime, von Hoth and his collaborators were doing everything possible to peddle their stock. Before the year was over three thousand wealthy businessmen had bought half a million shares. The city council recommended that the city buy the remaining two and a half million.

This very encouraging financial beginning enabled the stockholders to meet on March 13 and 31 to select a board of directors and a president. Besides those who attended that memorable dinner on West Walnut Street, the board consisted of the millionaires Robert Toland and D. S. Brown; the fascinating raconteur and Casanova, George Carpenter; financial speculators Thomas T. Lea and Christian Spangler; politically influential Henry C. Corbett; and the distinguished William C. Patterson, widely known for his finely stocked wine cellar. The president, quite naturally, was Herman T. von Hoth.

"In the selection of a chief engineer," wrote the Board of Directors in their first annual report, "our Railroad was fortunate in securing the services of Mr. Benjamin Edgar James, a gentleman of sound professional experience and equally sound judgment, who has earned a sterling reputation in connection with his activities in behalf of the Georgia Railroad, and in whom the Board of Directors has placed great confidence."

Their Mr. James was a small man with seemingly limitless energy. He had short legs and a rather large head, quite bald on top but with long hair toward the back, that curled over his collar. His delicate face was punctuated with luminous black eyes, shaggy eyebrows, and heavy sideburns. He had been born in Delaware County, Pennsylvania, but his speech and his manners resembled those of an educated Englishman. Although he was an American patriot, he was at the same time a great admirer of the technical progress of Great Britain and of Russian literature and women. In his youth he had spent a few years in Moscow as a British spy, where he married Nina, the daughter of a wealthy Russian merchant named Petrov. After three children by her and several scandals, James was expelled from the country by the czarist police. There were stories that he attempted several daring attempts to smuggle out his children. He was unsuccessful and was never reunited with his family.

He began his railroad career as an engineer on the original survey of the Philadelphia and Christopher Railroad. Three years later he was made first assistant engineer of the Camden

Railroad. After that he traveled extensively, as he said, "to obtain firsthand knowledge of European railroads." During this period he engaged in lucrative spying, buying and selling all kinds of intelligence information to the British, Russians, and Americans. On his return he accepted the position of chief engineer on the Georgia Railroad. Von Hoth and James became fast friends and, it was they, historically speaking, who were the founders of the CCRR, the greatest railroad in America.

On July 16, under the direction of James, the grading of the first twenty miles of the railroad began west of Harrisburg. A week later work started fifteen miles east of Pittsburgh. Hundreds and hundreds of Negroes and poor whites worked a sixteen-hour day sustained by bread and soup, which aided the pouring of their sweat and blood into the commonwealth earth. James lived with them on gold wages. He shared their experiences and occasionally indulged in their primitive pioneer-builders' life-style.

The Pennsylvanian described their efforts in the following terms: "The great railroad, that imperishable chain, destined to more closely unite the interests of the East and West of this continent, is rapidly progressing along the banks of the Juniata. Day by day the engineers and workmen may be seen surveying, arranging, digging, and blasting, as the highest, most rugged, and rockiest bluffs bordering the river crumble and are subdued, to form the foundation for this life-artery of profit and prosperity."

On September first, the first link was opened for passenger and freight business. Train movement was synchronized with transportation on the roads and canals. A year later the CCRR reached Harrisburg and absorbed the state-owned Portage Railroad so that travel through the Allegheny Mountains from Philadelphia became an easy matter. Not quite one year later, a twenty-one-mile stretch west of Johnstown was put into service. At that time Ben James was directing the building of the Gallitzin Tunnel and the Horseshoe Curve. Taken together, these improvements shortened the travel time between the two cities by almost a day.

Ben was called "the railroad genius" by his friends. He was a man of many talents. During the construction of the railroad and the development of an espionage system for the directors he also learned to cook; his specialty was English stew made from deer and rabbit which he hunted down himself. His knowledge of world architecture was thorough. He was also a charming storyteller. But at the same time he was an unprincipled goldbeater, and on more than one occasion was reported to have been unusually cruel to his subordinates, especially when they were black.

Herman von Hoth, on the other hand, was a more receptive person. In his old age he became an attentive listener. He was a connoisseur of German and English poetry, yet somehow never managed to tire of hearing Ben's stories about the railways of the world. After supper, the two men would closet themselves and a bottle of brandy in the study. Ben would tell stories while Herman placed logs on the fire and the two would smoke their pipes and sip brandy; in between tales they would calculate their wealth. After half a bottle, Herman would be moved to recite some poetry. One evening, following his delivery of Gray's "Elegy Written in a Country Churchyard," Ben remarked, "Did you know, Herm, that another Thomas Gray, in the year eighteen hundred and nineteen, worked out a most accurate plan, detailed and realistic, for a national railroad in England? He covered the whole country from one end to the other with railroads."

"That's very interesting," Herman said as he added more logs to the fire and poured more brandy for himself. "He must have been the contemporary of George Stephenson."

"Well, the story goes that Thomas Gray urged Richard

Trevithick, an ingenious fellow from a Cornwall tin mine, to try his locomotive on the Merthyr-Tydvil Railroad in Wales."

Herman rubbed his whiskers, stared into the fire and tried to recall. "Oh yes, this Trevithick chap was very interesting; a self-taught man. I remember now. A few years ago someone wrote an article about him in *The Pennsylvanian*. His locomotive made about five miles an hour."

"But it wasn't able to go up the smallest hill," interrupted Ben. "George Stephenson made the important improvement with his locomotive 'Rocket.' When he conducted a trial of it in eighteen twenty-nine, on the Liverpool and Manchester, it made thirty miles an hour."

"Ben, do you remember when the first track was laid in America?" asked Herman, whose forte was railroad finance, not railroad history.

"Oh, yes—I believe it was in eighteen nine, an experimental track built by a Scottish millwright who worked for the Thomas Leiper Company. It was only sixty and something yards long, the gauge was four feet, and the sleepers eight feet apart. To some extent the experiment was successful, because the next year Leiper built a mile-long railroad in Delaware County from Crum Creek to Ridley. This little railroad was used for twenty years by the Leiper Company for transporting stones from the quarries in Crum."

The sparks in the fireplace grew lively and the wood flamed red. But this was not distraction enough to divert the two millionaires so pleasantly occupied with their brandy and the past.

Herman turned his flushed face toward Ben. "You know, my sister's father-in-law was Colonel John Stevens. I know he presented a petition to the New Jersey legislature for permission to build a railroad. I thought he might have been first—in any case, he wasn't much later."

"Yes, I know, that was in eighteen hundred and eleven," added Ben. His memory fed on dates. "But nothing came of it."

"Oh, no, no," Herman protested, as he stirred in his chair. The heat from the fireplace had made itself felt. "Not this story. I know this story well because it's part of my family. Colonel Stevens got, or rather bought, permission, and a few years later he incorporated the New Jersey Railroad Company that was supposed to run from Trenton to New Brunswick. But he was a dreamer, like you, Ben. He knew everything about the railroad but nothing about banks. And that's probably what killed him and his project." He laughed cheerfully.

"Railroads, railroads, always plenty of trouble with railroads, but you and I made our fortunes on it." Ben smiled and continued his reminiscing. "Have you ever heard about all the difficulty the Columbia Railroad had with the farmers when they changed from horse power to locomotives? Country folk organized protests, running about with sticks after the locomotives."

"I have indeed. It was tragic and comic at the same time. Apparently it was popularly thought to be bad luck if a locomotive ran near your house or through your field. They even charged the railroad company with allowing sparks from the engine to set fire to the houses and fields and even injure their animals. I remember it well. . . ."

"Basically, I think this whole protest started with the horse traders." Ben James always looked to the concrete facts of a story. "The traders were losing their markets. Why, Edward Gay, the chief engineer, had all kinds of trouble trying to convince his own bosses to bring locomotives to the railroad, because the bosses were also horse traders. Finally they contracted for a couple of locomotives which were supposed to be on the road the following year, but then due to banker opposition the locomotives didn't begin their run until years later."

"I guess," mused Herman, "the bankers became convinced that they couldn't stop progress."

"Yes, you're right. Why, it was just a few years after the first run before the Columbia was using forty locomotives and . . ."

"Fire!" shouted Herman as he jumped from his flaming chair.

Ben began beating it with his jacket but to no avail. He seized and struggled with a tremendous rug, hoping to somehow smother the fire with that. Herman, uninjured but quite startled, ran about with his clothes smoking, crying "Water! Get water!" In his frantic desire to put out the chair fire he grabbed the brandy bottle and was about to use its remaining contents when Ben struck it from his hand. It shattered on the hearth and immediately formed a pool of bluish flame. The fine wood paneling in the old study became charred and discolored and on the mantelpiece a replica of the first CCRR engine melted into a lump of silver metal.

回 Chapter 13

When studying the saga of American growth, the historian is often puzzled by that human phenomenon, Benjamin Edgar James. This man, quite average in appearance, possessed all the canny shrewdness of the nineteenth-century businessman. He was president of the Coast to Coast Railroad for twenty-two years until a heart attack caused his death. His entire life of amassing millions, was reflected in the growth of the railroad. It is no exaggeration to say he planned and built the railroad which stretched from the Atlantic to the Pacific touching along the way the most populated and industrialized areas of the country. Under James's stewardship, the capital worth of the

CCRR went from six million to over two hundred million dollars. He knew that the best railroad equipment would increase the volume of business, so he was constantly modernizing and rebuilding the physical plant of the CCRR. Most locomotives utilized wood for fuel, but gradually almost all converted to the more economical and practical coal. James himself controlled several coal mines in Pennsylvania.

One of the secrets of Ben James's success was his ability to have his own people in the right place at the right time. He could continue to genuinely enjoy the companionship of William Patterson, even after the latter had taken the CCRR presidency away from him for a short while with the aid of some of the leading banker stockholders. Patterson was a handsome, black-eyed ladies' man, a financial speculator, with little knowledge of railroading. After von Hoth's death, he was appointed to the presidency by a distressed group of bankers who thought there should be more money for them and less expansion of the railroad. Patterson spent all of his time developing various schemes to save money on track, equipment and workers. He even organized the Union Trust Company, predecessor of the Union of Unemployed, which was supposed to build up a savings fund for the employees from their own monthly contributions.

The bankers were quick to notice their company's depreciation. They discovered that to survive and make a profit, a railroad must constantly build, improve, modernize. When William Patterson suffered his first heart attack, he was honest enough to recognize with the help of their banker and mutual friend, Tom Scott, that his position should be taken over by Ben. Following this physical shock, Patterson experienced two more personal tragedies. A mysterious explosion destroyed his house, and a week later he lost two million dollars in land and grain speculation. This last misfortune also brought the loss of his credit and the personal trust of people around him.

Overnight the debonair Patterson had become a poor man. The next months were a succession of downturns ending under the hoofs of his own horse presented to him a year before by Ben.

It was Ben who also arranged Patterson's burial. During the wake one of Philadelphia's more prominent bankers spoke in a deprecating tone of the deceased's railroad and financial speculations. Ben's answer was severe. "Patterson was a good man. His financial calculations were honest, but some people around him were not. And as for the railroad, it is like a woman: if you love her, you marry her for the rest of your life. And if you don't, don't think about marriage, don't think about the railroad, just use it for pleasure. And for a pleasure ticket, you have to pay with dollars."

An important side of James's life was his relationship with Willis Foster and his stepdaughter Charlotte. Many years later, William Wattson, a great-grandson of Charlotte, discovered among Ben's papers a letter written by Morris Foster, Willis' brother. "Charlotte was called Catharina, or 'Russian Girl.' She was very fond of my brother Willis, whose position as chief engineer on the railroad kept him away from home a great deal. Willis had a big, affectionate heart and his little 'Russian Girl' had many reasons for gratitude toward him— kind remembrances in the form of frequent presents and other tokens of affection. When she was about thirteen years old, Willis proposed to take her to Towanda, and there being a good school nearby, he stated that Charlotte might go to school if she wished.

"It was winter, and William drove all the way to Towanda in his own sleigh drawn by two horses. The distance traveled was over three hundred miles but the sleighing was good, and of course it was a jolly journey for a 'Russian Girl,' especially as brother Willis had for a companion Ben James, a man of great personal popularity who had many friends and acquaintances all along the road."

Later Ben James made Willis vice-president of the CCRR, and after he died Charlotte lived at Ben's home where she was treated and loved like a daughter. She was a fine-looking, intelligent girl with very large blue eyes and dark curls that shone against fair skin. It is difficult to establish who she loved more, Ben James, her father, or the railroad. One thing is certain, she had a positive influence on James, and to some extent was responsible for his drive to build and improve the railroad.

Quite often in the summer, Charlotte and her guardian took Sunday excursions on the Philadelphia-Lancaster line. At that time there was a lame porter named Samuel Jones serving the passenger cars. He was more popularly known as Grubby Sam and was one of the first Negroes to work on the CCRR. Sam was always smiling, ready with all kinds of information and proud of his job on the "Possum Bellies." That was the name he gave to the passenger cars with their baggage space under the floor. Besides serving the passengers, Grubby Sam was also in charge of the mail.

The Philadelphia-Lancaster was technically more advanced than any of the other lines. Passengers were even able to get food en route. For example, at the Paoli stop, Sam would, on request, bring sandwiches and milk aboard. At Downingtown, freshly made coffee and doughnuts were served. And in Lancaster, passengers could get cold cuts, gingerbread, pretzels, beer and other alcoholic beverages.

Charlotte was her guardian's eyes and ears. Conductors often spotted her traveling on one of the CCRR lines with her friend Grubby Sam. She observed the work of the train crews and discreetly asked passengers about their travels. She even acquired an advanced knowledge of railroad equipment and tracks. On her returns to Philadelphia she always gave Ben reports that were analytic and broad in scope. It was her idea to put uniforms on the conductors and trainmen. Ben was opposed to this kind of regimentation and expense, but Charlotte did not give up. She presented the idea to one of the directors, who found the suggestion very acceptable. In a short time, all passenger conductors were wearing brass-buttoned blue coats, buff vests, and black trousers. The brakemen wore gray suits with sack-style coats that had three outside pockets and one inside. Although Ben never showed his appreciation for Charlotte's observations, he nonetheless used many of them. Undoubtedly, it was love that impelled Ben James to leave Charlotte a sizable sum of money to live on and to provide a trust of over two million dollars for her, even after he learned of her marriage to Bullitt O. Wattson. On her marriage certificate she put the name of Catharina Petrovna James Wattson.

🏛 Chapter 14

Again the bombardment. The first indication was a sound like the rumbling of many trucks, accompanied by a steady grinding, persistent and gruff, that reverberated through the night. Then came a wild shriek as sharp as a knife. Only one who has heard the crack of Arctic ice in the stillness of a subzero night knows the piercing chill that this sound possesses. Finally the ugly noise of a wild animal as it bursts into the cellar room, flinging the water pail from its boxstand, brought Skobelev and Rosen instantly to their feet. Even before the water from the pail had splashed over Tania, she was rising and clutching her rifle.

"They're coming! They're almost here!" Skobelev uttered in a hoarse whisper. He was no longer drunk. Old Hryc began to fill his pockets with grenades. The four of them with their weapons poised, moved toward the door. Hryc was out first, then Skobelev. David Rosen turned around to beg Tania to stay in the cellar. It would kill him, he thought in sudden misery, to see her brought down by the fascist death. But Tania displayed no trace of fear. She was resolute. Without hesitation, she slapped Rosen. When he persisted in keeping his pleading hand on her shoulder, she kicked him in the shin. Then she ran out, and he, swearing and laughing, ran after her.

The walls trembled. Pellets of brick, stone, and mortar fell like sleet. Windows crashed. Chimneys crashed. The fire of a machine gun saluted the four as they stood, uncertain for a moment on where to turn. Bullets whistled. Denczenko struck off to the right, not boldly, but slowly and carefully. His brain remained clear and calculating. He fell to his stomach to crawl, face close to the earth. As he crawled and wriggled through the ruins he searched his pockets for grenades. And strangely, as he counted them, he chuckled at a recollection. Once, when he was a boy in the Ukraine, he had been chased from an orchard for stealing apples, and he had crawled away as he did now; counting his apples. Hryc, the Ukrainian, was cunning. He had a plan. He was going to crawl behind the oncoming Germans and give them a taste of his apples. "Such sweet apples," he thought, as he suppressed a chuckle of delight.

Rosen, with his submachinegun at the ready, went off to his left and swiftly jumped from one heap of torn earth to another. The night was made darker and thicker by the smoke, so the enemy snipers did not see him, or, if they did, could not tell whether he was Russian or German.

Skobelev and Tania remained in the doorway and opened fire. Their plan was as good as Denczenko's for they sought to attract the enemy's attention through their deliberate, constant fire. It was life or death with the odds controlled by chance. They were as indifferent as the night to the planes overhead, the shrapnel falling all around, and the streams of green fire that spat out from the cannon.

The enemy's fire became more furious. It came progressively closer. It was showing off a finer accuracy than it had had before. The thick wall against which Tania and Skobelev were leaning swayed and parts of it crumpled. Dust filled their eyes, their nostrils, their mouths and throats. A bullet scorched Skobelev's head. They picked up a machinegun hanging out of a hole that had formerly been a window. They could not retreat. They continued to fire. Fire! Dear Father, how long could they keep it up? The enemy detected the direction of their bullets and flung back a hello. Sweat and dust and snow blinded them. Soon now, surely, the shivering wall would fall and take them down with it.

Then something unexpected happened. Grenades began dropping from somewhere. But where? To their left, firing grew louder and louder. Ivan pushed Tania into a large earthen bake-oven. It would be the end of both if anything struck that oven.

"Crawl further down," Ivan begged Tania. "I'm going to try to escape."

"Stay where you are," she answered roughly. "There is no escape."

She got her rifle into position and began firing again. He did the same. Fire. Fire. Fire! There was not one second of respite. Tania was weary. Was it just an hour ago that she said Jan's name? She did not remember. No matter now. She was too tired for sorrow to tug at her heart. Yesterday it had been different. Yesterday she had cried because Jan had deserted her. Was it just yesterday that she had sobbed like a broken-hearted child? Well, no matter.

A fearful detonation snorted through the air; a powerful tremor shook the earth. Dynamite. Skobelev and Tania could not know that this was Denczenko's masterly achievement, just as he could not know that in the instant before the climax

133

of his coup, a nazi bullet had found Tania.

"What is it?" Ivan cried in deep distress. Up to this moment, he had been without feeling. Now he was in a sudden frenzy of fear, not for himself but for Tania. He struggled to her rescue.

"It is nothing," Tania answered. "A bullet scratched my legs, that's all. I wouldn't have fallen, but for the explosion."

There was silence now. Not an ominous silence, but a stillness that conveyed a sense of peace. Swiftly Skobelev began to thrust away the rubble that held them trapped. Once his hands had cleared a passage, he began to drag Tania out of the oven. They came out into the blue, smoky night to find Rosen pushing a prisoner before him toward the entrance of the cellar, which had not yet been destroyed.

"The only one left out of fifteen," Rosen said when he saw them. Then, seeing Tania leaning on Skobelev, he cried, "Wounded? You're wounded!"

"She says it's not serious," Skobelev replied.

Denczenko joined them, grinning like a delighted child when Rosen told him to look after the prisoner. "Ivan and I will take care of Tania," he said.

"Be careful of him, Hryc," Skobelev said. "They'll need him for questioning at Headquarters."

This duty pleased Denczenko. If the frightened German youth could have seen the glee that spread over Hryc's face and glinted like steel in his blue eyes, he surely could not have maintained his firm nazi bearing. While Skobelev and Rosen were there, Denczenko held his rifle pointed at the nazi's heart. Once they were gone, he put his rifle down, and with his two hands pressed against the nazi's shoulders, forced him to sit down. Then he, Denczenko, sat down in front of him.

"We'll talk," Hryc growled, and then he laughed boisterously. The German grunted. It was really only a sigh of weariness and fear, but the Ukrainian took it for a response. He leaned forward and looked up into the prisoner's face. In the night it looked starkly white and this pleased Hryc. He chuckled, and it was like water trickling through a tiny hole. Then he began to talk in a hoarse, suppressed whisper. He talked rapidly and as the words flowed from him, he shook his fist back and forth in front of the nazi hero. If for a second other words failed him, he muttered a refrain of *"Bachysh. . . . Sukin syn. . . . Bachysh. . . . Sukin syn. . . ."*

"I had a wife, a beautiful woman, as generous a creature as ever set foot on the earth," Hryc said.

The German nodded his head. He did not understand what Denczenko was saying, but he was a prisoner, and he acknowledged the words.

"I had a daughter. Her cheeks were like roses. Her laughter was as musical as organ pipes." Hryc said softly.

"My son! The man he would have been—strong, true, a good worker." He chanted gently as one would a lullaby.

There was silence for a few minutes, broken only by Hryc's refrain of *"Bachysh. . . . Sukin syn. . . . Bachysh. . . . Sukin syn. . . ."* The German continued to nod.

"Then you came, you mad demons of Hitler. You came."

Passion mounted higher in the Ukrainian. "Kraska died. My wife died. My young Hryc. Everything. My home, my lovely home with apple trees was burned, demolished. All Kiev was wrecked."

Another pause. The German cowered. He felt the saliva from Denczenko's mouth on his forehead. The hate in Denczenko's words vibrated in his ears.

"You killed millions." Hryc's fist fanned the prisoner's jaw. "You killed Ukrainians." The accusation was more bitter than Goering's torrents of hate. "You killed Russians and Poles, Jews and Gentiles. You killed . . . killed . . . killed!" This Ukrainian displayed the same frenzied wrath as the Führer himself. The German put his hands to his ears, but he could not keep out the voice. "Your tanks and your guns and your bombs have devastated the earth and all its people!"

Denczenko sank back on his heels. His teeth, which had decayed to stubs, chattered. His eyes, fixed on the German, glared with wild passion. His long, thick fingers were stretched out as if to show that they were eight unforgettable charges of cruelty. His whole body shivered with hate.

Bubbles of sweat rose over the German's body. Hryc put out his hand and felt the wet forehead. It pleased him. He muttered, *"Bachysh. . . . Sukin syn!"* over and over again. He clapped his hands together. He swayed back and forth, caught in a paroxysm of joy and hate, and laughed and groaned. The German cringed as if fire were scorching him.

Suddenly Hryc Denczenko leaped to his feet. He thrust out his hands, the fingers turned up like a beckoning, mischievous witch's, and caught and held the German's head. He pulled him up. The nails of the fingers clawed into the white face. Then they slipped down to the neck. They were soft for a moment, then became hard, like steel. They gripped; they clutched; they twisted. Three brief groans fell from the German's swollen lips. Three, and that was all. The prisoner's body curled up and fell to the hospitable Russian earth. Five times his legs stretched and twisted like those of a ballet dancer. But then his dance was over.

A slow, rumbling sigh of satisfaction issued from Hryc. He picked up his rifle and quietly walked toward his cellar home. Once he paused and looked back at the crumpled heap he had left on the ground.

"Do you know, nazi, that it was I who drove off your soldiers?" he asked softly. There was no answer and he continued, "You would like to know how I did it? Then I shall tell you, and maybe some day you will use my prescription."

Hryc chuckled.

"You must have at least eight grenades," he said, "and you must bind them together. Then you must slip very close, so close that the enemy can surely hear you breathing. Then you light all eight grenades and throw them straight at the heads. Straight, mind you. Don't bother about the legs."

Another chuckle.

"Simple, isn't it, son . . . of Hitler?" The Ukrainian laughed. "Now that I have told you, you will be able to fling grenades straight from Berlin to the Volga. Yes, you will. *Bachysh. . . . Sukin syn. . . . Bachysh. . . . Sukin syn!*" And Denczenko laughed uproariously. It was the kind of laughter that follows an excellent joke.

As Denczenko entered the cellar no one noticed him, for Skobelev and Rosen were busy dressing the wounds in Tania's leg and she, quite unaware of their ministrations, was staring up at the ceiling. Denczenko slunk into a far corner and watched them carefully. He saw David take a towel from a suitcase, dip it into water, and begin to wash the blood from the girl's face. When it blossomed clean and white from the smoke and blood, he washed her hands, then her legs. Her violet-blue eyes opened wide, and a shudder of returning consciousness ran through her body. Her uncovered breasts heaved and a tiny sigh came from her parted lips.

The dressing and washing were barely finished when the thunder of bombardment began again. Motors whirled and cannon wheezed. Planes, like so many infernal devils, soared and swooped. The supreme devil had taken control again. Or had he? Perhaps not. For now Mother Volga became furious and from her far bank a swarm of Stormoviks mounted into the air. Tanks rumbled up from her near shore; they were the heaviest tanks that had been made in Krasnyi Oktiabr. They were stronger by far than those which had hurled destruction on the attacking foe at Moscow. An onlooker, if there had been one, might well have thought that the Volga was rising up from her deep bed to beat back the assailants. There is an old legend that when Napoleon's forces marched into Russia,

137

Mother Volga broke from her confining banks and sucked the attackers into her thick mud. That seemed about to happen again, for the noise from the mother river was stupendous. She could suffocate, wash away in her gray-green waves.

The storm increased. The Volga and the planes and tanks she had hidden were not alone in the swift defense and bold attack. The earth split open and fire burst out. This inferno was the mighty military symphony to the twentieth century. The sounds were not of marching feet, horses' hoofs beating over frozen roads, or commands issued in ringing voices. The theme and refrain were of trees torn by their roots from the earth, of fat-bellied bombs boring through towns, of houses crackling with flames and falling, of villages being beaten into the earth by tanks.

"We must go!" David cried to Skobelev. "They need us out there. Where is Denczenko?"

Skobelev pointed.

"Where is the prisoner?" David asked Hryc, but he did not answer. He was staring at the bandages on Tania's legs and appeared not to hear the question.

Skobelev looked at Rosen, who nodded his head. They knew what had happened.

"You'll be brought before the military court for this!" Rosen exclaimed, and shook Denczenko roughly. But it was no use; he could not bring any look of intelligence into the Ukrainian's blackened face.

The two younger men hastily reloaded their rifles and stuffed the pockets of their cotton kabats with egg-grenades.

"Listen, Hyrc," Skobelev shouted into his ear. "You stay here and look after Tania. Guard her as you would the pupil of your eye."

A faint glimmer of understanding showed in the old man's face.

"We'll send someone to take her to the hospital," Rosen

said. "But don't you dare leave her before the ambulance comes."

"Afterward you must report to the factory," Skobelev told him. Denczenko nodded. The two started for the door. A feeble, imploring whisper reached them. "Jan, Jan, see . . ." Tania begged.

David turned back, then thought better of it. He and Ivan Skobelev went out together.

The candle began to sputter. The tremor outside increased. Denczenko was calm, very calm. Hardly a muscle moved on his face, but occasionally he raised one of his hands before his eyes and stared at it. Silently, he joined his two hands together as if he were going to pray. A soft murmur came from beneath his mustache. He choked a little as if he were searching for words. Then he was silent. He could not pray. There was too much hate in his heart. It had seared his brain, his whole being.

The candle went out, and darkness filled the deep cellar home. Denczenko, his prayer unsaid, stole back to Tania and lay down beside her. As he lay there he began to cry like a wounded animal. "She is my daughter. My beautiful Kraska."

Only the night, the bomb-infested night, heard him and when it made no response, his cry deepened to a sob. He beat his chest, pulled at his hair. Something, he did not know what, was coming at him out of the evil night and he implored God to save him and to save Tania who had become his daughter.

From supplication he turned to blasphemy. He cursed. He breathed deep threats of vengeance, and then with tears streaming from his eyes and perspiration from his brow, he shouted, "God, if you do exist, why are you so cruel? So unjust? God! God! Do you hear me?"

▣ Chapter 15

Five o'clock in the morning was fast approaching. The glow in the sky predicted a fine July day for the town of Glen Manors, Pennsylvania. The smell of fresh-cut grass, mixed with the scent of crushed grapes, drifted through the open windows into the bedrooms of the house.

Over the grass, over the flowers and grapevines, a pair of pine trees reigned in a court of half a dozen spruce. It was a pleasant setting for the small, bright-shuttered house.

A different smell was coming from the kitchen, where Richard De Jager, a young railroadman for the Coast to Coast Railroad Company, was eating a huge breakfast. The house was very quiet, and the only sounds came from outside, where the sparrows were jabbering in the yard. Bertha and the three children were sleeping upstairs. Richard didn't mind making his own breakfast; he wanted his wife, who was expecting another child, to have plenty of rest. She and the little ones were his whole life, his whole world, along with the house, the trees, and the birds.

He was a quiet man, not given to quarreling, drinking, or cards. He spent what little spare time he had helping Bertha, fixing the house, or working in the garden. Like his father and grandfather before him, he was a member of the Episcopal Church. His forebears had come from England; his wife's family, the von Hoths, had come from Germany. Bertha was Lutheran. Despite the religious and temperamental differences, harsh words or arguments were unknown in their house. It is odd to say they never quarreled, but it was true. They were simple, they worked hard, and they tried to bring up their children to be honest people.

Noise, Richard mused, was the only problem. The heavy contributors were Sigismund, who was five; Agatha, not quite four; and Richard, Junior, almost two. Bertha was expecting their fourth child at any moment. Richard would not be going to work this morning because he was starting the night shift. But he rose early anyhow, from force of habit. He thought he could do some gardening first, and then later he'd go to Pittsburgh and talk to the doctor. Although he was a man with more faith in God than in medicine, he thought perhaps the doctor could help his wife now. Her whole body had swollen unnaturally during her pregnancy.

"It would be all right if the baby came tomorrow," he muttered to himself, "but what will happen if we have to wait one or two more weeks?" His thin face grew somber at the thought.

As he got up to take a pot of coffee off the stove, Bertha opened the door to the kitchen. Though she was never considered beautiful, her warmth gave great charm to her light hair, blue eyes, and constant smile. Her hands were never idle. She was a woman who enjoyed the chores of her home.

"Good morning, Richard." She sat down gently next to her husband's chair.

He moved his full cup of coffee in front of her and said, "Why don't you sleep longer, Bertha? I'm not going to work this morning and can take care of things here in the kitchen myself."

She looked into his eyes. "So why didn't you sleep a little longer yourself?"

"Oh, I have much to do in the garden, and it's so pleasant to work in the morning. Besides, I have to go to Pittsburgh to take care of a few things."

She understood immediately. "If you are going to Pittsburgh

to see a doctor about my swelling, don't worry about it." She managed to keep smiling as she continued: "You know this is my fourth child and I have experience. The swelling must be connected with the pregnancy. I am sure that as soon as I have the child, I will be back to normal."

"Who told you that, a local witch? You know, Bertha, you've never had such enormous swelling with the other children."

"Richard, oh Richard, be sensible. I'm getting older, you know. And besides, every child is not the same. Somehow— and no witch told me, either—I feel this one will be very different from the first three!"

"I hope you're right about the swelling, that's all." He kissed her on the cheek and made his way out to the vegetable garden.

Richard De Jager enjoyed soil on his hands. His first job as a fourteen-year-old boy had been as a farmhand working around Glen Manors and nearby Shaftonwall. At seventeen he felt ready for bigger things and, with the help of the von Hoth family, got a job on the Pittsburgh branch of the Coast to Coast Railroad Company.

Now he owned a house and a garden. He grew corn, stringbeans, carrots, potatoes, and beets, along with his grapevines and strawberry patches. There were plenty of vegetables for Bertha to preserve for the family and to provide gifts for the neighbors. Richard was a happy man and he thought about it very often. He had a good, honest, hard-working wife who was not only a good cook, but was fine at neeedlework and sewing too.

"She gave me three healthy children, and now a fourth is coming. Oh, God, help her so she won't have any trouble with this one."

Richard spoke softly to himself as he stood near the front porch. In the distance he saw the muddy waters of the Ohio

River. On both sides of it the light green and yellow fields of wheat and rye were cut by ribbons of trees. Suddenly he was recalling that spring, many years before, when he watched this same river ravage the land, and he remembered his uncle and the others who perished in its rampaging waters.

▣ Chapter 16

Willie the Whistle, son of Richard and Bertha De Jager, had an old bachelor granduncle. Although he generally avoided people, everybody, everywhere, called him by his first names, Leonard Peter, probably out of respect. He was well over six feet tall, possessed unheard-of strength, and looked like a wrestler. Granduncle Leonard Peter lived in Harrisburg, Pennsylvania, and worshipped Abraham Lincoln. He was a fireman on the CCRR and during the war between the states he was one of the hand-picked men who took part in transporting "valuable cargo" from Harrisburg to Washington.

Neither Richard nor Bertha De Jager ever mentioned any of their important and influential relatives, including Leonard Peter, to their friends, neighbors, or even their own children. They lived in the present, thought always of the immediate, and used their influential relatives only in emergencies. They were much more inclined to keep busy with the work at hand than to sit and talk about the past; and, besides, the well-paid but long hours of labor each day and the bringing up of five children consumed all their time. Yet occasionally their children came home with questions about their relatives and ancestors. The stories the neighborhood playmates heard from their families promoted this quest for information. Ultimately the De Jager children had a story of their own to tell.

It was early evening on February 22, 1861. A light snow was falling on the tracks of the railroad in Harrisburg. A locomotive stood hitched to a single passenger car. The locomotive, one of the newer types, was equipped with tires of steel and fireboxes. Great-uncle Leonard Peter was dutifully following rule number seventeen, which said that "the duty of the fireman is to see that the locomotive has enough fuel and water and that vital parts are well-oiled." He looked down the tracks that stretched out before him unto the feathery whiteness and sincerely hoped that the snow would not affect his vision in the light of rule eighteen, "The fireman will assist in keeping a constant lookout upon the track, and must instantly give the engine man notice of any obstruction he may perceive."

He had a feeling something important was coming. During the day at the engine shop there was talk that Mr. Enoch Lewis, general superintendent; Thomas Scott, vice-president; and Herman Haupt of the CCRR, along with some other influential people, were in Harrisburg. Leonard Peter was neither frightened nor more interested than he would be if he were dealing with any of the more normal passengers. He was just one of the many railroad men who performed their duties according to the rules and their abilities. He was grateful to the Von Hoth family for giving him a job and was loyal to his railroad despite the twelve hours' work under heavy discipline which it required.

Instead of the regular man, engine man Jack Shoemaker appeared at the side of the locomotive. He was accompanied by the road foreman of engines, the conductor of the train, and two other men Leonard Peter did not know. He did, however, quickly deduce that they must be about to transport some extremely valuable cargo.

The light of the conductor's lamp showed Leonard Peter

the faces of the two men he did not know, one of whom spoke. "I am Enoch Lewis, and this is Mr. G. C. Franciscus, superintendent of the division." The long, gaunt face of the second man, mustached and gray-bearded, was indistinct in the shadow of the lamp.

"Indeed, I am pleased to meet you, gentlemen," Leonard Peter answered quietly, vigorously wiping the oil from his strong working hands.

"Riding in the car with the two of us," Mr. Lewis continued, "will be the vice-president of the railroad and a few businessmen from Chicago. Because we would like this ride to be without incident or unforeseen events, we selected the two finest men on the division, the best engine man and the best fireman."

"Thank you, sir," Leonard Peter replied timidly, and before he had turned his head Mr. Lewis and Mr. Franciscus departed with the conductor, who guided their way with his lamp.

Leonard Peter climbed back into the smoking locomotive after Jack Shoemaker and asked, "What does all this mean? Why are such big men going about at night and talking to a little fireman like me?"

"Politics, my friend, politics. Perhaps they will make you the chief engineer of the entire system, or maybe the president." Jack threw his friend a smile as he shook off the wet snow from his cap.

Leonard Peter did not respond to the joke but looked back to the end of the car and saw the silhouette of a very tall man, about six feet four in height. He was wearing a soft cap and was surrounded by six men. They all looked like mushrooms around a tree.

Shortly thereafter, the conductor gave the go signal. The new locomotive, as impatient as a young horse, leaped into its gait and rode out into a night that darkened with each passing moment. The snow gradually ceased and the wind gained speed, as if the elements themselves were trying to hurry the train and its precious cargo forward.

It was a famous night and a famous train that carried Abraham Lincoln to Washington. And there was good reason for all this precaution. Allen Pinkerton, the shrewd detective hired by the Philadelphia, Wilmington and Baltimore Railroad, had discovered a plot by Southern sympathizers to kill the newly elected American President before he would take his oath of office on March 4.

On this secret trip, Mr. Lincoln was accompanied by Lewis, Franciscus, and Colonel Ward H. Lamon, who later became the President's chief bodyguard. The group also included T. E. Garrett, general baggage agent of the railroad, and telegrapher Bob Pitcairn. At the very last moment Tom Scott decided to stay in Harrisburg and take care of the telegraph lines. He wanted to be sure that no contact was made with Baltimore or Washington that might alert the potential assassins. To be doubly safe, he even cut all the telegraph wires.

The short train made a stop in Downingtown to take water and then went on to the West Philadelphia station. It arrived there at five after ten and was secretly met by Allen Pinkerton and several other people whose direct concern was for the safety of the President. The story goes that Abe Lincoln, dressed in a gray suit and gray cap, first went to the locomotive to thank the engine man and fireman for his safe journey. Then, accompanied by Pinkerton, Lamon, and H. F. Kenny of the Philadelphia, Wilmington and Baltimore, he rode in a carriage that went to Market Street, a time-killing precaution. Once on Market they continued on to Nineteenth Street, then turned toward Vine, then down to Seventeenth, and finally around to Carpenter Street, having by that time used up the minutes until shortly before eleven when a special train was due to take them to Baltimore and then to Washington.

President-elect Lincoln objected to this extreme secrecy saying that he did not want to hide like a thief. But Colonel Lamon and Detective Pinkerton counseled him by explaining that it was the only way to prevent a tragedy. On February 23, at six in the morning, Abraham Lincoln arrived safely in Washington. A few minutes later Scott received a telegram on the restored lines at Harrisburg which read: PLUMS DELIVERED BY NUTS SAFELY.

This was but one of the many ways the CCRR and its people worked for the Union. During these particularly turbulent years the railroad spent an extra thirty thousand dollars for the special protection of bridges and tracks against saboteurs.

Herman Haupt, a resourceful railroad engineer, organized the Northern army's construction corps. When examining the delicate wooden bridge spanning the Potomac Creek, President Lincoln commented, "I have seen the most remarkable structure human eyes have ever rested upon. That man Haupt has built a bridge four hundred feet long and nearly a hundred feet high, over which loaded trains pass every hour, and upon my word, gentlemen, there is nothing in it but beanpoles and cornstalks."

Other railroad men like Pitcairn and Andrew Carnegie organized the Union Military Telegraph System, while Tom Scott was in charge of military transportation. In 1863, on very short notice, railroad men transported twenty thousand soldiers in full gear including horses over a distance of one thousand miles from the Potomac to Louisville in three days. It was probably the earliest and biggest military transport by railroad. As a consequence President Lincoln personally conferred the rank of colonel on Tom Scott. Behind Scott's achievement was the teamwork of many ordinary people like fireman Leonard Peter De Jager, engine man Jack Shoemaker, and others long forgotten by history.

▣ Chapter 17

"As far as you could see all over these hamlets, all over the whole valley, there was water, gray-brown water," Richard De Jager remembered.

"Coal mine buildings and houses were wrecked. Everything floated like shells down through Conemaugh Valley. Men with shovels and axes tried to save the railroad tracks that water had not yet reached by covering them with soil and gravel and packing it tightly down. Workers pushed cars and tried to start up the engines to bring them to safety. Among them was my uncle Leonard Peter." De Jager wrinkled his eyebrows and closed his eyes, trying to recall the exact scene.

"Doctors and nurses attended the injured townspeople and railroad workers. They used artificial respirators, trying to bring life back to drowned victims. Women and children screamed and ran toward a round hill that was shaped like a great upside down frying pan. But instead of fire, water licked at its sides and enclosed it inch by inch. The nurses and railroad men tried to launch primitively built barges. I don't know what happened to them, because at that moment I received orders to start moving my train."

These are the fragments remembered by an eyewitness to a horror story. It was May and very rainy in the commonwealth of Pennsylvania. The last four days of the month recalled to the minds of many the biblical deluge. Wagons, horses, and people were half-swallowed in the mud. Even the high fields were so drenched that farmers lost all chance to do any spring work.

In their beds of mire, the railroad tracks shook as if built on gelatin hills. Trains moved very, very slowly. Hundreds of workers tried to save the main line of the railroad, particularly that part between Pittsburgh and Harrisburg. Animals and birds escaped up the hills and into the Allegheny Mountains. But people were so distressed at their damaged property that they lost their senses and the wisdom to leave.

From the Alleghenies and the small surrounding hills, thousands of streams poured down into the South Fork Dam, into the Conemaugh River. Even the Ohio on the west and the Susquehanna on the east were dangerously swollen. Between the two, dozens of small but treacherous rivers, including the Monongahela and the Juniata, became restive. From four to eight inches of water had even fallen in localities well downstream. Tragedy hung in the air.

On the afternoon of May 30, a severe storm developed in the western part of the commonwealth and gradually moved east. The rain, in competition with the wind, increased in intensity each moment. Powerful gusts pulled trees up from their roots, houses from their foundations, people from each other, and swept them all away.

On orders from the president of the CCRR, thousands of railroad workers were mobilized on all divisions and four engineers left Philadelphia late Friday morning, May 31. They were told to save the railroad properties and try to keep the tracks open on all main lines. Telegraph wires buzzed twenty-four hours a day with reports of flood conditions.

The people of Johnstown, Williamsport, South Fork, Milton, and Renovo prayed hard and fortified their communities by building walls of rock and debris. Everyone thought that God would protect them from approaching tragedy. But no one really grasped the immensity of the threat. No attempts were made to move to higher places.

The well-organized railroad workers with their fresh telegraph reports warned inhabitants to evacuate. From their Johnstown and South Fork stations, they sent messengers on horses to alert and plead with citizenry to leave their places of work and their homes. But the Conemaugh Valley was loved and its poor people did not want to desert it for unknown regions. They stayed on stubbornly, moving about as usual, feeding the livestock and waiting to see what would develop. The rain poured. The water rose. Word of disaster came in from other areas. Some of the less trusting began to build barges or to push rocks and soil against the walls of their houses.

At two-thirty on the afternoon of May 31, as if on a signal, the old South Fork Dam burst under colossal pressure. Huge waves, like a pack of mad wolves, ravaged people, devoured homes, farms, railroad buildings, tracks, and trains. In a few minutes everything was rolling wildly through the Conemaugh Valley. Amid the screams of people and animals were heard the strange sounds of locomotive blasts and the explosions of steam engines. A passenger train standing at Conemaugh station was pulled off the track by one tremendous wave and dragged four hundred feet downstream like so much rubbish. A number five iron bridge, one hundred and sixty-five feet long, burst apart like a box of crushed matches. A number six bridge, with telegraph lines, a station building, roadbed, and tracks vanished. Mingling in this watery hell were stores, factories, and two thousand homes. Even the Conemaugh viaduct, a solid stone structure eighty feet high, simply disappeared. The flood claimed the Conemaugh roundhouse, sidings, yards, forty locomotives, twenty-two passenger cars, and three hundred and fifteen freight cars that stood on the main track between South Fork and Johnstown. Twenty-nine miles of track and seven hundred thousand yards of roadbed were destroyed with it. Three thousand human beings, many of them railroad workers, perished in the floods.

"I saw the four locomotives lying on their backs," Richard recalled. "I just noticed the wheels sticking up from the water. The fifth one, number one twenty-seven, was the old diamond-stock type, but I could only see part of it. Leonard Peter was touching the cab roof with his head. I don't know why, but he had the engine whistle blowing constantly. In front of him were piles of debris; behind him were passenger cars and water that gradually encircled him. I don't know what happened to him. He was trying to save the locomotive, and he went with the debris. . . ."

▣ Chapter 18

"As we know, the CCRR never runs behind time. And for a punctual, prompt road, I'm sure this story will not meet with your approval. However, the emergency in which I am placed at this moment compels me to punish you as severely as the managers of this railroad did to me the other day."

And with these words, the prominent Washington lawyer and railroad man, Herman Theobald von Hoth the Third, began his speech at the fiftieth anniversary celebration of the CCRR. It was a sunny April afternoon. Present at the Philadelphia Academy of Music were dozens of Von Hoths, and a multitude of other powerful representatives of American industry, including Rollons, Abdollers, Meynemars, Vanderflitts, Jameses, Smalls, and Seymours.

From the dais von Hoth fondly presented one more sweeping glance at a sea of well-groomed heads filled with holiday spirit and tobacco smoke. Red and white carnations dotted the entire scene; every buttonhole had a flower in honor of the birthday.

He continued his speech, which though light in tone, accurately defined the present rosy state of the CCRR.

"I set out from Washington on the four o'clock train for New York, and in the dining car I met the wife of a great statesman of our land. She was also going to New York. She was alone. I was alone.

"Said I, 'Madame, don't you think it quite unsafe that you travel alone to New York so late in the afternoon?'

"'Oh, no,' said she, 'we are on the CCRR, and nothing ever happens on the CCRR.' I congratulated her on the correctness of her appraisal. By and by the train came to a halt on the near side of Baltimore. It was discovered that we had a hotbox. We arrived in Baltimore two hours behind time.

"We started out again from Baltimore, and before we had reached Philadelphia we had endured another hotbox. We arrived four hours behind time. Then, lo and behold, before we had attained Jersey City a cylinder blew out. I visited the lady, and consoled her by saying, 'you see, something does happen.' When we finally arrived in Jersey City, I asked, 'Well, madame, how will you be getting uptown?'

"She said, 'I shall take a cab.'

"When we had crossed the river to the New York side, she came to me in great distress and said, 'They don't provide cabs here after midnight.'

"I said, 'Madame, what are you going to do about it?'

"She replied, 'I am going to throw myself upon you.'"

Von Hoth took a deep breath, sipped some water, and proceeded.

"Well, I got her to her hotel in the upper part of the city at half past one o'clock in the morning . . . and we have never once met since that day when she does not say to me,

'What jolly fellows those managers of the CCRR were, to give us such a nice long evening together!' "

The hall rocked with laughter, though the junior members of the company snickered enough to draw the attention of President von Hoth the Second who was seated on the dais. However, he too smiled, so as not to appear unsociable.

An ascetic, quiet, serious-minded man, von Hoth the Second ultimately died of coronary thrombosis, though he was expected to die of the stomach trouble that had beset most of his life. He was educated as an engineer and was a graduate of Rensselaer Polytechnic Institute. Probably his most important achievement was purchasing the Wilmington Railroad, on which he made a handsome private profit. Most of his presidential years were spent fighting the competition of railroad tycoons like Jay Gould, William H. Vanderbilt, J. Pierpont Morgan, and their families.

The struggles between these giants centered around the fixing of rates for passengers and freight. Rate wars were common before the Civil War. The tactics employed by these railroad barons were ruthless and reached a dangerous peak for the country in the 1870's and '80's. For example, in April of 1876 Commodore Vanderbilt ordered his railroad to reduce its rates by as much as sixty per cent. Thus passenger fares from Chicago to Boston dropped from twenty-five to fourteen dollars. Freight rates on agricultural products from Chicago to New York dropped from fifty cents to eighteen cents per hundred pounds. It was not until the passage of the Interstate Commerce Act and later bills that attempts were made in any way to establish some equitable standards.

But no trace of these conflicts was going to be allowed to mar the festivities on this happy fiftieth anniversary afternoon. Von Hoth the Second now rose, and speaking in a quiet voice, surveyed all fifty years in fact and figure. The guests listened raptly as his low, monotonous voice conveyed an appealing sketch of the workers. ". . . Then there is the fact that each man stands closely alongside of each other man, sharing his prosperity and adversity. As evidence of this, some ten years since they combined to organize their Relief Fund, and that Relief Fund today numbers fifty-two thousand members, and had distributed among its membership a sum of money over six million dollars—caring for the sick, for the widows, for the orphans, for those who in the performance of their duty have sacrificed their lives or their limbs. Today the Relief Fund is distributing from those who are blessed by health and freedom from accident to those of their fellow employees who have met with misfortune a sum of money equal to two thousand dollars for each working day."

These last words were lost on some of the minor employees because of their feeling that the railroad companies were making tremendous profits and did not give labor a fair share. But the faces remained expressionless.

In the corner of the hall sat Richard De Jager with a group of other men from Pittsburgh. He had made the trip at the invitation of the von Hoths, and Bertha had come with him. She had never been in so great a city as Philadelphia, which was four times the size of Pittsburgh and much more beautiful. The Philadelphia trolleys extended farther than those of any other city in the country, and everyone found them a delightful excursion; Bertha seemed to enjoy them more than anyone.

That afternoon the program of festivities listed a concert by a sixty-piece orchestra under the baton of Charles M. Schmitz. But Bertha could not attend the jubilee in the Academy of Music, because ladies were not invited. Later, Richard faithfully related to her exactly how and what Maestro Schmitz had conducted. Bertha was most delighted to find out that the works of Franz Schubert and Robert Schumann were played. She had particular admiration for the latter, both for his music and his love for Clara Wieck. To Bertha, the famous composer and his wife exemplified an ideal love and marriage. She had read and been greatly moved by a magazine serial on their life together.

As planned, Bertha De Jager spent that afternoon with a friend, touring Philadelphia and shopping. She bought woolen cloth to make the children suits, cotton for Richard's shirts, and a piece of silk for herself. She even had time to visit the various offices of the CCRR. At those places she found you could buy ordinary or sleeping car tickets to any part of the country, send your personal baggage, and even arrange for a carriage that would await you at your destination. To Bertha the whole city was a marvel of complications and efficiency; she would have much to talk about back home.

When the jubilee had finally drawn to a close, Richard returned to the home of his host and a supper of chicken, pork, red beets, potatoes, and an elaborately decorated fruitcake that Bertha had baked especially for the occasion. Over the meal the men spoke about their railroad work. There was always plenty to do, and it was always done under military-like discipline. Salaries were middling for jobs that were so hard. The host, a distant relative of the von Hoths, raised some critical points about the president's speech, which in his opinion was a bit too bombastic. Richard thought that their relative should have given more credit to the backbone of the railroad, the hard-working employees on the lower levels. He talked openly, quietly, but with a dozen interruptions from Bertha, who kept asking about the orchestra. How long did they play? Which selections were most enthusiastically received? Did anyone sing?

It was getting on in the evening when the subject of music led the hostess to leave the room and return with a violin, which she placed in Richard's hands. He tuned it deftly and played an air which they all recognized so well that they began to sing along.

155

Up in Ninth Street Station there's a man
Whose hist'ry shows the prizes to be won by working.
Filling well a dozen diff'rent places,
He's risen to the top by never shirking.
Many years he helped to handle freight and made it pay—
Then boss gave him milk to haul in many cans a day.

The song, of course, referred to George Nixon, who with his wife's help rose from among the ranks to become a vice-president of the railroad. As Richard discovered that the singing was better than his playing, he put down the violin and joined them in the chorus.

Mr. Nixon! O, Nixon!
He's a man you can't play tricks on
And there never is a minute
Our v.p. isn't in it.
Biz for breakfast
Biz for luncheon
Biz for dinner too,
Asking statements by the millions
Every day or two.
Mr. Nixon! O, Nixon!
You are getting fine increases,
And you'll soon show us
The passenger crew
Has been making the sauce.

▣ Chapter 19

If you are not a wife, you feel helpless when you see that some men fear life itself. They are afraid of all things, but above all they fear new things. It is difficult to find the cause; the easiest explanation is that they are born with this chemistry of the mind. Richard De Jager was one of these people, and as is typical of the species, he was a hard worker and a good family man.

The von Hoths had been quietly grooming Richard for a better position on the CCRR, and for that reason switched him from job to job to give him the maximum railroad experience. But Richard, though he was a conscientious worker, was not sufficiently aggressive or ambitious. Lost in the crowd of von Hoth's relatives, he was finally settled as a telegraph operator. His general superintendent on the Pittsburgh division was Samuel Fogg, and a Carl Wilson was in charge of electrical matters. Both men were fair but exacting superiors. This made little difference to Richard, whose native intelligence far surpassed his courage in practically every situation.

One evening he returned home late from work. His wife, Bertha, was putting wood on the stove when he came in. Instead of sitting down to supper he went over to a chair in the kitchen corner, sat down, put his head in his hands, and began to cry. The children were asleep and the house was strangely silent. Bertha turned her face toward Richard to greet him. When she saw his slumped figure in the chair she quickly wiped her hands on her apron and ran to him.

"What's wrong, dear? Did something bad happen in the yard?" She put a strong hand gently on his head as if speaking to a child. "Dick, what has happened? Tell me."

He looked at her, his eyes wet with tears, his voice hoarse. "I have worked on the railroad for many years and now I have to look for a job somewhere else."

Bertha stood quietly in front of him, her face pale.

"You are my wife, how can I fail you? What will happen to our children while I look for another job?"

"What are you talking about? Why do you have to leave

your job?" She sat down on a chair beside him. "You are a good worker. Everyone likes you at the yard. I've heard many times that you are the best employee on the railroad. . . ."

Silently Richard looked at his wife's delicate face, and then he pulled the *Evening Times* out of his pocket. On the back page was an article almost torn out by his fingernails. Bertha scanned it, puzzled, and then began reading it quickly.

"As stated by us yesterday, the experiments with the telephone were continued in the afternoon by the railroad officials in this city. One instrument was attached in Samuel Fogg's private office and was operated by Carl Wilson. The other instrument was placed in the office of Mr. Pitcairn, Pittsburgh, and operated by Frank Hollister, Mr. Fogg superintending the operations at that point. In the office in this city a group of people were seated, each of whom took a turn talking, or singing a song, to the gentlemen in Pittsburgh. 'Can you understand?' asked the men in this city, and the answer came, 'Yes.' 'Sing us a song,' Pittsburgh then asked. 'Hold the Fort,' 'America,' 'The Old Gray Colt,' and 'Three Crows' were sung, which Pittsburgh answered by saying, 'We heard that splendidly; do it again.' The long metre doxology was sung by Pittsburgh, and received quite distinctly in this office."

Bertha, now composed, looked up and asked softly, "Well, what has this to do with you? You are a telegraph operator."

"You don't understand what it means yet," he responded tensely. "Read further and you will see for yourself."

She began reading again without even glancing at him. It was the story of the first telephone on the railroad.

"Professor Alexander Graham Bell was not in Pittsburgh yesterday, as previously reported, but is in New York lecturing on the telephone. The words on the short circuit of fifteen miles were easily understood, but as the circuit yesterday was over one hundred miles they were rather hard to hear; the sounds came plainly but were very faint. Practice in listening is required to separate the sounds of voices from the noises that are made by the vibrations of the wires on the lines or from induction.

"Contrary to general belief, there is no battery used on the wire. The sounds are carried by only that amount of electricity that is generated by a permanent magnet in connection with an iron diaphragm, which, being spoken against, is caused to vibrate and thus alternately approach and recede from the magnet. The electricity thus generated is the power carrying the sound waves. One of the most satisfactory recent experiments with the telephone was that of a trio of voices singing, each part being carried so plainly that the listeners were enabled to hear distinctly and recognize the parts, the harmony being perfect."

As Bertha lowered the paper and looked up, Richard knew what she was going to say. He jumped up from the chair before she could speak. "Read the last paragraph and you will understand that in a few months, or perhaps a year, every telegraph operator in the country will be out of a job!"

To satisfy her husband and her own curiosity, she read the last paragraph.

"It is proposed by the officials in this city to make numerous future tests by placing the telephone under different conditions and also to test for electric currents by using a sensitive galvanometer. The instruments are quite simple and are of like shape for both transmitting and receiving. Professor Bell is now working to perfect this method of transmitting information and we hope to see an important facility for all businesses, and especially for the railroads, grow out of his untiring efforts."

She had hardly finished when Richard began talking again. "Our boss said yesterday that soon the operations in the yards, shops, offices, and even the disposition of trains and single cars will be conducted by telephone. My place is going to be the first to install these changes. With the changes will go all the telegraph operators—and where will we go, please tell me?" Richard was almost shouting. "Where can I find work? What kind of work?" Bertha quickly tried to hush him, gesturing toward the upstairs. Richard only looked more frantic. "And how will I be able to support my children?"

For a few seconds the sudden stillness rang in Bertha's ears. She recognized the problem now but there was, at the moment, nothing to do but find some weak points in her husband's argument and relieve some of his despondency. There was no advantage in developing a tragic story before all the facts were known. She walked toward the stove to see how the wood was burning and calmly said, "I think you are capable of learning a different job, and I am sure the bosses will give you an opportunity." Bertha had never been openly affectionate toward her husband, but now she made every effort to draw him out of his despair. She continued talking as she put the lid back on the stove and placed a kettle of water over it. "Do you know what we will do?"

He gave no answer and she continued. "If you lose your job, I will ask mother to take care of the children and I will work myself while you look for another place."

Richard went back to his chair and sat down. "This is not a solution to our problem. I worked hard for the railroad. Who is going to teach me new things, and who will start me off with enough pay to support my family?"

Bertha was quickly realizing the seriousness of the situation, but she tried not to show her fears. Coming over to him, she soothingly put her hand on his head again and suggested that he go to sleep. Richard sighed. Tomorrow he had to rise early and go to work—who knew, perhaps for the last time. He had never been late for work and he did not want to be late on what he supposed was to be his final day.

Neither of them slept well. The same thought turned over and over in their minds. Richard lay on his back, stared at the black ceiling, paralyzed by his worries, unable to reach any satisfactory conclusion. Bertha was different. She loved her husband for his sincerity and honesty, but she was also a practical woman who knew how to confront daily problems. She would find the solution to this one too.

Before Bertha had been married, she had worked as a nurse-maid in the home of her relative, President von Hoth the Second. Now perhaps she might go see him secretly the first thing in the morning, and let him know how they felt about the railroad and Professor Bell's invention. Yes, Bertha decided, she would go. She never told her husband what she had done to keep him in his job. She knew that Richard would lose all pride in his job and perhaps leave the railroad for good if he ever discovered her interference.

Richard went to work as usual that day, and his wife dressed and went to see von Hoth, to ask if Richard might be trained as a telephone operator or be sent to another job where he could use his knowledge of railroading in some way.

▣ Chapter 20

It was a warm Sunday afternoon in May. The four-story Union Depot in Pittsburgh shone brightly in a sun whose rays invaded the building through the windows to flood its many arcades. Shrill whistles, puffing locomotives, chattering passengers, the cries of the conductors and porters, the excited voices of children, all enveloped in smoke and steam, made the railroad station a bustling, festive place.

Richard De Jager had promised his son William that they would take an excursion to Pittsburgh for his birthday. William, whose nickname "Willie the Whistle" came about because of his lisping pronunciation, looked exactly like his father and possessed the same intense family feeling. He had asked his father to take the four other children with them. Richard liked to spend every spare moment with his family and readily agreed to Willie's suggestion. This would also provide Bertha with an opportunity for a little rest. Only little Rudolph would stay at home with his mother.

After an early, hardy breakfast, the four little De Jagers and their father left for the wonderful city of Pittsburgh. Once there, they asked to see City Hall, the Customs House, and the Arsenal. Besides, Willie the Whistle had homework for school; he was writing a story about Pittsburgh for his class. And, oh yes, they must not forget to go to the top of the Courthouse so that they could view the entire city and all its hills and rivers. Because it was Sunday, little smoke was visible in the warm May air.

Willie the Whistle, as good in history as he was in athletics, knew the Indian names for the three rivers. He was more than pleased to show off his knowledge. The Ohio River meant "fair water" in the Seneca language; while the Delawares gave the Allegheny River its name because it was "nice to look upon." Willie couldn't remember which tribe was responsible for the Monongahela, but he did know that it meant either "falling in banks," or "river without islands." His fund of information surprised and impressed his father, though it was probably more broad than it was accurate. Agatha, Sigismund and Richard, Junior, listened attentively, accepting Willie as the family expert even though he was younger. Didn't he know everything about football and baseball?

On this particular Sunday afternoon he surpassed himself. He quoted Arthur Lee's description of Pittsburgh in 1784: "The city is inhabited almost entirely by the Irish and Scots, who live in paltry log houses, and are as dirty as in the north of Ireland or even in Scotland. There is a great deal of small trade carried on, the goods being brought at the vast expense of forty-five shillings per hundredweight, from Baltimore. They take, in the shops, money, wheat, flour and skin. Pittsburgh, I believe, will never be very considerable."

It was hardly necessary for Willie to point out how today's Pittsburgh contradicted Mr. Lee. All they had to do was just look around them at the many factories, mining buildings, church steeples, and large public structures. Thousands worked in those factories and mines, building these industrial monuments to Rollon, Abdoller, Meynemar, Small, and von Hoth.

It seemed amazing, as Willie pointed out, that Pittsburgh production had originally begun with whiskey sold to the Indians for skins and furs. This, of course, was during Arthur Lee's time. He and his contemporaries knew very little about the treasures lying in western Pennsylvania. There was underground wealth waiting for the hands of the bankers to stretch out to promote their full growth and exploitation. Coal, iron, copper, oil, sand, and clay deposits were hidden from view along with granite, slate, limestone, kaolin, and even silver and gold. Navigable rivers and canals aided the developing trade and commerce. Later the railroad came, an iron horse to build and carry fortunes. Most important were the poorer sorts of people with their industriousness and will to build. The Scotch, Irish, German, Polish, and French workers were represented along with many other nationalities and races. They all labored to raise American business to its high level of power and wealth. They paid for it in sweat, blood, and lives, but there were few regrets and no looking back.

Willie the Whistle knew all these exciting facts and it delighted him that his family had been part of them all. The railroad interested him so much. Union Depot did not; he went along with it because it was part of the excursion plan. Besides, his father had promised that he would show them a giant steam locomotive.

When they reached the platform between the tracks, a new type of train had just arrived from Philadelphia. Even before Richard De Jager had a chance to tell the children to stay close together in the crowd, Agatha discovered that Willie the Whistle and Sigismund were lost.

Richard, Junior, was eager for excitement. "Maybe they are playing hide and seek."

"This is not the place to play games!" his father said firmly. He looked around quickly and then told the two remaining children, "You, Agatha, look to your left and you, Richie, look to the right, and I shall look in the front and back. We certainly must spot them." He held their hands tightly and walked toward the end of the last train.

Passengers with suitcases, packages, and bundles shuttled back and forth. Their bustling and their cries added to the confusion. It took Richard De Jager fully ten minutes to reach the last car of the train. Suddenly he saw his two boys. They were standing on either side of a tall, handsomely dressed older man, whose two arms rested on the boys' shoulders as he spoke to them. The trio was studying the last car, a private car used by high company officials.

Richard was astounded. He easily recognized the distinguished-looking man as Herman von Hoth, Bertha's relative, and the president of the CCRR. Richard immediately recalled all the stories and gossip he had heard concerning this well-known figure, the boss of the whole gigantic railroad. Mr. von Hoth was a wealthy megalomaniac with aristocratic habits, a stern man whom even his relatives found hard to soften. Although he had been born and raised in Pittsburgh, he did not visit the city very often. His wealth had afforded him the best American and European educations and the opportunity to be anything he wanted. It was a mystery to many why he chose the railroad. Perhaps it was because of his father's investments or because of his own early work on the railroad. There were those, including Bertha, who said Herman von Hoth was tough on the outside but mellow on the inside; he was, at least, romantic enough to be an ardent traveler and he did seem to regard the railroad as a means of diversion and amusement, as well as of hard profit. Other controversial opinions circulated around the famous Mr. von Hoth, but one fact remained certain. He did have many powerful friends here and abroad, including the American President.

In personal contacts, von Hoth was difficult and often unpleasant. But as the years sped by, he became more understanding, and his relatives did find him more accessible. He had a rare talent for multiplying his millions while improving the railroad. The first task he accomplished, and with great success, was to stop rate-breaking. This was an abuse condoned by many big shippers. They would demand, using various threats, unjust cuts in the cost of shipping their freight by rail. Von Hoth, with the President's aid and federal legislation, effectively halted such practices and saved the railroad from bankruptcy.

Although he behaved like a Prussian with his employees, von Hoth did have one great weakness—children. He seemed to love them all, whoever they belonged to. Richard De Jager was now a witness to this himself. It took a few minutes before he mustered enough courage to approach the president and speak. Finally he did, and in a brightly joking fashion at that, "Mr. von Hoth, the railroad is yours, but those two boys are Bertha's and mine." He removed his hat, nodding to von Hoth, and then stretched out his hands for the boys to come.

Von Hoth was a bit taken aback at the remark but managed to answer quickly. "Hello, Richard, hello. Are you sure they are yours? They are very bright boys indeed!"

"Yes." Richard seemed unsure whether to be proud or embarrassed.

"Well. Are you and Bertha thinking of making railroad men of them?"

Without much deliberation, De Jager answered, "One railroad man in the family is enough."

Von Hoth's round face became thoughtful. "Do you think it is so bad on the railroad that you won't want your children working on it?"

"Oh, no!" Richard began his retreat. "But Bertha and I want our children to select their own occupations. I wouldn't want to impose anything on them that would make them unhappy or regretful later."

"That's the right approach," the president said. "But in spite of everything, I think Bertha's sons will be railroad men." Touching the fair heads of Willie the Whistle and Sigismund, he concluded, "But you'll have to be good baggagemasters and learn how to take care of your baggage, so that you don't lose it. Am I right, Willie, Sig?"

The boys nodded their heads in unison and their father blushed. Von Hoth laughed at his own joke. He patted the boys' heads once more and said, "Good-bye, baggagemasters, and my warmest regards to your mother."

He started up the steps of his private car, but turned back to ask, "Do you know what your son Willie the Whistle wants to be?"

Richard De Jager was still holding his hat in his hands. "What, Mr. von Hoth?"

"He wants to be in my place. He wants to be nothing else but president of the railroad!" Von Hoth vanished into his car and they could hear laughter behind the door.

▣ Chapter 21

Tom Tripple was a contented but somewhat perplexed farmer. His young and conscientious farmhand had requested that he be paid half in cash and half in farm products: cheese, butter, milk, meat, flour, and vegetables. The latter was all to be delivered sometime in the second part of December. Farmer Tripple was even more confused because the boy had asked him to keep it a secret. Naturally he respected all his conditions; it was quite convenient to pay his seasonal helper in produce rather than in money. But still he wondered. The young ones certainly had their own way of doing things, and especially Willie the Whistle De Jager.

"To bring up children to be real people you have to give them opportunities to learn and you must teach them to fear God, obey their parents, and keep constantly occupied." In one sentence, railroadman Richard De Jager expressed his whole life's purpose. His wife Bertha was in complete agreement. As a result, when school was out, the three older De Jager boys worked at farming or gardening for various landowners in Glen Manors. Agatha stayed home with her mother, taking care of little Rudolph, helping to prepare meals, and washing and ironing for the working men of the family.

During the evening, the family sat around reading aloud to one another, playing games, or discussing family problems. On Sunday after church, Bertha, accompanied by Agatha and Rudolph, would visit friends or stay at home with Richard if he had that Sunday off. The three older boys would go down to the field near the school to play baseball. Of the three,

Willie was the original thinker. Even as a small boy he made plans without the benefit of the grown-ups' advice. At times this independence was astonishing; anything he did he did well, but in his own original way. Although afterward he was just as likely to lapse into a period of indifference. He was shrewd, quick, and realistic. When someone gave him ideas he would listen politely, but usually later follow his own judgment.

Tripple's farm was some two miles up the hill from the shady road where the De Jager family lived. Every morning at six, Willie finished his breakfast and went to work. He helped feed the chickens, water the cows, and often led the horses in plowing. The Tripples were fond of Willie. The tall farmer liked the boy because he knew how to handle things and his very short wife liked him because he was always smiling and willing to do things. Besides, he had found a way to put the chickens' nests high enough off the ground so that the fox couldn't get to the chickens, which was enough to make any farmer's wife happy. Mrs. Tripple also enjoyed going on climbing hikes with Willie.

One summer day when Willie had finished his tasks with the animals, Mr. Tripple said, "The boards on the side of our well are completely rotten and the dirt is starting to fall into the water. Perhaps today we can do something about it. I have some new boards lying under the barn."

"Don't you think it would be better to make brick walls?" suggested Willie. "Then you'll have no problems with the well for the rest of your life."

"A fine suggestion," the farmer said, "but for bricks we need money and we also need a bricklayer. At the moment we haven't enough bricks to spare nor a bricklayer available to do the work." Laughing, he took Willie aside and led him by the arm to the well. "With your help I think we can replace the top today."

Willie brightened and stood up straight. The praise and display of confidence made him feel almost as tall as the farmer. Mr. Tripple, still holding him by the arm, frowned a moment, hesitated, and then asked his question. "My boy, tell me, what are you going to do with the money I pay you, and especially with the food I will be delivering in December?"

Willie paused, looking directly at the farmer, and said, "I will tell you, Mr. Tripple, but you must keep it a secret. No one must know."

"Willie, you know that a secret with us is as safe as something thrown to the bottom of the well. No one will ever draw it out."

The boy searched the farmer's wrinkled face and looked again at the well. "Part of the money will go to my mother," he said, "and part of it I'll spend for baseball equipment for me and my brothers."

"That's a good and generous idea. I know that all the De Jager boys are excellent baseball players."

"I like it better than any sport. I'm not as good as Sig, but I'm not too bad either," Willie responded with assurance.

"But why did you ask me to deliver all the farm goods exactly on December twenty-second and to keep it a secret from everyone, even my wife?"

They approached the well and Willie absent-mindedly kicked his foot against its side. "It wouldn't seem important to anyone else, but it is to me."

"I'm sure it's very important," the farmer said, smiling down at him.

"Well, December twenty-third is my little brother's birthday. Usually, the day before, mother goes to town to shop for his birthday and also for Christmas. I wanted everything to be there waiting for her when she comes back. I planned it so it would be a surprise and right in time for the holidays, too." Willie stopped, but looked as if there was something more he wanted to say. Then he went on quickly in confidential tones,

"My parents have always given me things, but I feel I'm getting too big to be so dependent. I wanted to try to pay them back in some way, to settle my obligations to them."

Farmer Tripple was a quick thinker and was seldom at a loss for words. At this moment he said nothing. Finally, in a low voice, he replied, "I will do my best, Willie."

It took them the rest of the morning to measure and cut the boards which were to replace the rotten ones. Just as they were finishing up, Mrs. Tripple called them in to lunch. Their appetites were hardy and their conversation enthusiastic, as they discussed a topic that was a favorite with both the old farmer and the young boy—Indians, especially those in Pennsylvania.

Farmer Tripple was telling his young listener a favorite story of his about the Mingo chief, Logan, "It seems that old Judge Brown, Jim Reed, and one of the McClays were wandering around Big Spring to bear. They spotted one about a mile from the spring and split up to get a shot at him. When Judge Brown got to the spring, the bear was nowhere in sight, but the hunter didn't care. He was thirsty enough to consider it his very good fortune to discover so fine a spring. When he put his head near the water, he saw the reflection of a magnificently tall Indian. The hunter jumped for his gun, but as he did so the Indian gave a yell, knocked up the pan of his own gun, threw out the priming and extended an open palm.

"Judge Brown had been the first actual settler in Kishicoquillas valley. He had known many Indians, but of Logan, the friendly Indian whom he met at the spring, he said"—Farmer Tripple stopped in the middle of the story and closed his eyes to remember the Judge's exact words—" 'This was Logan, the best specimen of humanity I ever met with, either white or red.'

"Logan and the hunters became friends and when the men visited Logan's camp, Mr. McClay and the renowned chief shot at a target for a dollar a shot. McClay, a dead shot, was the victor. The Indian, moments later, emerged from his hut with as many deerskins as he had lost in dollars. McClay felt it was only a game, and refused the payment, but the remarkable Logan said, 'I bet to make you shoot your best; I gentleman, and I take you dollar if me beat.'

"McClay took the skins for one reason only: he would not insult the dignity and honor of such a red man."

Willie, who knew and loved the many stories about Logan, had never heard this one. He listened with rapt attention till the very last word. Mrs. Tripple, too, listened with quiet pleasure. But the boy's delight was yet to be increased. He admired the Indians, as many young people do, and his father had often recounted stories of the many red men who had toiled on the railroad, aiding the progress that would lead to their own extermination. Now Farmer Tripple was foraging in a big oak chest near the window and finally returned with a yellowed paper. It was the original letter written by R. P. McClay to a friend, the authentic basis of the story that the farmer had just told Willie. The boy was thrilled, and spent the rest of lunchtime poring over the old document, written in a large, careful hand.

But the well had to be completed, and so the farmer and his young helper returned to their work. They labored all afternoon in the hot sun, and as they worked Willie related some Indian stories he knew. The wind died, and the sun beat down more intensely. Then, just when they felt the job was about finished, and Willie reached for the last few nails, Mr. Tripple slipped and with a shout fell into the well.

Willie grabbed the heavy well-rope and bucket and began, with difficulty, to unwind it into the well, at the same time calling for Mrs. Tripple. She came running out of the house and together, she and Willie strained to roll up the heavy rope and bucket that Mr. Tripple had grasped and was clinging to tightly.

When the wet and shaken farmer reached the top, he gasped, "Thank God the rope was strong enough to hold me. Thank you, my dear. . . ." He leaned against his tiny wife.

"Don't thank me, Tom. You should thank Willie."

"Yes, I know," said the exhausted farmer. "Willie, I owe you my life."

That day Willie the Whistle returned home with his pockets full of money that the grateful farmer had pressed on him. When his mother asked about the unusual amount, he mentioned nothing about the accident or his part in it. "Mr. Tripple paid me my salary for the previous weeks," was all the young man said.

The story came to light the afternoon of December 22, when Farmer Tripple delivered the second half of Willie's salary.

回 Chapter 22

It was the first Sunday in June, and at the De Jager home in Glen Manors the family was collected together to pass judgment on young William's future.

The round kitchen table was covered with a flowered oilcloth. No one had made any move to clear the dishes. Bertha and Richard sat next to each other with their backs to the china closet. William sat opposite them. Agatha and young Rudolph were on one side of him, Sigismund and Richie on the other. They had finished dinner a few moments before and now everyone waited for someone else to start the conversation.

The silence persisted and the tension grew. Willie sat there in an open-collared shirt. He knew everyone was thinking about him. All he could do was roll a green apple between the palms of his hands.

It was Sigismund who started. "Well, we all know the principal of Woodville High School offered to arrange an athletic scholarship for Willie, but he says he doesn't want it."

"But why not, Willie? Why not?" exclaimed the ten-year-old at his elbow.

"Rudolph, let the oldest speak first," their mother said calmly.

The little fellow's face reddened and he lapsed back quietly.

Sigismund, considerably better dressed than his brothers, chose his words carefully. "Such an opportunity is hard to come by, especially for a member of our family." At twenty-two, Sigismund was working in the general store in Glen Manors.

Richard, Junior, scratched his freckled nose and picked up his brother's thoughts. "I have spoken to Willie several times, myself, but he wouldn't listen. Here he has an excellent opportunity to get a college education, perhaps he's the only one in our family who'll get one, but he refuses to follow it up."

"Why not, Willie?" his father asked. "Why don't you want to accept? The principal has promised to help you, and you know he is a man of his word."

Willie looked around at all the anxious faces. His eyes stopped at Agatha, very pretty in her blue dress, her hair neatly combed, her face concerned. Slowly and quietly he directed his explanation to her. "I have thought about this night and day for a long time, and I came to one conclusion—a college education is not for me."

His mother impatiently exclaimed, "What are you saying?"

"Yes, mother, not for me!"

"But why?" his father asked tremulously. There was a trace of anger in his voice, usually so mild. "Tuition will be free. You'll get your room and board. All you have to do is play baseball."

"I like sports, but I don't have the patience to be a learner. I like people and I'd like to manage them. I won't learn this in college. Don't you see that for me it's a waste of time?"

Sigismund jumped up. "In college they teach you things like government and philosophy and a lot of subjects about people —what they've discovered or accomplished. With that knowledge and a diploma you can get a position worthy of your managerial talent."

"He's right, Willie," Agatha confirmed. "With a college diploma you might even become the president of a big corporation some day."

"But Agie, I believe I must get firsthand experience by doing things as I go along. I'll manage somehow."

"How?" his mother asked flatly.

"Yes, how?" repeated his father. "I don't understand you at all, Willie. This is a great opportunity for the son of a minor railroad employee. You have a sports talent and the principal is willing to help. And yet you sit here and throw away a wonderful future."

"I don't want to go to college. I want to start working and earn some money. I'm not going to be a doctor, or a professor, or a politician—I don't need a college education!"

"So what do you want to be?" his father exclaimed in disgust. "Do you want to be a railroad man and spend the rest of your life on a job as a freight brakeman, or maybe if you're lucky, and have some pull with the von Hoths, get a job as a conductor? If you have a college background and a head on your shoulders—as you do—you'll be able to get any job in the country."

William did not give in an inch. "I don't think much of this magic word, college, and I don't believe every door is open to anyone who says the word. Character and a lot of determination and hard work are a lot more important, as far as I'm concerned."

When he had finished, everyone just sat there, still, each one silently groping for a new argument to get Willie to see their side. They were six against one, but the one stood firm. Given Willie's temperament, there seemed little hope of changing his attitude toward education. His mother got up from her chair and made a fire under the coffee. She stood staring for a while at the white enameled pot. The room was so quiet that they could hear the perking of the coffee. Bertha lifted the pot and poured out some for her husband and herself.

He took a sip and said abruptly, "I see no reason to discuss William's future any more. He seems to have made up his mind, and we agreed long ago that the decision would be his. This is the life he wants and it is out of our hands. Everyone here is witness to the fact that we all urged him to go to college, but he refused."

Willie pushed his hair back from his forehead. He felt very badly, but tried to smile gratefully at his father, who continued to speak in a voice now heavy with resignation. "You have to find yourself a job now, Willie, a job that you can get ahead on and make some money so you can eventually marry. You mentioned love for people. Well, it takes more than that to live and support a family. You'll need to make some money."

"I understand, and I've thought this over too. I've decided that I want to work on the railroad first."

"On the railroad?" his father asked in surprise.

"Yes," William said, as emphatically as he could.

His father looked directly at him. "And what do you think you are going to be on the railroad, president or general superintendent? Most of the big bosses on the railroad have a college degree in engineering. What chance will you have? If you get no education you will be a brakeman. That's the top position for those without college!"

"It's not as tragic as you make it," William answered calmly. "I will start as a clerk, and if I don't like it, or I can't move up,

175

I'll go into some other business."

"You can take everything coolly now, without much emotion, but the years go by very fast, Willie, and you can't start all over at thirty when you have a wife and children. Naturally it will help if you are lucky enough to find a wife like your mother, who can manage on a small salary. But if you can't, you are in for plenty of trouble."

"I'd like to try the railroad first. There are so many people there and so many different technical and human problems. The business is so complex that I'm sure eventually I'll be able to find a position where I can make some progress. With the help of friendly people, I think I can manage to succeed. I'm sure I can."

"God help you," his mother said, with a kind of desperate finality. Everyone sitting around the table lowered his eyes in agreement.

"It's your own life, son," his father added, "and from now on you are on your own. The only help you can expect is from God and yourself."

William looked out the kitchen window. It was already dark. The Sunday afternoon had ended.

It took little time for him to get a job on the Coast to Coast Railroad. Herman Theobald von Hoth the Third said to him during the interview, "Or course, your father's unblemished record of never missing a day's work was considered. It has helped to get you, Willie the Whistle, a job as a clerk in the trainmaster's office."

After six months of work his boss sent the personnel manager the following confidential memo, which he in turn forwarded to Mr. von Hoth: "I think anyone who works with him and knows him feels that he is about tops. He's humane, he has a full understanding of the other fellow's feelings and gives him every consideration. He has the happy faculty of having people do things for him. He's keen enough to grasp the problems of money-making on the railroad and to understand them after a short but thorough analysis."

Perhaps Willie the Whistle had also seen things this way that Sunday afternoon at the old round table in his mother's kitchen.

▣ Chapter 23

Miss Gusty Mary Higginbottom had a fine figure and a charming smile. There were a few who suspected that she smiled so frequently in order to show off her row of lovely white teeth. But most people just smiled back. She dressed elegantly and enjoyed doing so. Under her fashionable, large-brimmed hats was an extremely clever mind, one that instinctively knew how to deal with men and sex. Perhaps that's why trainmaster John Victor Casevant selected her for his secretary.

The job of trainmaster was an important one. According to the railroad rules, the trainmaster was to supervise all employees in the passenger and freight service, and be directly responsible for those connected with freight trains. He was required to report promptly to the division superintendent all failures or negligence on the part of the employees, and anything else that came into his sights that could interfere with the prompt and safe working of the railroad. He and his assistants had to be in continuous contact with the trainmen, to see that they were furnished with all the necessary signals and that they used those signals according to the rules. The trainmaster also gave special attention to the speedy movement of freight trains and to the proper distribution of cars for the stations on their division. He saw that all cars were promptly loaded and unloaded, and forwarded without delay. Finally, in case of accident or detention of a train, the trainmaster and his assistants were to see that every precaution was taken to insure the safety of approaching trains and to protect property and people under the charge of and belonging to the railroad company.

For Gusty Mary, there was a good deal of both work and pleasure in the office of the handsome, newly married, trainmaster. It was a delicate kind of work, involving men under constant pressure. But Miss Higginbottom was unusually astute and well qualified for her job. By her second day on the job she had established an aura of friendliness that was at once disarming and immediately effectve. She was cheerful, but could also be quite direct and objective in dealing with railroad men whose problems flowed like a river into John V. Casevant's office. Behind her back everyone called her Gusty Mary. No one quite had the courage to call her anything but "Miss Higginbottom" in her presence, except for her boss, and even he reverted to "Miss Higginbottom" most of the time. He quickly recognized that she knew how to manipulate men better than most railroad people knew how to maneuver trains. And as John knew, she was discreet.

Gusty Mary was born in McKeesport, Pennsylvania, a town containing about two hundred and fifty people. It was located southeast of Pittsburgh, not far from Glen Manors. When still a very young woman she had taken stock and determined her limitations. Although she was good-looking, she did not have the formal education that would have enabled her to hold an advanced position. Besides, even with whatever connections she had or could develop, it was very difficult for a woman to advance at all. It was especially difficult on the railroad, where the policy seemed to be against employing them in the first place. But Gusty Mary had a persistent dream, much like any other girl's, but a bit more specific. She went to the railroad to find a young man whom she could love, marry, and make into a great man.

One day such a man walked into the office. His name was William De Jager, and he had come to work for Mr. Casevant. Gusty Mary looked directly at him and said, "Welcome to the CCRR family." This was the rather simple beginning of their life together. She knew nothing about the fair-haired young man from Glen Manors except that he spoke little, worked hard, and had a ready smile. An exhilarating sense of possibility came into her life because of Willie De Jager. She knew that very well too. She soon learned that he readily tackled anything he wanted to do, and usually in a perfectly admirable way. And he had patience, great patience that never tired of waiting for results. She had instinctively recognized his greatest assets.

As if not to disappoint her, Willie somehow managed to advance from clerk to car tracer, from car tracer to car distributor, and later to the position of chief statistician. He was gaining experience rapidly in passenger and freight operations. Everyone knew Willie the Whistle; he went about with notebook in hand jotting down his observations. Nothing escaped him, except Gusty Mary's relations with Casevant. He watched, listened to, and read everything pertaining to the railroad, and particularly to the CCRR. His memory was phenomenal, and not only for facts and figures; he knew the first names of the wives and children of all of his co-workers. Willie was cooperative and helpful, and in a year's time everyone, from the redcap to the trainmaster, thought of him as his friend. And what is more, the trainmaster's secretary was in love with him. But his resistance was strong. It took him two years to make the final decision. Then, on a brisk October day, Willie the Whistle and Gusty Mary were married.

I, Franklin Kapistrot, the accidental chronicler of this saga, knew Willie the Whistle personally only many years later. I was riding home to dinner with him one evening, and as we were nearing our destination, I said to him, "The stories about your intelligence and your reputation as a clever businessman can't be unfounded, Willie. You've succeeded in becoming a legend in one of the toughest businesses going."

Willie smiled knowingly and then said, "Trifles, trifles. You are coming to my house and you will see who the intelligent and clever one is. You shall find out who is really responsible for all this."

 # Chapter 24

I was so busy working on the virtues of Gusty Mary De Jager, *c'est toujours l'inattendu qui arrive,* that I forgot about Bill Wattson and the novel he was writing on his Russian relative, Tania. Presumably, he was doing this, I thought, to justify his own existence in the world of the De Jagers. I soon discovered, however, that the novel had remained in dramatic outline for a long time, while his creative life was being tapped by the dulling sensationalism of American youth in the 1960s.

It was a winter evening in a cozy nightclub: humming noises, an orchestra playing rock 'n' roll, couples dancing. Suddenly the rock 'n' roll ceased and the orchestra launched into the sentimental melody of an Argentine tango; the singer crooned. Everyone looked startled, and searched to see at whose request the sudden change in mood was occurring. Miss Julienne Small, daughter of Jack V. Small, and a brunette in her early thirties, was sipping her extra dry martini and staring at Bill Wattson, who reacted by saying, "I assure you, Julienne, I am guiltless in this matter."

"Evidently. But you have to admit that there is something." She put her hand lightly on his knee. "It certainly is astonishing, you know—I dreamed about you not just once, but three times in a row!"

"Julienne, I never think of you. . . ."

"You know. In a way . . . you could be more polite."

At that moment Elton Call, a young man of twenty-five, head of the improvement department in the Union of Unemployed, walked over. "Oh, I hope I'm not disturbing, Bill?"

"Not at all. Have a seat."

"I'd better not."

"Well, good luck to you," said Julienne. She called the waiter to bring her briefcase and turned back to Wattson. "What good does it do to hold somebody by force? Now . . . I had something to tell you. The articles. You don't contribute enough to our *New World* magazine. There should be a story from the department of cooperatives at least twice a month. It pays well!"

"If you remember, I wrote more in the beginning, but you returned all my articles. If you think they aren't good enough . . ."

"How childish you are! Your writing isn't bad at all. Why don't you come see me with the manuscripts I returned to you? Most convenient would be at my house. We could argue about it. I would help you, or my father would. We could rewrite the material together—you and I. Please come see me, Bill. Give me an argument, make a hellish scene. Is that a deal, dear Bill?"

"All right."

"Remember, we'll work it out." She looked again into her notebook.

"An excellent way to remember, to make a note of everything."

"You do that too?"

"Sometimes."

"Now, I want to boast a little."

"Yes."

"I am starting something new in the *New World*. It will undoubtedly stir up a great deal of interest among the unemployed readers."

"Tell me about it."

"I will. Aside from the directors, only you and my genius father will know about it."

"I feel flattered."

"Well!" she resumed in coquettish tones. "We shall announce shortly some very important, fundamental, and far-reaching news concerning the souls and spirits of the unemployed."

"You certainly are the first one who would think of such a project. Don't be modest about it. It's true. Nobody does anything for the unemployed."

"Do you have a girl?" Then, seeing in Wattson's startled face that he had, she went on more coldly, "My project has been approved by William De Jager!"

"That is something indeed. The referee of agricultural adjustment has been denied the execution of his pet project."

"How about your own?"

"About three weeks ago I submitted it for the president's approval. Since then I have redone it several times. It was considered too good for the unemployed, so I tried to work it out with Mr. Abdoller. Maybe De Jager will accept it now."

"He will accept it."

"Mr. Abdoller told me the last time . . ."

"Do you know what they say about De Jager?"

"No."

"This is to remain between us. . . . People say that he is a tool in the hands of the Abdoller brothers and their oil empire."

"A tool for a good cause, let's hope."

"Of course. What do you think of Joseph Cianfarra?"

"That simple fool? Well, I suppose it's untrue, but I hear that he has something to say about all our programs. Mine is now . . ."

"Certainly. Now Bill, you really worry too much."

"Solomon himself couldn't be more confused. Look what happened to the chief of the Agricultural Department."

"He's a radical! All of them, they're all fools. Only you, you're so different, so deep and unusual. . . ."

"Thank you." He seemed embarrassed by her compliments. "Thank you very much. You haven't yet told me anything about your new program. You merely indicated that it will reach far, and deep, into the hearts and souls of the unemployed."

"It will be a series of articles based on my father's philosophy with the general title, 'The Joy of Life.' "

" 'The Joy of Life?' "

The orchestra started to play rock 'n' roll again and Miss Small persevered. "You'll see what a fantastic response it will get! The first article will be 'The Joy in Family Life,' followed by 'The Joy of the Social-Minded Individual.' After that 'The Joy in Childhood,' 'The Joy in Entertainment,' 'The Joy in Youth,' . . . adulthood . . . old age. . . ."

"In other words, a joyful cycle of joy to joy for the unemployed."

"We'll push this through our entire organization, then among all the unemployed in the country and the rest of the world. It will be done on the grand scale with our own and with government funds. The Abdoller Brothers Foundation will have a hand in it."

"Ho, ho."

"I want your opinion. How do you like the idea?"

"It's hard to tell. You've only given me a very general picture."

"Do you want to hear details? Very well, come see me at my house. I'll give you all the information. You ought to know, Bill, that I'm quite influential with my father and his Catholic friends, and we are very influential in the circles where the De Jagers, Abdollers, Seymours . . ." She saw Bill raise his hand for the check. "What, are you leaving?"

"Well, serious obligations. You know, my mother."

"Too bad, Bill." She leaned forward and spoke close to his ear. "You won't be sorry. I have everything, including connections in Washington. All this for you. . . . You won't be disappointed."

The orchestra changed its tune again. In spite of this appealing musical turn of events, William Wattson went home to work on his Russian epic of World War Two.

ꙮ Chapter 25

A sense of the immediate returns to Denczenko. The overwhelming desire to gratify his hate returns and then ebbs swiftly. His anguish has reached a climax and his mind now seeks release. But the present soon vanishes. His gaze falls on Tania and he thinks he is once more in his native Kiev. Tania is Kraska. He laughs wildly as he imagines Kraska chatting and joking with soldiers in the canteen. Kraska's beauty and popularity bring him a surge of pride. The fevered brain that had turned the writhing Tania into a vivacious, happy Kraska, now transforms Kraska into his wife. He is her youthful, adoring husband. He murmurs endearments, and pours out promises to be faithful, to be strong, to achieve skill in his trade. Insane fervor leads him to call on God to witness his vows. He groans. He pleads with the Almighty. It is an all-powerful God that he must propitiate. Suddenly God is calm and majestic imbued in a golden aura and rosy splendor. Denczenko sobs like a baby. He stoops to kiss the feet of God. He kisses Tania, caresses her legs and runs his fingers through her tangled hair. He remembers: These are the hands that killed the nazi officer. They are stained with blood.

⌗ Chapter 26

Jan does not come for Tania, as she in her pain had begged. An ambulance does arrive, and with Denczenko muttering and crying out protests, Tania is removed to a clearing station close to the bank of the Volga. The ancient truck rumbles over the road and lurches through deep holes. Tania is roused from her stupor. She thinks that she is in a bus on her way to the city of Lwow and to Jan. A smile crosses her lips as she thinks of resting in his arms. They shall walk in the park and talk softly of their love and of the promise of their future life together in peace, plenty, children, success, and faith in each other. The ambulance moves more slowly; then stops. Two other stretchers are put in next to Tania's. Through the open door she catches a glimpse of the horrible debris that strews the roadside. She cries out, then sinks into a stupor again.

As the ambulance bumps over the torn driveway to the hospital, the attendant sees a large, stooped, hulking figure running madly behind the vehicle. It has white hair and a flowing, tobacco-stained mustache. It is Denczenko and he is proclaiming wildly that the ambulance has stolen his treasure. He calls out for Tania, then for Kraska. He raises a desperate wail for his wife. When he reaches the steps, he can be heard to beg God to save him from the fury of the guns.

🐾 Chapter 27

The German forces have been concentrating their efforts on taking Krasnyi Oktiabr. The devastation of the thoroughfare that leads to this immense factory is expressed in the brotherhood of death, the only brotherhood that the German and Russian dead share.

The attackers are ultimately driven back, and for a time at least, this military stronghold is secure. Tanks are being assembled in the cavernous depths of Krasnyi Oktiabr, and after each battle, they are repaired along with the guns and planes that can be salvaged. An underground passageway leads from the factory to military headquarters.

After the bombardment has subsided, Rosen and Skobelev return to their work in the factory. The latter opens a battered tank and finds the swollen bodies of five crew men. Their dead eyes stare at him.

"Look, David!" he calls out. "How is this possible? Dead men cannot drive a tank!"

But Rosen, shuddering and green with sudden sickness, has an answer. "One man, see, still trembles with life."

A courier comes to summon the two of them to General Headquarters.

Headquarters is east of Krasnyi Oktiabr, and as they trudge through the underground tunnel, the two men hear the steady, rhythmic lapping of the Volga. It gives them courage; and just like a mother's lullaby, provides reassurance.

Military court is in session and the case of Lieutenant Horst Kraussgrell is being heard. He has come by parachute, as a spy, and probably would have gone undetected if a wary Russian soldier had not seen that a map had been stuffed into his shoes. Lieutenant Kraussgrell is quickly disposed of and the case of Jan Kowalski is called.

Jan Kowalski is also charged with spying. He maintains, under interrogation, that his name is Wolski and that he was the assistant to Lwow Polytechnic professor Jozef Dobrowicz, who had worked with the Russian scientist Semen Tarasov. With obvious reluctance, Wolski admits that the two scientists had been engaged in experiments to develop an indestructible tank. When questioned further, he acknowledges that he himself participated in those experiments and that he has in his possession the formula for the making of bulletproof steel and the plans for making the tank. When the chairman of the military court asks Wolski why he has not volunteered this information to the Soviets, the Pole becomes surly. When he is accused of hating Russians, he exclaims, "The system! The Soviet system, I hate it."

At this point, Skobelev, who with Rosen has moved up to the front to testify, tells of his experiences with Wolski. He has found him a stolid but good workman. He has watched Wolski carefully, as Headquarters had ordered him to do. He has never observed nor have any of his confidential assistants ever observed Wolski do anything that might indicate he was betraying his special knowledge to the enemy.

Rosen interrupts to exclaim, "This is the man Tania Petrovna knew in Lwow. It was the man she cried to see when she was wounded!"

Wolski hears the exclamation, as Rosen meant he should, and a change comes over the Pole. He is noticeably tense.

The court adjourns soon after. Rosen and Skobelev are called in for a conference with the general. The decision is made: to free Wolski but keep him under even closer surveillance, and to bring him and Tania together as soon as possible.

🔃 Chapter 28

In the clearing house for the wounded, the awkward figure moves through the dim aisles of stretchers. He walks softly, and bends down often to peer into the face of one patient after another. The busy nurses and attendants see him but they are too engrossed in their urgent work to pay attention to him. Finally, he comes to a stretcher set in an archway. A sound of delight springs from his lips. He has found the one for whom he has been searching. Swiftly, with no more than one hurried glance around him, he winds the patient in her bed sheet and lifts her up. Stealthily he moves to a side door and is immediately outside. Denczenko has kidnapped Tania from the hospital. Totally deranged by now, he knows he is not carrying Tania. Rather it is the elixir of life in human guise. A treasure of untold value. He makes his way rapidly through dark streets. Great joy wells up in his heart. He has no need for God. No need for anything but his own strong hands to hold this treasure.

⌘ Chapter 29

A conversation is taking place between Rosen, Skobelev and Wolski in a small office in General Headquarters. It begins in restraint, for Wolski has nothing but contempt for the two Russians. He has no confidence in their avowals of interest in him. When Rosen asks him to go to Tania, he firmly refuses. Even when Rosen begs him to do so, pointing out that Tania is in pain and is crying for him, he refuses. Rosen is effusive in his pleas. It is Skobelev, less emotional and more discerning of character, who makes real progress. He states frankly, "We love Tania, both Rosen and I, but it is my belief that she cares for neither of us and that it is you she wants."

Bit by bit, with Skobelev taking the lead, Wolski is persuaded. He will see Tania, he says, but even as he agrees to do so, there is doubt and perhaps fear inside. These two, he knows, are planning to use Tania, or she may already have become their tool. He will go to her with this resolution implanted in his mind: "I will tell her nothing of the formula, nothing of the plans."

⌘ Chapter 30

Cannons roar. Tanks rumble. Planes buzz like hornets. The walls of the cellar house tremble. The shudders alternate between the mighty crashes of bombs and falling timbers. Tania, who has been lying in a stupor on her straw pallet in the cellar with Denczenko standing guard over her, stirs. She sits up suddenly, wild-eyed, and cries, "Jan! Jan! Find Jan. Jan can save us."

"*Do chorta, do chorta,*" Denczenko shrieks. "*Do chorta* with Jan. We do not need him. We need only each other." With each word, the Ukrainian's vehemence grows. He seizes Tania and tells her in desperation that he loves her, that they must have a child, a child to live after all this destruction is over.

Tania does not protest or shrink back in fear. Instead, she speaks softly. She reminds Denczenko that he, although a strong and skilled worker, is nevertheless old, and cannot hope to live for many more years, while she is young. . . .

Denczenko's passion is somewhat calmed by her reasoning, but he does not cease his insistent pleading. Finally Tania says with quiet conviction, "Denczenko, I already have a man and a child." These words conquer Denczenko. He sobs like the weary old man that he is.

⌐͞͞ Chapter 31

The character of Skobelev can now be fully revealed. He is found to be deliberate and calculating in his thinking. The instant Wolski agrees to see Tania, Skobelev commands Rosen to take him to her. The two leave the office a few minutes before the bombardment is renewed with even greater force. Simultaneously Skobelev rushes over to his repair shop and takes a military car. He will reach Tania before the other two proceeding by foot can get to her. He will convince her to draw Wolski's secret from him.

The bombardment begins. Air-raid sirens howl. Antiaircraft guns rip open the night and Skobelev, hurrying to get to a safe shelter, is caught in a crevasse made by two crumbling walls. He is pinned but not injured, held there like an animal in a trap. For a few moments he struggles frantically to extricate himself. Then realizing the futility of his efforts, he lies down to think. Rosen and Wolski may be caught as he is. Even if they do reach Tania, his cause is not lost. Wolski, he is confident, will tell Tania his secret, and she will reveal it to her people for she is loyal. Wolski will be taken care of after the indestructible tanks are built. It will be an easy matter to lure Wolski to his death. Death is simply arranged in a factory. With Wolski gone, he Skobelev, not Rosen, will have Tania, because he is the stronger.

⊞ Chapter 32

War has many faces; not always is its course irrevocable like a set clock. The faces of war can be ridiculous. That some of the leaders of the Stalingrad defense should become suddenly preoccupied in the search for a young canteen worker, Tania Petrovna, might well seem foolhardy. Yet they did. Tania, it appears, is an integral part of Stalingrad's security, and she is now lost. Yes, she was last registered in the hospital, and there is no record of her departure. Officials empty their desks. Police on motorcycles and on foot make their way through streets

that lead from the hospital to the cellar. Civilians who personally know her are pressed into the hunt. Tania Petrovna must
be found.

Chapter 33

Still rubbing his eyes, Denczenko climbs out of the cellar; the
disappointment that has replaced his passion makes him anxious to get away from Tania. Moreover, animal fear surges in
him with the increasing force of the bombardment. He has
become obsessed by the implications of two acts: the theft of
Tania from the hospital, and the killing of the nazi officer
whom he should have handed over to the authorities for questioning. His lust for blood is overpowering.

Once out of the cellar he runs anywhere. He is a forest animal pursued by fire. When a guard tries to stop him he shouts
that he is a messenger bound for the first line of defense. As he
runs the conviction grows in him that he should die. Death
would be a release. Yes, he will die, but before he dies he
must kill again, as many times as possible. He is well-prepared,
for he carries many grenades in his pockets.

When he reaches the enemy line and sees a detachment of
tanks approaching, he jumps into a deep hole. The tanks
come close and with keen precision he flings grenades, three
at a time. Like matchboxes the tanks collapse; and the enemy,
seeing their progress impeded, send infantry. At the same time,
the Russians begin a counterattack.

⊞ Chapter 34

Tania is found in the cellar, and she and Wolski have a conversation. It is restrained at first, because the Pole is set on keeping his secret. Tania asks for it and is refused. She pleads and points out that two scientists, one a Pole and the other a Russian, had worked on the project, and that by right of experimentation it belongs to Russia quite as much as to Poland. Wolski is adamant, until Tania tells him that it is their individual and mutual responsibility to vanquish their common enemy, the nazi. He may hate the Russians; he may scorn their way of life. Yet together the Poles and Russians have this foe in common. Wolski is dubious and still antagonistic. There is little lessening of his resolution until Tania tells him that their mutual responsibility is centered in the child that she will bear, his child. Then, still reluctant, still dubious, Wolski agrees to give up the formula and the plans. He and Rosen leave for Headquarters.

⊞ Chapter 35

Thousands of hands work on tanks. Into their making go all the hope of the country. These are no ordinary tanks that will crush like matchboxes. They are stronger than any previous tank ever built, based as they are on the plans of Tarasov and

Dobrowicz, and their aide, Jan Wolski. Krasnyi Oktiabr, the bulwark of the city of Stalingrad, becomes the mighty defense of them all. Within its deep underground chambers, the strength of the people is being renewed.

Ivan Skobelev, engineer at Krasnyi Oktiabr, works feverishly. He has no time to sing now or to play tunes on his harmoshka. There is fiery light burning in his dark eyes. He issues commands in a staccato voice. Workers and friends alike look on him in amazement; one whispers that the old blithe Ivan has been suffocated by the new tanks. Now, he says, Skobelev thinks nothing but tanks, tanks made of indestructible steel.

But no one knows that the engineer holds a secret locked deep in his heart. It is a plan to rid himself of Jan Wolski. It is going to be a good plan, without any possibility of a flaw; and when he has carried it out he will have Tania.

Chapter 36

Life looks golden to Tania Petrovna. Jan Wolski, whom she loves, has become one with her people. He has made an essential contribution to victory. With the achievement of indestructible tanks, the battle will be won. She will have a home; she will have a husband and a child. Once more there will be peace and faith in her heart.

⌗ Chapter 37

David Rosen is a philosopher; his ability to survey himself objectively may at times sap his initiative, but it never causes him to lose his ambition for great achievement. The character of his accomplishments changes, however. Now that the cooperation of Jan Wolski has been secured and his relationship with Tania revealed, David realizes that he may never win her. So he turns his thoughts to statesmanship. David is a rationalist. Once the war is over, the party will need farsighted men who are willing to sacrifice their lives in the country's organization. Through such efforts, he might conservatively gain renown. With renown will come public acclaim, feminine interest and adulation. With women striving to win his favor, he can demonstrate to Tania that he is great in two things, statesmanship and love.

⌗ Chapter 38

Chief engineer Ivan Skobelev is convinced the new world emerging from the war will have no need for a Polish *svoloch*. Neither will he have any need for him; in fact he has none now. He wants to see the last of Jan Wolski. The man's very presence in Krasnyi Oktiabr is stifling. Ivan decides to put his plan into action. He will ask Wolski to observe the first of

the new tanks in action. He will also invite Rosen and Denczenko to participate. Once all four are in the leading tank, he
will suggest to Wolski that he open the tower and peer through
his binoculars at the enemy positions. This will be the signal
for a man at the rear. Wolski is to be shot the instant his head
shows above the tower. The assassin shall be amply rewarded.
When Wolski's death is investigated, it will be easy, Skobelev
reasons, to convince the authorities that an enemy sniper
picked off the stupid Pole.

⌗ Chapter 39

The hour for testing the new tanks arrives. Everyone is nervous and excited. The smudged faces of the workers in Krasnyi
Oktiabr, sour and grim during the weeks of the siege, are
once again smiling. There is an eager spring in their footsteps.
Voices radiate hope. "The moment is at hand," one whispers
to another.

The general attack begins in the hazy dawn. It is as Skobelev had planned it should be. He is in one of the leading tanks,
accompanied by the brave Denczenko, acclaimed a hero for
the grenade destruction of enemy tanks. Two soldiers and Jan
Wolski are also in the tank. Only Rosen is absent, detained by
a command issued at the last moment.
Tanks roll forward with lightning speed, awesome in their
pulsating power. They approach the enemy lines, and Skobelev
makes his request. Jan Wolski opens the tower, and one of
the enemy flings a grenade at the tank. It enters by way of

the tower, and all are killed. Hundreds of other tank crews see
this as a signal for action.

▦ Chapter 40

Just one is left now. David Rosen. All the days of the siege,
death has dogged his footsteps. In the hour of the great attack
it tore his heels, yet he has managed to escape. With tears in
his eyes, he stands up before his fellow-workers and tells them
of Skobelev, Denczenko, and Wolski. In this speech David
Rosen, safe from death's jaws, reveals himself as a powerful
orator. He gains his first public supporters.

▦ Chapter 41

Tania Petrovna learns the news of the deaths from David
Rosen. She takes it as a strong person would. She does not cry
out. When Rosen whispers that she can find security with him,
she barely listens. He has to repeat the words, and he does so
with dignity. But she shakes her head. With equal sincerity,
she explains that although her man, Jan Wolski, is dead, their
child will live, and through its life she will learn of the new
world to come.

Chapter 42

On a long corridor in the Union of Unemployed Miss Marah met Frederick Tribbe, a referee of the Agriculture Department.

"Good morning, Miss Marah!"

"Hi, Fred."

"Is Mr. Wattson in?"

She looked at him starkly. "Yes, he is. And you might ask him . . ."

"What?"

"If he had a nice time last night with our editor Julienne Small."

Entering Wattson's room he called back, "I will, Miss Marah." He saluted Bill. "Long live the cooperative movement!"

"Long live agriculture! Very good of you to come, Fred. Please sit down."

"What is it?"

"I've several new ideas in connection with yesterday's discussion about agriculture and readjustment of the unemployed. We must enlarge this department."

"We'll have to hurry on with it, too. Revolution's in the air and we can't say we've done a thing to prevent it. In this union we're working for the future, granted. But when in the devil's name are we going to put all the wonderful plans into practice, into real life?" Fred apppeared harried.

"I suppose as soon as our plans are accepted by De Jager and his people in the capital."

"But when? When is that bound to happen?"

"Then," Bill went on, "can you imagine? The very thought made me feel so good that I forgot all the unpleasantness here."

"And all the nonsense and thieveries, and all the lies as well?"

"You're a pessimist, Fred."

"Then listen to just one bit of reality, Mr. Optimist."

"Okay, let's hear it."

"There was another referee here, before me, in Agriculture. He worked out in great detail a plan for resettling all the unemployed in this country. He had it down even to the education of their children. He did everything that had to be done in preparing a blueprint. What happened? Not only was his project not accepted—the next day he was fired. . . . I knew that the plans of my predecessor had been rejected, and that he had been bounced, so I started from a different angle. I based my program on various theoretical principles and used a more practical method. Well! What do you know—Mr. Lawrence Aldrich Abdoller and his four siblings rejected my project five times."

"The reason, Fred?"

". . . 'It was entirely different from what my predecessor had done.' "

"So what then?"

"I incorporated all the ideas of my poor predecessor with all of mine in a new plan. Mr. Abdoller graciously admitted, 'This plan is almost perfect.' Approved by the five brothers it went through Mr. De Jager to the capital. After three months it was returned with the following remarks: 'Inadequately worked out; style negligent; indication of socialism. The whole project far from being complete.' "

"So what? You can now adjust your project to Washington's ideas."

"And the Abdollers will then reject it through Mr. De Jager!"

"You're a pessimist. I've discussed my cooperative plan with Willie De Jager, and submitted it to the Abdoller brothers about two months ago. It hasn't been rejected."

"Was it accepted?"

"Not yet, but it will be within the next few days."

"Are you sure?"

"We shall see," said Wattson, lighting a cigarette. At this moment Elton Call, referee of the Improvement Department, stuck his head through the door.

"Hi! What's going on here? International conspiracy?"

"We're planning an assault against Abdoller power in the country," Wattson said ironically.

Tribbe laughed. "You'd better watch your step and not enter these premises. CIA is listening."

"If that's so, then I will enter. I'm courageous and know how to face the danger. Especially if the threats come from supermen like yourselves. But this time I'm here to ask for a match, Mr. Agriculture. I want a cigarette and have no one to assist me in this problem."

"Please."

"It's just that you seem to be the only light around here."

"The only real light in this great institution," said Wattson, giving him a light.

"Be careful, you'll burn your mustache," laughed Fred.

"Yes, I forgot all about that."

"Why didn't you come in before? You just showed your head and were gone," said Wattson.

"I didn't run away. I'm courageous. But I didn't want to disturb you."

"With whom?"

"Miss Small."

"Our expert on improvement is fond of jokes, isn't he, Bill?"

"Yes, he's a cunning one." He turned to Call. "But lately you seem sort of downhearted."

"Yes. It's too bad, but you see, gentlemen, in connection with my project, I had to organize several courses all over the country—library courses, directing of shows, self-government, singing. If we want a real cultural life in those future settlements, in those communities of that new perfect society, as our honorary president puts it, we must nourish civilized life: sports clubs, theaters, libraries, orchestras. We have to prepare our future settlers for all this. Isn't that true?"

"Clearly," nodded Wattson, and Tribbe after him.

"We received a special subsidy for that purpose from the Atomic Bank. But that's not really much to talk about."

"That's true," said Fred.

"And what happened?" asked Wattson.

"De Jager bound me tight, hands and feet, and didn't permit me to spend any money. He said the whole matter has to be thought out once more, researched further, the figures reviewed again, to see whether my project does not require more money and more planning. I have to make damn sure that I don't overdraw the budget. Contact with workers is forbidden —might give them too many smart ideas. Contact with unemployed is forbidden; they're socialists. You know, gentlemen, I sometimes wonder whether we are an institution of eternal reflection and deliberation upon someone else's cash or an eternal, national brotherhood of swindlers. What has the Union of Unemployed done, this organization for the achievement of a better social system, either for working people or for the country?"

"You should fight for your plan," Wattson told him. "Try to convince others. Without fighting nothing will ever be accomplished."

"Fight, fight, that's why I'm on the black list here and in the capital."

"Is that why you're so depressed, then?"

"I'm not really depressed. I'm actually quite furious. So furious that I'm looking for somebody to kill." He noticed a fly on the wall. "Hah, I'll kill that fly. Killing this fly will also mean that I have accomplished something today."

"You're murdering my live inventory. Three flies flew around peacefully. . . ."

"Now there will be two, and the next day, one," said Tribbe, "and the day after that the honorary president will have him arrested for being antisocial."

"Well, gentlemen, don't let me keep you from your work, or the pretense of it. Comfortable, isn't it, to have the job of doing nothing? Good day, gentlemen." With a bitter smile he walked out.

"Wonderful."

"You mean it's good that he left?" asked Tribbe.

"Yes. We can finally start on some productive work. Where did we stop yesterday?"

"Here," said Fred, looking at the papers he had brought along. "Here is the paragraph: 'The reduction of city unemployed for work on our farms.' "

"Let's put that away. We should discuss that later and separately."

"Okay. Here, this paragraph: 'The matter of transferring the unemployed to those farms whose owners are considered radicals.' I'll read the last sentence: 'We have so far three thousand farms which can be taken over by the Union of Unemployed at almost any moment, on the grounds of unpaid taxes, because their owners are radicals.' I suppose the government would now need the hard legal justification to demonstrate to the public why it must be done?"

"Well, that should be easy indeed, with the help of Tom Karl and his squad. Furthermore, as De Jager says, 'unemployment is as serious a menace as war.' "

"And what if somebody very important in Washington does not consider the question of unemployment in the country a menace equal to war?"

"That argument, Fred, will require the help of Mr. Karl."

"Two problems would be solved at the same time."

"Precisely. How many radical farms are there in the South?"

Frederick Tribbe searched through his papers. "One thousand and fifty-four; in other words, three hundred thousand acres."

"In the South? We could settle one hundred thousand unemployed families there, in that case."

"But we originally said that even five acres for one family would be too little!"

"No."

"What do you mean?"

"The cooperative," Bill explained, "with the support of the Atomic Bank offers the possibility of rationing work. If we take one hundred thousand separate and individual farms, each having three acres, the work on those farms will require a minimum of nine thousand horses."

"Ah. We're regressing from agricultural machines to horses."

"But if we were to create agricultural cooperatives, we would need only five thousand horses."

"Yes."

"We would save four thousand horses, and because one horse eats as much as one and a half cows, we could gain so many more cows."

"Right, Bill. Then we would have milk and plenty of beef."

"And now from here let's go to the world figures," said Bill, as he pushed a chart in front of Fred. "Here are my plans for the preservation of sovereignty in the world of free enterprise; changing weights and measures, et cetera. After this little smoke-screen we can easily adjust everything we do to the preservation of the supreme doctrine. Let's take, for the sake of argument, the maintenance of an unemployed family consisting of four persons—I'm figuring on two children to a couple—we would need yearly two hundred kilograms of rye, wheat, and barley."

"That amounts to one hundred and seventy quadrate meters of land."

"What soil?"

"Third class."

Wattson twirled his pencil. "One hundred kilograms of potatoes."

"Plus one hundred and a half quadrate meters of land . . ."

"Let's add one pint of milk a day for each person. In other words, one thousand, four hundred and sixty pints yearly . . ."

"In order to produce that much milk, seven hundred hectares are necessary. . . ."

"And cows?"

"Cows we have, thanks to the metamorphosis of horses."

Both were thoughtful. After a while Wattson asked, "Did I convince you?"

"Yes, why yes," replied Tribbe. Then after a short silence, "The way matters are in the Union of Unemployed . . ."

"The unemployed are starving to death."

"Unproductively."

"And the capital is in the hands of Abdollers, Rollons, and Seymours," said Wattson. "I only hope that we can shake them off of the U. of U."

Miss Marah walked in and announced to Frederick Tribbe, "Abdoller wants to see you, Mr. Agriculture!"

"Yes. Right away." He turned to Wattson as Miss Marah walked off. "Well, we have to stop again."

"Perhaps we can postpone our discussion until tomorrow. I want to read all the letters in the Question Box."

"Of course. Tomorrow in my office."

"Very good."

"So long, then."

"Good-bye."

The referee of the Agriculture Department left. Taking up the Question Box, William Wattson followed him out.

 Chapter 43

The bachelor apartment contained portraits of Christ and Marx on one wall, above a small table on which was propped a photograph of Tessa De Jager. A large window looked out to winter dusk falling on the bare branches of trees lining the front of the house. William Wattson was musing over a pile of papers, reading in a loud voice.

" 'I am twenty-four years old, have two healthy hands, ready to work. My wife, twenty-three, has to mind the childern. One child is three years old, the other, eighteen months. That is my family. After I lost my job in my town, I came here and am now completely hopeless. Whose face deserved to be pushed in for all the misery? What should I do? From your lectures, Mr. Wattson, one learns that it just happens in a democracy to be the way it is. . . .' "

Wattson stopped and took a second letter from the stack. " 'People do everything for a purpose, especially those who are rich. Every philanthropist, whatever good he does, does it out of boredom or for publicity.' Hmm, possible." He took up a new letter. " 'If I don't meet him, I'll lose my mind.' To hell with it! Those women, all alike, whether they work or are un-employed. Here—'And I hear somebody calling. . . .' This one has hallucinations." He returned to the previous letter. " 'If I don't . . .' Who is that? Who? 'If I don't meet him

. . . what may I expect? Who needs me? Who will miss me after I die?' A suicide candidate, poor soul. But who is he? Which one of them? 'If I don't meet him'—who is she?—'I'll lose my mind . . . lose my mind . . . lose . . .' "

Reading the mail and reflecting, Wattson did not hear Tessa enter the room. Approaching on tiptoe she covered his eyes with her gloved hands.

"What's that?"

"If you wish to meditate," she said, taking her hands from his eyes, "Lock your door."

"Tessa, darling."

"Ex-darling. Be exact and sincere."

"I said darling, and I meant it. What is it you are referring to by 'ex'?"

"You're avoiding me."

"What gave you that idea?" He pulled her to him.

"When did we see each other last? Since you have become a social worker, I no longer exist for you."

"That's not true."

"It is."

"It's not so. You wanted me to become a . . ."

"Not I, it was Margie's idea."

"Well, it makes no difference. Sit down, sweetheart."

Tessa sat on top of the table.

"That's good. I'll sit next to you." He pushed the papers away and embraced her. "My only girl."

"But not your only love."

"Let me explain. With this work, I'm really finding myself. It absorbs me completely. Look, I'll show you something." He took up the question sheets.

"What's this? A collection of dirty paper?"

"These are the letters from the unemployed which we receive after each free lecture. I'm talking to them now about the economic crisis, inflation and the government projects.

Those people have such sad souls, even morbid. They don't know how beautiful love is and how hopeful the country's future really is. Of course, everything is going to change for the better, but they don't believe it."

"I'd like to know what they write."

"I'll read it to you. Perhaps we'll read together."

"All right."

"Here, for instance. 'How should a worker'—just a moment, not this one." He grew confused. "We'll take this one instead."

"Why? Why not this one? Read it. I won't be shocked, not even by revolution."

"I'd rather not." He hid the letter behind his back. "Let's take another. Here!"

He read while Tessa watched him curiously. When he had finished she observed, "That's very interesting. That was written by an intelligent person who knows all the dirt in the U. of U. and in the capital." She cuddled closer to Wattson.

"I told you, you see."

Tessa imitated him. "You see."

"An ordinary laborer. Those people think a lot and come to their own conclusions. 'What are the government and the Union of Unemployed dignitaries doing for the people? Zero.' " Then he changed the subject. "I have in my lecture audience one very interesting young man. It's painful to see such an imaginative and patriotic mind going to waste."

"Read me more, Bill."

"Well then, just one more. 'While we walk around with our heads down like tired mules and our bellies grow into our backs, you in your lectures call for a flower day all over the country.' "

Tessa sat cross-legged on the table, laughing hilariously. "This one told you off! Hahaha, social worker! haha!"

"He's quite right." Sliding from the table, Bill turned to face her. "That doesn't mean, however, that the job of a social

worker is worthless, that social work is without foundation."
He stammered slightly. "We, the young people in the Union
of Unemployed and in the Social Corps, shall rebuild the nation. We *will* liberate the world! We only need the right leaders."

Tessa jumped to the floor and half-danced around the room.
"Bill. I didn't come here to listen to your explanations of social
work, especially since I've realized that the unemployed you
worry about have consumed my love. Tell me, isn't it so? If it
is really true, I'll take my coat and run."

"Why run?" He sat on the couch. "Come here."

"You come to me. Wouldn't you like to take a walk in Main
Park?"

"Tessa, sweetheart, I have to study all this mail, think about
it, answer it."

She approached very close. "Throw it in the wastepaper
basket."

"You're a child, dear."

"Let's go."

"You must understand. My duty . . . I have work to do."

"Duty? Well, all right. Will you have dinner with me tonight
at my house?"

"Just a moment, let me think. What is today? Oh, too bad.
I can't make it. I have a meeting."

"Again it's too bad. You seem never to have any time"—she
was about to leave—"for me."

"Wait a moment, Tessa!" He jumped from the couch and
grabbed her hand. "Sweetheart, wait, how could you? How
about tomorrow? Let's have dinner at your house tomorrow."

"Tomorrow?" she asked sadly. "Tomorrow I'll be ill . . .
wait, let me see . . . tomorrow, yes, I'll feel lousy—my period. I don't think I can make it."

"Oh." He took off her coat. "You know?"

"I'm planning on it."

"Now what is it? Tessa, look. In a week or so I'll have time and you all your health."

They were sitting on the couch. Tessa's mood had completely changed. "Wonderful. I'll think up an interesting program for Sunday."

"Splendid. Don't forget to call me." He clasped her in his arms and kissed her.

Tessa murmured caressingly, "Of course I'll call you. Tomorrow? Today, however, I shan't disturb you any longer, you're so busy. . . ."

"No, no, it's only because I'm so tired. . . ."

"All right. It's all right." She touched his hair. "I have my moods too. Fine."

"Dear, my dearest . . . darling . . ." The embraces and kisses led them to the couch.

"Bill, my sweet social worker . . . dearest . . . Bill, not so fast! Fast and hard . . . you're hurting me. Bill, please slowly, you're hurting me . . . I'm still a virgin in some spots!"

⊕ Chapter 44

The next morning Wattson was still busy with the Question Box when William De Jager entered his office. "Good morning, Bill."

"Good morning, Mr. President."

"How do you like your work?" De Jager sat down.

"Okay, thank you."

"I heard some very flattering things about your lectures to the unemployed from Tessa. You're doing a fine job smashing socialism."

"Well, I try to reach those people."

"Naturally. You have what is called 'spiritus socialis.' I noticed that as soon as I met you."

"You're very kind."

"I've brought you . . . your project." De Jager put several pages of typewritten paper on Bill's desk. "It's good thinking. No question about the quality of your intellect. However, there are some mistakes in the working out of the subject matter."

Wattson with some uneasiness played with a pencil, but his voice remained cool. "Concrete fact, sir."

"The first part, in fact, is nothing else but the standing order of our organization, which no one intends to put to work. You were not able to differentiate, subordinate, or eliminate unimportant matters. And the second part—well, first of all, the title is something that could be mistaken for something else. And it's not catching at all."

Wattson rubbed his chin and gazed at the papers on his desk.

"As far as the subject matter is concerned, I have not much to say. You'll find my notes in the margin, as well as the notes of the Abdoller Brothers Foundation."

Wattson jumped up from his chair, but De Jager continued talking. "The layout of the third part is chaotic and the style not very consistent. Repetitions, too much leftist moralizing, no arguments. I am forced to consider your work far from excellent or complete." He concluded forcefully. "You'll have to rewrite your project completely, Bill, in the spirit of the Union of Unemployed and of the great democracy which we are presenting to the world."

Wattson, pale and furious, stood and bellowed, "Is that so! Is that so!"

 **Chapter 45**

The library of the Union of Unemployed was impressive: mahogany doors, grand windows, long bookcases along the walls, and portraits of film stars, sportsmen, national politicians and benefactors, including the five Abdoller brothers. In the middle of the library a long table covered with green cloth was set for a meeting.

Before the open bookcase stood Frederick Tribbe, referee of the Agriculture Department of the U. of U., leafing through some books on the topmost shelf. After a time Wattson entered and Tribbe went over to him.

"I see you too are getting educated."

"I don't like to be backward."

"Yes, yes, what can we do? All through life one is forced to accumulate so much garbage in one's skull. Those few dollars we need for our daily bread require us to be versatile in capitalistic and socialistic dialectics."

"As the Holy Scriptures say, 'man does not live by gold dollars only.' "

"Certainly not. My father and De Jager and the Abdoller brothers and Small and Seymour and the whole pack, they all live by fraud and swindle. But," he continued after a pause, "it won't be long before we'll celebrate your first anniversary in the Union of Unemployed."

Wattson replied indifferently, "Oh yes. Do you have a catalogue somewhere near you?"

"Here it is."

"Thank you." He sat at the table and went through the catalogue, stopping to read some titles. " 'The American Farmer,' 'The Downfall of Cooperatives in American Republics' . . ."

"You should read this, 'The Cooperative Movement in Madagascar.' "

"I know that. An old story." Bill studied the catalogue again. "J. J. Houser: 'Indian Corn and Its Usefulness in the Army,' W. Chaplin: 'The Work of Law Enforcement in the Adjustment of Agricultural Youth' . . ."

Tribbe put the book back in place. "Do you know that yesterday honorary director Abdoller came to see me."

Wattson read on. " 'Pigs and the Cooperatives,' 'Pigs and the Encampment of Pigs.' " He stopped. "And what?"

"And asked me whether I had written my yearly report for the chiefs of staff."

"Have you?"

"What the devil should I write about? What has been done in that time? You know yourself. Plans, programs, projects . . ."

"So you're not going to write anything?"

"What do you think? If I don't submit the report they will fire me immediately, Celine will be upset, my mother will become most awkward with me, and my father will get mad and cut my allowance."

"In other words, you're writing it."

"I have to."

"You have to." Bill smiled. "A man is even being engaged by the Union of Unemployed to write a special plan for the chief of staff on resettlement of the unemployed after an atomic war."

"Do I have to rewrite many times?"

"Four, five, maybe six. After that, submit it for approval to Honorary Director Abdoller and a few more directors, including the Chief of Intelligence. . . . You know, we have to follow democratic procedures!"

"Once it was even suggested that I send a report to Cian-farra."

"Mr. Last-but-not-least."

"At the end of the year, you go and write your account. What? Why were you so inactive? What? You want to transfer your own responsibility to the Abdoller brothers? Create! Create! Well, such a regular, extensive, and colorful account of nonexistent activities is all that is being created. Everyone is satisfied. Subsidies, grants, and loans from the Atomic Bank, from the Abdoller Foundation, from big companies come in the millions. But nothing has been really done. Nothing accomplished Still, everything is fine, just fine. De Jager is a genius of purism!"

"Well, is this how you understand it?"

"Our superiors know what they are doing. They are experts on the moral and economic problems of the great democratic world strategy. Bah! If one had as many dollars as one has reasons for intercourse with the girls . . . if only one were independent!"

"At liberty to change girls and rich fathers?"

"In these times? All is a joke, Wattson my friend."

"You're a pessimist."

"Am I? These methods of our fathers! In our society thieveries begin at the highest rank and end at the desk of the little county clerk. A chain, a golden chain . . ." He heard footsteps and stopped talking.

"From this bulletin"—Bill took a paper out of his pocket and gave it to Tribbe—"I can judge, today's conference will be different. We are on the threshold of a world atomic crisis. Something has to be done."

Tribbe read the bulletin. " 'Honorary President William S. De Jager will speak on the most important tasks for the Union of Unemployed in the near future, connected with the changes in our world atomic plan. . . .' Indeed, something quite unusual for our organization."

"I expect we shall now finally view reality on a global scale."

"There is nothing to prevent the Russians from taking over Europe, not even dollars. I was told so in confidence by Mr. Meynemar. He may have been butterflying with women under Roosevelt, but now he's a big power in political intelligence for the new Democratic administration."

"Our superminds in the capital will surely have a remedy for that 'Russian bull shriek,' as Mr. De Jager would say."

"Super in size, but empty inside. Well, let's hope, let's hope."

"You're a pessimist." Bill returned to the catalogue. "Nine hundred and seventeen."

"You have your number?"

"I've got it."

"And I've got mine."

"Then we can go for a drink and talk."

 Chapter 46

Joseph Cianfarra, executive secretary of the Union of Unemployed, glanced around the library with the disapproving look of a person who likes order.

"Too much confusion!" He went toward the bell to ring for Joseph Col just as Elton Call, referee of the Improvement Department, appeared.

"Is Director Abdoller here? Oh, you. Good. At least I have you."

"What's the matter, Mr. Call?"

"Tell me, Mr. Cianfarra, what kind of jokes are you making with my money?"

"I? Cianfarra?"

"Yes, you!"

"Jokes?"

"Today, I received word that my project has been withheld for the fourth time. Do you think I don't know your part in all this?"

"Calmly, sir, calmly. Sit down, please. What kind of part am I supposed to have played?"

"You gave your approval for my project. You were the first."

"Yes?"

"I took all your suggestions under consideration."

"Calmly, sir. Calmly."

"I know that your opinions are decisive in my department."

"I'm pleased. However, not in everything, not in everything. I am confident of that."

"Then don't suggest poor ideas to other people. I assure you, it won't help. None of you here or in the capital can force me into any dirty business." He paced the floor in front of Cianfarra.

"Mr. Call, don't excite yourself. Here." Cianfarra took a piece of paper out of his folder and placed it in front of Call. "Here is your account. I am not surprised that it has been rejected and held back."

Call picked up the paper and stared at it. "Why?"

"You're asking me? Why, your account states that your expenditures in the last year were seventy thousand, eight hundred dollars."

"What of it?"

"For our work in the Department of Improvement we received over half a million dollars."

"But we didn't spend it."

"The account of expenditures, however, cannot and must not be lower than the subsidy received for that purpose. It is advisable that such financial statements be higher than the allowance, or else the subsidy will be lowered for the coming year."

"But the monies have not been exhausted. There is a considerable sum left over."

Cianfarra raised both of his hands and his voice. "What does that mean? We had over half a million dollars, that's what we received, that's what we have to account for. Otherwise, what will you do with the difference between seventy thousand and half a million?"

"Return it, of course. You don't think I'd pocket it!"

"Are you insane?" Cianfarra hit the table with his fist. "You haven't accounted for the courses you wrote so explicitly about in your working project, have you?"

"But those courses weren't held. Mr. Abdoller didn't approve them. He was afraid that the budget would be overdrawn if I went ahead with my plans."

"Still," Cianfarra went on in a milder vein, "you should figure those courses . . . into your account."

There was a knock on the door. John V. Casevant entered carrying a red briefcase.

"I beg your pardon, gentlemen, but in a very short while a new meeting will be held here."

"Therefore, Mr. Call, it is advisable for us to leave."

"If you would be kind enough," said Casevant.

"Of course. Mr. Call, let's go to my office."

"All right."

"I'm very sorry, gentlemen." Casevant always displayed unusual politeness for a man of his importance in the world.

"Perhaps Mr. Casevant," started Call, "would tell me . . ."

"No, no, sir," protested Cianfarra, "don't waste your time, sir . . ."

Chapter 47

"Howdy, Willie the Whistle! Howdy, Lawrence," John V. Casevant called to De Jager and Abdoller as he caught them entering the library. With his love for Scotch whiskey had survived his love for Scottish expressions.

"Your servant, old man," said De Jager. "Perhaps we'd better start right away."

"Good morning, John," said Abdoller, removing several books from his briefcase. "Very good. Everything is ready."

"Tell me, John," asked Willie the Whistle, "when is the revision committee supposed to arrive?"

"Saturday."

"If you please, gentlemen," started Abdoller.

Casevant nodded to Willie the Whistle. "Mr. President De Jager, the floor is yours."

"Okay, old man. I hereby call to order the meeting of the Board of Superintendents of the Landing Place Company. Present and accounted for are the president of the board, secretary Abdoller, and director Casevant, in charge of the management of the company." He paused and then continued, "Next I will announce the agenda: first, examination of the balance account; second, use of profits; third, the reduction of debts of the Union of Unemployed."

Abdoller, who was taking notes, looked up. "Clarification, Willie, please."

"Yes?"

"I noticed that in the order of matters to be discussed, the matter of additional payment to the *New World* magazine has been omitted."

"Point three covers that," interrupted Casevant.

"Yes, we shall talk about that. We shall deliberate. Now, what about you, John?"

"I have nothing to add, thank you."

"So let us then take up point one." De Jager turned again to Casevant. "Will you be kind enough to inform us on the balance account."

"The year has been . . . started by us under . . . not very fortunate circumstances and we are presently accounting . . . for the crisis inflation. . . ."

Willie the Whistle cut in. "I beg your pardon." John stopped. "John, we are informed as to the particular conditions and circumstances in the world. We realize them fully. Thus let us call the balance account closed."

"Yes, indeed," said Abdoller, fingering a glass of water.

Willie the Whistle continued. "Let us therefore assume that the balance account has already been examined."

"Good," agreed Casevant happily.

"Self-understood," Abdoller chimed in.

"Therefore, John, let us approach point two. Summarize, please."

"The statement of profits and losses, business expenditures, personal expenses, printing costs, commissions, amortizations, real estate, all on the right side—in other words, clear profit of one million, nine hundred eighty-two thousand dollars."

Abdoller was curious. "Is this the sum arrived at after the deduction for the reserve funds?"

"Yes, it is, including additional payments to all publications and the *New World* magazine."

"Not bad," said Willie De Jager.

"If you please."

"We are listening, Mr. Abdoller," said Casevant politely.

"I wanted to ask if you gentlemen have any suggestions to offer."

"May I have the floor?" asked Casevant.

"Talk, John. As my brother Lloyd would say, 'Talk fast, John, you're the best in that business!' "

"Thank you, Lawrence. I have done my share for the Abdollers. But here, now, we must act in accord with the statute, so I suggest the full transfer of clear profit from the Landing Place Company to the Union of Unemployed."

"Impossible! My brother was wrong about you, John. Doing that would jeopardize all future subventions. The Union of Unemployed has to operate constantly at a deficit, in the red! A social organization is not a business. . . ."

They whispered briefly while De Jager, looking unconcerned, scanned the shelves.

"However, after deliberation, I consider the suggestion of Mr. Casevant as accepted, up to the sum of one million, eight hundred and twenty-two thousand." He turned to De Jager. "Please make a note, Mr. President."

"There remains a sum of one hundred and sixty thousand dollars in my books."

"Willie, may I have the floor?"

"Please, Lawrence."

"As you know, John, the Union of Unemployed was invited to several important conventions of the Atomic Plan for Europe. All this will be done on a grand scale, on an international scale. As director of our organization, I find it pertinent that our delegate be sent to Europe. I am thinking of William S. De Jager going abroad as our representative."

"Oh, yes," Casevant nodded wisely. "His observations will be useful to the government and to the Union of Unemployed, as well as to the Atomic Bank." They both turned toward De Jager.

219

"Thank you for your kind words, gentlemen. My trips abroad and contacts with French and German manufacturers and bankers have always allowed me the possibility of study and comparison of the social work of highly democratic governments—which make those experiences very educational for me and very useful to our Union of Unemployed."

"I suppose a hundred thousand dollars will be adequate for this trip?" asked Abdoller. "Lisbon, Madrid, Paris . . ."

"A convention week in Monaco," De Jager added.

Casevant came in with his own suggestions. "London, Geneva, the Vatican."

"It would be worthwhile also, I think, for me to consider Berlin and Bonn."

"Will a hundred thousand dollars be enough, Willie?" asked Abdoller. "If not, the Abdoller Brothers Fund will give you fifty more."

"Well, thank you, but a hundred thousand, now that's definitely too much. I suppose ninety thousand would be quite sufficient, maybe ninety-five."

"John and I agree that a representative trip is a representative trip, and you're a great citizen of a great country. Money cannot be a determinant."

"Therefore," stated Casevant, "I suggest a compromise at ninety-five thousand dollars, to be allotted for the trip abroad of William De Jager in the matters and interest of the Union of Unemployed."

"Is there any objection to our director's proposal?" asked De Jager. There was silence. "The motion has been carried."

"There are sixty-five thousand remaining," said Abdoller, looking at his notes.

"Mhmh, mhm, yes," murmured Casevant.

"Please, gentlemen," encouraged Willie, "ninety-five for me. But you—John, Lawrence?"

"Mr. President, that's all right. Let me think. . . . Oh yes.

Perhaps ten thousand will go to Lawrence in the form of additional dividends?"

"I suggest that John also be paid ten thousand."

"Splendid idea. John, Lawrence, is everyone agreed?"

"Thank you," said old Casevant, straightening his tiepin. "Well, gentlemen, there are still forty-five thousand dollars. What are we going to do with them?"

"As honorary president of the U. of U., I would like to offer a suggestion. Some time ago, if my memory doesn't fail me, I proposed a reserve fund for the top executives of our organization."

"Yes, I remember 'some time ago.'" Lawrence smiled. "So I will propose to transfer all remaining funds to the account of a special reserve, in case any of us should fall ill."

"Precisely, Lawrence."

"But that . . ."

"Any objection, John?"

"Hmhm." Casevant patted his temples thoughtfully. "There is one question now: How are we going to include it in the books?"

"Well, in general, John, there is no need to give particular account of what need not be known in detail. You think it over, and tomorrow morning advise me as to how you will arrange the matter over in bookkeeping." Willie glanced at his watch. "The staff meeting will start soon. Let us therefore take up point three, the last issue before us today." He turned to Casevant. "If you please."

"That, hmhm, that is the matter of the newspaper. You know, how much for us, for each of our areas?"

De Jager got up to pace the floor. "Indeed, I don't know," he remarked to Abdoller, who was pouring water into a glass and from the glass back into a jug. "How much did the Abdoller Brothers Oil Company pay us for advertising in the *New World?*"

"I don't remember, but the paper's subsidy is fixed. It will be enough, it will be enough."

"Well then, as president, I adjourn the meeting."

John V. Casevant put the finishing touches on his own notes, assembled them, and stood up. "My compliments, Willie the Whistle. You are my best student! Lawrence, his brothers, you, and hundreds of your friends and supporters of the U. of U. are the real builders of America, a new and better America."

"John, old gun, you are the greatest genius in the history of the railroad—and I might add, in the history of social and educational work."

"Thank you, Willie, and thank you, Lawrence. Now I have to go." He shook hands, bowed to them and left.

Lawrence Abdoller remained, still signing papers, closing books, and occasionally staring at the water that he had spilled hitting the floor drop by drop.

"Willie, you have always maintained that if the problem of unemployment were solved, the great organization we have created would still remain in existence. For, you say, we have created this magnificent U. of U. in order to convince the world how matters of social importance are being handled by right-minded Americans."

"That's the policy, Mr. Abdoller, our policy indeed. Besides, the instinct of self-preservation on our part and the part of our institution demands faith and confidence in the democratic way of life."

"Wouldn't it be a fine time now to . . ." Lawrence rose and took a few nervous steps. ". . . Shouldn't we do something about the anti-American movement among the students, intelligentsia, and some workers? The capital is working ever so hard on this problem, and we? Even in our own offices— you are in only occasionally, Willie, you have no time to see. The CCRR takes most of your time, the Atomic Bank. I understand. However, maybe you haven't noticed. All those questioning glances, sharp words, the strange psychological atmosphere in our offices may explode any day in our U. of U., in the capital, in the whole country. I think you and I should talk to the board of directors and then see what the security forces have to say about the situation. Abdoller Brothers Fund will supply money and facts, names. . . ."

"The situation is serious enough, I know. However, in the capital, a huge new two-billion-dollar expansion of security is under way. There is nothing to worry about. It will eliminate the threat of rebellion as easily as a strong man squeezes a lemon. But Lawrence, here in the offices of the Union of Unemployed, among these gossipers and castrated intellectuals and revolutionaries of ours, you are in charge. All the questioning, threatening glances and words, whatever—all this is your responsibility. Psychological atmosphere? Bah! Think up something new to keep the organization in order and loose mouths shut."

"What?" Lawrence looked alarmed.

"These poor, dreary intellectuals! And you, a member of the greatest and richest family in the country, you frightened? Nonsense! Tell them to write some more brochures, books, articles. Get them to serve on some more committees."

"New projects involve new expenses." Then, after a bit more reflection, Lawrence said, "Very good," and sat down to rest in the corner of the library. "We have to transform them into solid candidates for our social work. They have to live, and they are used to big wages. They must be channeled, or the F.B.I. will be made to deal with them. Well, then!" He spoke considerably relieved, "What will happen to the newcomers? That is, those we must engage, the recommended people?"

"We'll find a way, don't be overly concerned. New offices, new publications. They will talk and write to their hearts' content—under supervision, of course. They will learn to write

223

skillfully enough, and like good lawyers will know when what they write will lose them their jobs. Remember, we have two billion dollars a year to draw on, just for those purposes. You will be in charge, but with the help of trustworthy people, your job will consist mainly of supervision. Thus there need never be any fundamental change in the political or economic system of our great country. No revolution. No restitution."

"Very good, Willie. Lloyd was right. You're the greatest American philosopher since Ben Franklin! You give us all confidence in our way of life."

▣ Chapter 48

The Coast to Coast Railroad was built and developed by strong and farsighted men with a terrifying hunger for profit and power. According to some American theories, some more scientific than others, further progress and extension of our society depends on economic conditions in the world specifically linked with the world market. The adherents of such theories rarely consider the working masses, but depend on the character and will of a few men who exert a strong and definite influence on society. Sometimes these men perform the impossible.

On such matters I was meditating the morning I received a phone call from John Casevant. The former president of the CCRR told me that he had just arrived from Rich Acres and suggested that we have lunch. I accepted, in the first place because my dislike for the man always seemed to amount to fascination, and secondly because a talk with Vant is almost certainly a profitable experience for any researcher. You can learn more from him in half an hour about life, history, and the railroad than most books can give you in months of study.

In the CCRR Restaurant I began by asking, "You're over eighty years old, and you've spent much of that time gaining wealth and political power. Of all that you have seen, what would you say is the most interesting thing you have observed about human nature?"

Vant closed his eyes for a moment, his sculptured gray head bent over the table in thought. Then, slowly directing his attention to me, he replied, "Mr. Kapistrot, an incident with a native American. It happened when I was working in the engineering department of Consolidated Railroads, a major division of the CCRR. I remember as if it happened this morning. The day was clear, no chance for any accident, but we had one, a bad one. A number of workers were killed and many others were hurt. I was helping to place the injured on stretchers."

He paused for emphasis and resumed speaking. "Accompanied by another railroad worker I went over to a big man who was lying down beside the tracks. He was an Indian, one of the finest looking I'd ever seen. He had been badly hurt. His right leg hung by the skin just below the knee."

Vant rubbed his chin. "I quickly removed my belt and wrapped it above his knee to stop the bleeding. Then I did what I could for the wound. The pain was so severe the man could say nothing at all, but he managed to smile thanks. We carried him to the railroad car which was to take him to the hospital. He remained fully conscious the entire time. Then he reached for his dangling leg, and lifting it up said to me, 'See . . . nice leg Indian have. See nice leg Indian have!'

"I was astounded by this heroic man. I couldn't utter a single word. We lifted the stretcher into the car and put it down. Our victim, summoning his noble traditions, repeated again, 'Strong leg have son of Logan, chief of the Mingo.' My helper stood beside him and cried uncontrollably. I turned quickly away and went to help the others."

This proud Indian actually did recover, Vant told me. As soon as he was physically able, he returned to work with a wooden leg, bought for him by the other railroad workers, of which he was very proud. "By the way"—Vant looked up suddenly—"this is a favorite story of Willie's, too, though I was the source of it."

We sat silently for a few moments. Then a new thought struck him. "That story was the most amazing single incident. But for mass courage, I would have to acknowledge the sandhogs, in the days when we built the Hudson River Tunnel.

"To build the Hudson River Tunnel, the men worked ninety-three feet underground, digging in rock, mud, and water. They labored under appalling air pressure with no safety devices, and somehow they managed to successfully dig the tunnels that connected the city to the rest of the country. I genuinely admire those workers, each and every one of them." Vant lifted his fork, then put it down and pushed aside his pie. "I'd better not," he smiled. "The doctor wants me to stay trim."

I related how, until 1900, there was no direct link between the city and the state of New Jersey. The city was isolated by the Hudson River with the only connections being a few bridges to the north. Every day thousands of people journeyed from New Jersey over the same water their colonial ancestors had used. In summer, the ferryboat ride was pleasant, but rather long; in the winter it was a most difficult trip.

Toward the end of the nineteenth century, Abdoller, von Hoth, Meynemar, and several other families combined with other interests and commenced construction of the Hudson River Tunnel. They were later forced to abandon the project because of inadequate plans and insufficient data. In the early twentieth century they sent one of their youngest engineers,

John Casevant, to Europe to study tunnel-building methods. Vant was an enthusiastic, almost fanatical exponent of railroad electrification as well as of anything else that smacked of the new, the modern, and the practical. To an extent his stubbornness and pride were akin to that of the son of Logan. But fate was kinder to Vant. When he returned from Europe he helped organize a working group of English, French, and American engineers. This team made up plans to build two single-track tubes under the Hudson River, as well as a large coach yard and a train terminal on the Manhattan side. Everything was to be run on electricity.

Needless to say, the project was quite expensive. The cost was in excess of one hundred million dollars. The legal problems, such as who had the right to grant permission to build an underground passageway ninety feet below the city, were unbelievably complex. Railroad baron William Gibbs McAdoo was particularly helpful in guiding the project through a labyrinth of state laws and bribes. McAdoo later became Secretary of the Treasury in Woodrow Wilson's cabinet.

The tunnel work was performed in stages. Each section to be constructed was under the direction of a separate team of engineers and workers who labored day and night. In some areas there were tremendous rock beds. Dynamite had to be used and it posed an extreme danger for people both above and below the surface. An entirely different problem was created by the presence of clay and mud. Water pumps became clogged with the sticky brown ooze. Safety devices often failed to give sufficient warning of trouble.

To every brigade of sandhogs was attached a squad of men whose special task was to install heavy cast-iron rings. These rings were over a foot in diameter and their separate parts had to be bolted together and stretched across the tunnel to prevent it from caving in. Work was hard and slow. So many long hours of human labor soon added up into years; ten, to be exact, before the tunnel was finally completed. John Casevant's skill in love and finance was just as easily transferred to engineering management. His stubborn will and capacity for hard work won out again just as it had many times earlier in his life.

After all, he had had a most heart-rending childhood. His father died when he was thirteen and he went to work to support the rest of the family. Lucky enough to secure a job in the engineering corps of the CCRR, his determination and hunger for wealth and knowledge spurred him to enter engineering school, where he did exceedingly well. His luck at meeting the right people at the right time, when combined with his industriousness and criminal shrewdness, marked him as a sure success in the business world. The railroad family of von Hoth grew to like him personally after they recognized his railroad ability. They also actively encouraged his interests in the direction of any one of the von Hoth girls. They were grooming him for the position of president of the company. Vant was smart enough to recognize their intentions early, and he cooperated fully. His sponsors were not to be disillusioned.

One of the members of Vant's work force, unknown to the von Hoths and to history, was the very same son of the Indian chief Logan. Many years after the accident, Vant told me, he discovered the Indian working as one of the sandhogs in the Hudson River Tunnel. Shortly thereafter, there was an accident involving massive water seepage into a section of the unfinished tunnel where men were at work. When the water was finally pumped out, one of the rescuers found a wooden leg, but there was no sign of the Indian. Today the legend runs that between the sound of trains speeding through the tunnel, a voice can be heard. Men at work down there never cease to joke and say it is the son of Logan, searching for his wooden leg.

▣ Chapter 49

John Victor Casevant was much admired during his tenure as president of the CCRR. He made himself wealthy and influential not only on Wall Street, where he set up young Fletcher as the head of the New York Stock Exchange, but also in the glass, steel, oil, and electric industries. In his long managerial career he gave out only two jobs for love. He made Willie the Whistle president of CCRR because of his affection for Gusty Mary. He also gave a minor position on the railroad to his painter cousin Charlie Todder because he was flattered to be called upon by Charlie to pose as his model.

Casevant usually opened his business conferences with an appropriate anecdote. He was relating one such story the afternoon I watched him preside over a board meeting in his Philadelphia office. "One day, a woman approached me on the street and asked me how much a freight car cost. I was surprised at such a peculiar inquiry and asked her why she needed the information. Said she, 'My husband is a freight-train conductor, and every month now he comes home with ten dollars missing from his pay. When I ask why, he says that he was responsible for the destruction of one freight car and the railroad decided to take ten dollars out of his salary every month until he had paid for the car.'" Casevant's directors were highly amused by this tale of one man's way of getting pocket money from a grasping wife.

But even under Vant's presidency, there were not that many opportunities for hearty laughs, for he inherited more than his share of uncompleted railroad programs and labor troubles.

The Depression, state restrictions like the two-cent fare laws, and the ignorance of a people fed by a press controlled by big shippers all contributed to the widespread belief that the railroad was little more than a get-rich-quick scheme. Casevant spent most of his years in financial conferences with bankers and businessmen, attempting to sell property, arrange loans, and locate other sources of funding that would help keep the CCRR solvent. His financial preoccupations and the general shortage of ready capital, he said, made him truly appreciate the story of another man, an engineer, who also came home every month with a shortage in his pay. To his wife's questions he innocently replied, "I am getting paid less for a very simple reason. I haul solid trains of empty cars, and as you know, they pay less for empty cars than for full ones."

Nothing publicly shocking occurred during Casevant's reign that would fill front pages of hungry newspapers, but inside, the view was a little different as seen through the eyes of his cousin Charlie Todder. Charlie was the same height as Vant and possessed the same delicate face. He also displayed a confident manner and a facility for words. Only their dress and financial status were different.

"When Vant was elected president, I was hired as an assistant baggage agent," Charlie began. "My duties consisted of running as an extra between Overbrook and Parkersburg, a distance of thirty-nine miles. My very first year I was furloughed for six months because of sickness. The next year, I was reinstated and sent to Narberth, and from there, to various other stations. While I was working out there my supervisor was Willie the Whistle, then an energetic young man. He became the president of the road, as you know, after Vant."

Charlie scanned my eyes searchingly, and said little more about Willie, because he was aware of my connections with him.

"I was later transferred to Bryn Mawr, one of the busiest

stations. There we had Bryn Mawr College, Miss Wright's School, and the Baldwin and Shipley private schools, all of them for rich girls." Charlie smiled pleasantly at the thought, but then continued recounting his railroad experience.

"Oh, there was plenty of work with those girls. We started off each day at seven A.M. and didn't stop until twelve midnight. The pay was forty-eight dollars a month plus two-fifty from Adams Express. When the schools closed for the summer we used to check as many as three hundred trunks a day, and many a girl had more than one trunk. We also billed all express shipments and became thereby well acquainted with the travelers. They in turn always remembered us at Christmas with presents.

"While working at Bryn Mawr a severe blizzard blew up. The trains were stalled for days. I remember distinctly on that morning we started work as usual at seven, but our train couldn't get out of the station until one P.M. There were a number of accidents and many cases of frostbite along the way, but since we didn't have medical care, we had to fend for ourselves."

Like any other railroadman, Charlie possessed a repertoire of unusual experiences. One day he was working on a train going west. It was loaded down with Italian, Polish, and Russian immigrants and a stop was made at the Ardmore station. The coaches were constructed entirely of wood and Gordon Mitchell pinch gas supplied the light. The engine was an old D-sixteen. West of Ardmore there was a freight wreck, a rear-end collision. The engineer of the train, Walt Walton, informed Charlie that the two freights were loaded with dynamite that had not yet exploded but might at any minute. The railroad workers immediately transferred the bewildered immigrants to trains going back to Philadelphia and evacuated the entire station and the surrounding area. What would have been a terrible tragedy was averted.

Charlie lit a cigarette and continued. "On that same run, a few months later, I participated in an incident of a slightly different type. An extremely intoxicated man decided to walk across the railroad bridge instead of waiting for a train. In the middle of the bridge, he grew tired, lay down, and went to sleep on the tracks. Shortly after, a man on a bicycle rode across the bridge and ran over the drunk. When the cyclist reached Wrightsville, he reported the incident to me. Me and the cyclist immediately went out on the bridge to investigate. We shook the man and told him to get up or he would be run over by a train which was due very soon. The sleepy drunk was not disturbed in the least and mumbled, 'I just lost my job on the railroad and there's no place for me to sleep.' Rolling over, he added, 'Besides, one of the damn things just ran over me a little while ago and nothing happened. So why should I get up?' "

▣ Chapter 50

It was a raw March day in Cleveland. The snow had been falling continuously for three days, and the temperature was still dropping. An icy wind cut through to the bone, the number of clothes notwithstanding. The trains were very late or not running at all.

The day before had been an unusually important one for CCRR president John Victor Casevant and his assistants. On March first the federal government had returned to their original management all the CCRR properties it had taken over for military use during World War Two.

Vant, a friend of the nation's Presidents, had been director

232

general of transportation for the American forces. His railroading knowledge and organizational abilities in the transportation field served him well in his wartime duties. Since railroad problems and money came first in his life, taking precedence over family, women, and even his own personal needs, sharp-tongued Vant was superbly equipped to take on any task. His verve was not always appreciated by those around him, but one thing was understood by all: Vant's climb to the top would be rapid and sure. He was extremely capable, and intimately familiar with every facet of the business. He possessed definite talent for making friends among important stockholders, who expressed complete confidence in his abilities. And when he chose, he could make the most delightful enemies. He utilized every bit of his native shrewdness in selecting the men who would work for him on the railroad and in his private dealings.

The day the Cleveland office was unheated and snowbound Vant decided on an inspection trip. Most of the employees were absent and no trains were running. He was facing real trouble, for there was not a capable man around who would know when to resume passenger train movement. He stared out the window at the thick blanket of snow that covered the sleeping yards. He was aware that if he failed to streamline the equipment and overcome the confusion and work stoppage that occurred during weather such as this, his railroad would fall way behind in service and profits.

While he stood pondering, Gregg Cunningham walked into the room. Gregg, ostensibly a railroad clerk, was actually one of Vant's spies on this division. He knew Cleveland like the back of his hand. Still quite young, he understood the workings of railroads in this part of the country, but had not yet learned to use this knowledge to his advantage.

His boss turned from the window to ask in imperative tones, "Gregg, I have a few men in mind to take care of passenger-train movements. If you were in my place, whom would you select?"

Gregg, who had come in with a problem of his own, was momentarily dumbfounded. Besides, his opinion had never been sought before, and he wondered now if Mr. Casevant was serious.

"Anybody, select anyone," Vant said, "except yourself." With an ironic smile he added, "We need you here ourselves, Gregg."

The young clerk stood in the middle of the room, trying feverishly to think of something to say. He knew that Mr. Casevant required an answer. Finally, he mustered his courage and began very slowly. "I am sure you know his wife and her shrewdness, but I don't know what you would think about this man, the one I have in mind. . . ."

"Speak up, Gregg, speak up," urged Vant. His impatience sped the words off Gregg's tongue. "He's a young statistician, with an ambitious wife who everyone around here says is helping further his career. I don't like him personally, but I know he is a smart fellow and can handle anything well."

"A statistician," Vant mulled. It didn't seem right to him to mix pleasure with business. He fingered the watch chain on his vest and sat down. "All right," he asked, "what's his name, Willie the Whistle?"

"Yes, Willie the Whistle De Jager," blurted Gregg. "But mind you, I don't recommend him to you."

"All right, all right, Gregg. You're my best pair of eyes out here. I know you said before he is a statistician and you don't like him, but I like his wife."

"That may be, sir," Gregg continued, trying to extricate himself from a tangle of words. "I said I don't *like* him, but it doesn't mean that . . ." Here he stopped to search again for the right phrase. "But he will make the best passenger man you ever had, perhaps later even a major officer."

His triumphant conclusion inspired him to speak out also for the underprivileged men in the office—for the clerks, the brakemen, the trainmen, the shop mechanics, everyone he could think of. Somehow, perhaps because of Casevant's confidential manner or the strangely idle building, a Gregg that no one had ever known was revealed. For the first time he was talking to someone really important about his innermost feelings on a management that didn't show any concern about the people at the bottom of the organization. "And probably," he blazed forth, "that is the reason why we have so much trouble on the railroad."

"Go ahead, Gregg, speak up." Vant balanced himself on the back legs of the chair and listened raptly.

Gregg was still standing in the same spot in the middle of the bare office. "I don't have much to say, but I think if management would look down into the lower ranks, they'd find plenty of capable men who should be given encouragement and support. I'm sure in a few years we will have many experienced and self-sacrificing workers who could put the CCRR out in front of all the railroads in this country."

Vant had his own ideas about the railroad and its people. But the supervision of passenger movement did finally go to Willie the Whistle and Gusty Mary.

Soon thereafter, a serious train mix-up occurred in the middle of a night. Three divisions were tied up completely in Cleveland. Traffic coming from the east, west, and north was blocked. Willie the Whistle appeared from nowhere, and in no time had taken things into his own hands. He himself took charge of the eastbound and westbound passenger traffic. Then, with his characteristic cool-headedness, he directed the CCRR trains to Cleveland onto the tracks of the independent railroad companies. Inbound trains he put on the tracks of the Big Three Railroads. Everyone was aware of the rule that a passenger-movement man of one railroad had no authority to put trains on another railroad's tracks. But there was precious little time to look for authorization, and Willie the Whistle took the chance, though it probably would mean his job.

Casevant could not be found anywhere. When he arrived home, messages were waiting for him from a dozen important railroad directors. They all wanted to know what was going on, why it was going on, and did he personally know it was going on. He rushed to his Philadelphia office to find a message on his desk. It was Willie the Whistle's report explaining that to prevent financially serious delays he had acted without authority and rerouted all trains. Casevant examined the facts and then called the directors to say that the situation had been handled properly. In fact, better than anyone, including himself, could have done. The matter was completely out of his hands. Casevant hung up the receiver, left the office, and went to a nearby hotel to meet Gusty Mary. Willie the Whistle was assured of a future presidency.

 Chapter 51

Julienne Small, editor of the *New World,* came into the library escorted by Stanley Kieb, referee for Spiritual Adjustment. From his chair at the head of the table Willie De Jager offered a warm welcome. "Ah, good morning, ladies and gentlemen!" His voice was unnaturally appealing. "Julienne, how is the joy campaign getting along? Any responses?"

Abdoller shook hands with Kieb. "How are you? I heard you were ill."

"The air in the capital, you know!" Stanley laughed weakly.

In quick succession entered Margie Maxton, referee of

Women's Affairs; Elton Call, referee of the Improvement Department; Frederick Tribbe, referee of the Agricultural Department; and William Wattson and Joseph Cianfarra, huddled in close conversation.

Miss Small whispered to Mr. Kieb, "I'm really anxious to know what the honorary president will talk about today."

"Let's hope he brings out nothing new; let's just hope nothing new. I'm always afraid of something new from him. When he stops to think, our president reveals a profoundly un-Christian philosophy."

"You know, I dreamed about you last night."

"I'm married."

"For the second time."

"And happily. I'm not looking around for any change. Any change!"

Two honorary referees sauntered in, Bart Leach of the Abstinence Department and Aquarell Meynemar, Junior, of Physical Education.

Margie Maxton remarked in an aside to Elton Call, "That communication intrigues me. Have you read it?"

"Of course."

"Isn't it fascinating?"

"Thrilling. Heavy print on soft paper."

"Hehehe."

"That's the most distinctive thing about it—legible, if not comprehensible."

"What can this meeting be all about?"

"Ladies and gentlemen, I'm calling the meeting to order," announced De Jager. "Let's not waste any time."

Abdoller rang the bell. "Please be seated." Everyone took a seat behind his respective nameplate.

"Mr. Cianfarra, who is taking the minutes today?"

Cianfarra looked into his protocol book. "Miss Small, our editor."

"Brr, I love it."

Cianfarra smiled at her with smooth good humor. "Social work demands self-sacrifice."

Abdoller began. "I hereby open the meeting of the executives of the Union of Unemployed. Have any of you ladies and gentlemen any suggestions to offer? No one? Well then, let us get down to business. The honorary president, Mr. William S. De Jager, if you please." He exchanged solemn nods with De Jager.

"Director Abdoller, ladies and gentlemen: Through the system of an intellectually adjusted sociology, we try to capture the complex of circumstance by which the realization of the goal of human life is best made possible. The greatest endeavor of adjusted sociology lies in the methods of applied social work, whether executed by an individual or by groups. In the smaller circle of everyday life, natural talents alone are adequate, as well as home proxies; however, methods of social activities supported by scientific principles make it possible to achieve the goal with less cost, less work, and less time lapse."

Margie Maxton poked her neighbor, Stanley Kieb. "God, that was a learned entry. I haven't any idea what he said."

"At least it's nothing new. The same mental Coca-Cola."

"But I didn't understand a word!"

The honorary president continued, "Ladies and gentlemen, do you know what I mean?"

Voices murmured, "Yes." "Of course—quite clear." "Good . . ."

"Therefore it is evident that a practitioner who does not build his social work upon theory only, but once in a while attempts to experiment with material and time, may harm future well-intentioned successes of the whole complex, which again are very important for the expansion of our country and the Union of Unemployed."

Wattson leaned toward Tribb. "No matter how hard I try,

I can't make out what Willie the Whistle means. . . . ."

"Neither can I."

Margie Maxton whispered with the referee of Spiritual Adjustment. Elton Call drew a caricature of a yawning Cianfarra. And even Abdoller, with a profound expression on his face, toyed with his water glass. De Jager spoke on.

"Unfortunately, as far as our office is concerned, we have to tell ourselves in all sincerity, the functioning of the Union of Unemployed has so far not been operating on a scientific basis. Therefore, it is not surprising that I have noticed shortcomings and mistakes. A fundamental reorganization of our work, supported by scientific principles of the new, more streamlined democracy and free enterprise, is awaiting our great organization in the near future."

"Here you have Willie's apple pie," remarked Wattson to his neighbor.

"That's what I was afraid of."

"This reformation and reorganization on a grand scale will undoubtedly influence the whole country and the expansion of our U. of U. as well, regulating its whole working system. The individual referees will study and then distribute their documents according to the folders of subject matters. Those folders, alias briefcases, a most important factor in our organization, have to be of identical form and color and will be differentiated only by small colored stickers with the name of the individual department, the number, and the date of the inauguration of the particular folder. One of our important phases of reformation will be a new division of departments for the unemployed. We shall also be changing the names of some departments; for instance, instead of Referee of the Agriculture, I would prefer Agriculture Referee. Besides that, each referee will be given an exact plan of his activity and his authority from the capital. Not without importance is that, besides change of title, departments will have, after their reorganization is effected, different colors and signs. For instance, the Department of Organization will have the sign number one, color green."

"I beg your pardon, Mr. President," interrupted Frederick Tribbe. "I only wanted to take issue over the fact that green is the color and symbol of agriculture. The color green, therefore, belongs to my department."

"Yes, Fred, you are quite right. We shall adjust the color scheme in light of your observation."

"Almost every agricultural party in the world carries a green banner, the green international."

"Yes, yes, Fred, you are right. But may I say that I *do not* like the word 'international' associated with the Union of Unemployed!"

"Mr. President," started Miss Small, "I would like to know when and how these colors will be used."

"You took the question out of my mouth, Julienne," said Margie Maxton

Abdoller rang his bell. "Meeting come to order! We have interrupted the president."

"That doesn't matter, Lawrence, that doesn't matter. It shows a lively interest in my reformation. I shall answer the ladies' questions, for I too am most concerned about the correct color of the stickers on our briefcases."

"Thank you," said Margie.

"Thank you!" echoed Julienne.

"As long as a discussion has started, let us continue it."

"Who would like to take the floor?" asked Abdoller, and his shadow, Cianfarra, added, "Kindly enter your names in order for discussion." After a short silence he went on, "In that case, perhaps I'll talk."

"Please," invited Abdoller.

"I would like, as executive secretary of the U. of U., to point out that I too recognize the necessity of reform and I consider the change suggested by our"—a bow in De Jager's direction—"great honorary president a vital, timely, and excellent concept. We hope that a further discussion will clarify many more worthwhile proposals of our 'farsighted chief.' "

"Thank you, Mr. Cianfarra," said Abdoller. "Now who else would like to communicate with Mr. De Jager?" There was no response. "As long as no one feels inclined to enter into a discussion, we shall continue and go on to the next point. Miss Small, if you please—"

"At present on the *New World* we are working on the third article, 'Joy in a Man's Life.' Last week we already had some response. The replies are most revealing, and even sensational. It is evident that present times, in spite of the distinguished work of the Union of Unemployed, are very short on joy.

"It is absolutely necessary that the unemployed be shown the way to enjoy life, so that the phantasmagoria of boredom and revolutionary thoughts resulting therefrom should not spoil their lives completely.

"Most difficult, it seems to me, is how to teach our young people of the U. of U. to enjoy life. For instance, here is a typical letter from one of them: 'The African youth is vacationing today in Switzerland, enjoying the beauty of Europe. But the joy of life is not for us, American hoboes; that's the domain of the privileged class in our country. My share is job hunting, trouble, poverty, and in the end, who knows, a premature death from starvation or alcohol.'. . ." Julienne Small grew sad. "I think about joy, this burning problem of our country, with a great deal of concern." She wiped her tears. "That is all."

"Who else, ladies and gentlemen," Abdoller went on in a lowered tone, "would like to make a remark?" Silence. "Then I shall ask the referee of Agriculture to report on his project."

"Unfortunately, I have nothing new to communicate. I shall, however, repeat once more that it is high time to start resettlement." He became enthusiastic. "The funds for it have been given us by the capital, the Abdoller Brothers, and the Atomic Bank. Soil in the sparsely populated areas of our country begs for workers' hands."

De Jager jumped up from his chair. "May I have a word?"

"Certainly, Mr. President," responded Abdoller most charmingly.

"I agree with you, Fred. It is time that the sad comedy of unemployment in our country be ended. Yes, indeed." There was excitement stirring among the referees. "We can't wait any longer."

Wattson nodded to his friend Fred Tribbe. "Didn't I tell you about Willie the Whistle?"

"Just be patient with me and with your conclusion about De Jager." Fred spoke up. "I feel that if the people lose hope in a better future, they will rebel against the government of the De Jagers—result: anarchy."

De Jager cut in, "Nevertheless, Mr. Tribbe, although I will not solve yours or Mr. Wattson's problems, and although our work seems to linger, it is not because of any bad intentions on my part as president. . . ."

"I didn't say that."

"However, there is deep truth in what you say. The whole world is in the process of evolution, if not revolution, and we are trying to create a noble and democratic association. Right now the international crisis is being fought from the capital with dollars and our best former top executives of the large corporations. We in the U. of U. have to withhold all action entailing major expense until there is no doubt in our mind that the program which we wish to employ is absolutely, from all viewpoints, perfect."

"Well," Wattson said loudly, and Tribbe insisted, "My plans, Mr. President?"

"Your plans are almost perfect, yet there is a new complication. The United World Office of Labor in the capital, as we hear, will take over the problem of resettling the unemployed in South Africa. That will give us, according to Capital's directives, a wonderful opportunity to try out our plans and projects. Therefore, for the time being, we simply have to wait."

"That will take endlessly long. Such a governmental institution will help only financial speculators in the international arena, but never poverty-stricken workers."

Here Abdoller stepped in. "However, if we wish to create something perfect . . ." and De Jager finished, "We must not be hasty."

"May I have a word now?" asked Wattson.

Noticing his excitement, Abdoller began, "Perhaps not . . ."

But Bill went on. "I do not agree with you, Willie . . . pardon, Mr. President!"

"Have you a suggestion to make?" asked the president softly. "Yes."

"Then go ahead."

"No," Abdoller prompted.

"Oh yes. I am of the opinion that to look for perfection in social work is a gross misunderstanding. To strive to achieve the best social system in our country is certainly not our goal. There has never been and, it seems to me, never will be an entirely perfect social and political system in this world. A man is often too small for the ideals he creates, but the world is constantly in motion and we have to bargain with our permanent tendency toward the unreachable. How dull it would be if the world, all of a sudden, became perfect! Our life would no longer be interesting. It would lose all its charm and beauty and even the right to exist, for there would be nothing to look forward to, nothing to wish for. Beauty is not a matter of perfect form but a matter of creation, imagination, and individual taste—progress and development in one—and a social

243

system is like art itself, a creative and everlasting search to find new ways and forms. However, to begin to fashion this work of art, will-power is needed, as well as resolution, action, honesty."

De Jager smiled ironically at Abdoller. "So far very nice."

"At the present pace of our country's competition with the communist ideology," Wattson went on strongly, "there is no time to rework and rework plans and projects for years in order to make them perfect. The success of our strategy does not depend on absolute faultlessness or the perfect ideology. Even the insufficient return on our honest work and sacrifice will turn out for the best in the end. In the meantime, let us do something now. Let us work hard for our fellow men."

"How can you be sure everything will turn out for the best?" inquired Abdoller

De Jager reproached him. "Bill, you make such utterly un-scientific, sweeping statements. Your reasoning is purely inventive."

"Time will tell. If you're honest and work hard, you don't worry about results. Presently, we are guilty of all the misery around us, for we're afraid of honest work!"

"You just talk and talk," complained Cianfarra, irritated, "and don't say anything."

"Even for poor results, honest workers are needed. But here we are constantly designing a great action and don't do a thing to accomplish it."

"I don't like your tone of voice, Mr. Wattson," said De Jager. He turned to Abdoller. "He is to stop this talk."

"Mr. Wattson, you are to stop talking immediately."

De Jager looked around the table. "I hate outbursts, ridiculous scandals like this!"

"I apologize for the tone of voice I used, but . . ."

"Don't think for a moment we won't find plenty of willing and agreeable people for your position, and you'll quickly find yourself on the capital blacklist of those who foment rebellion, thereby disturbing the peace that is real progress. My wife and Tessa will not help you then."

Wattson got up. "I have the feeling I am getting rid of the remnants of any illusion I might have had about you, Mr. Willie the Whistle, and this organization. Your last words, Mr. Honorary President, remind me of someone, to be precise, an informer for the F.B.I., who is presently among us and who also tries to do social work. It certainly would be better for social work if the police were kept out of it. A social worker must have, above all, one qualification besides modesty. He must have a great deal of idealism, and clean hands, which you gentlemen of railroad, oil, steel, glass . . ."

"Mr. Abdoller!" cried De Jager. "What does this mean? He is not to speak. We told him to stop talking. Why has he been permitted to speak after he was denied the floor?"

Consternation is followed by the soothing words of Lawrence Abdoller. "Please, gentlemen. Let's not lose our tempers."

Wattson summed up from the middle of the library, "All of you and your dollar benefactors are a group of national traitors. You are all nothing more than a den of thieves and cheaters, whose hands reek to high heaven with the distinctive fragrance of the oil and gold of the Atomic Bank!"

Suddenly Stanley Kieb, referee of Spiritual Adjustment, was on his feet. "Come to think of it, I have enough too. All you goddamn hypocrites and parasites, all of you should be transferred to the moon, so the globe would breathe easier!" He looked almost happy. "I've meant to say this for a long time. To hell with you!"

Wattson and Kieb walked out; behind them ran Julienne Small. The rest looked paralyzed. After a moment De Jager looked at Abdoller. "That," he said, "Gusty Mary did not foresee. And where is my Tessa?"

Chapter 52

On Broadway, in front of the skyscraper where the Union of Unemployed had its offices, gray figures waiting for work crept along the glittering marble wall. Men smoked pipes and cigarettes, and women talked quietly to each other, while the young kept close to their parents. The line moved forward slowly; but never got any smaller as more unemployed stepped into place at the end of it. At regular intervals policemen swaggered down the street. New York's pigeons and sounds grew in volume. The city was getting up.

A man spoke. "There are a lot of us here today, thousands!"

A second answered him. "Every day the same story. Thousands and thousands . . ."

"Look," someone interrupted, "something is going on in front of the entrance."

"According to the papers," the first man continued, "all over the country things are getting worse. . . . Oh! Look at those two women, huddled on the corner. They look like they could be planting bombs!"

"I know the older one. Her husband was injured on the job. He's paralyzed now. He's been that way for over three years now."

The conversation grew louder. A woman wearing a man's black topcoat and heavy men's shoes was complaining, "We are seven people at home. One daughter with three children under the age of four years. My husband's in jail. Our second daughter twenty-two years old has an eye disease. The Union of Unemployed doesn't want to help her. They say she can work with her hands and doesn't need eyes. The third daughter works part-time for forty dollars a week in the Biggis Department Stores."

"Still, you have some help."

"What kind of help is that? She earns forty, and I make about twenty selling old clothes. That's not enough for seven people. She's just nineteen. . . ."

"Pretty?"

"She is, but always talks about death. She has no strength to live. Goes to work without breakfast in sneakers. We eat once a day, only the children get something more. But today even the children . . ."

On the other side of the street Tessa De Jager and Bill Wattson approached.

"I'm quite glad it happened that way, although perhaps . . . I should have some pangs of conscience."

"Why do you say that, Tessa?"

"Because of me you wasted that time in the U. of U., instead of working on your novel."

"Not at all. I had no idea. Today at least I know how this bunch functions and who supports them in the capital. That's something."

"I was afraid."

"Afraid of what?"

"I was afraid for you."

"For me?"

"Somebody told me—yes, it was Fred Tribbe. He told me that when a man's energy is absorbed in the great social goal he has set for himself, it can rob him of the desire to love his woman, and he will come out with nothing. You know, the idea of doing good, the social mission. Fred said this preoccupation of mine makes you feel that you don't need me. It upset me very much."

"You had no reason to upset yourself."

"You were wrapped up in your work with your 'Brothers.' I had the feeling that I was expendable, not necessary to you. . . ."

"My dearest one!"

"I know, but I felt it."

"And now?"

"I'm no longer worried, because I have you with me. I'm so happy to have you back! Never again will you be a social worker, will you, Bill? I have premonitions about that."

"But, darling, I will always remain a social worker."

"What? After what you told me? After what happened to you? I don't want that."

"There isn't a thing anybody can do about it. Not even myself. I have to return to this kind of work, only approach it in a different way. My heart and mind got into a furious fight. Now that it's over, I'm positive that I will be doing social work on honorable principles!"

"Bill, how about a job on my father's railroad, or in the Atomic Bank?"

"Sorry, darling, I'll have to . . . I must expose them, point out those thieves, call attention to them."

"Don't play Hamlet on Park Avenue."

"I should. Why not?"

"Come on, Bill. Come home."

"Perhaps the same fight, but from a different perspective— along with them, with the poor . . ."

"Come home, Bill."

"All right, let's go. These people are looking at us. They don't know me. They don't know I'm on the blacklist. They don't know I belong to them, unemployed too. Let's go."

"Come home with me."

"Or let's go with them."

Meanwhile the line of unemployed had grown into four long rows of people, arguing over their places in line, over politics, over everything.

"All this is the fault of machinery," one offered. "As long as there were less machines, there was more work. Let's destroy the machines and we'll have work again."

Another unemployed man tilted his cap and looked scornful. "You're crazy. Back to the farm? That's stupid."

"I am not!"

"Of course you are! The machine makes work easier and better. In one hour a linotypist does now what one did before, without a machine, in one day. I'm a printer. I know what I'm talking about."

"From what you say, we should be working less and earning more. So why are you unemployed in such a rich country, where you got so many linotypes?"

A third man, better dressed, spoke up confidently. "I'll tell you something."

"What?" asked the other two.

"When a certain product sold for a hundred dollars, the worker got ten and the manufacturer ninety. Then, when the same product, with the help of machines, brought a thousand dollars, the earnings of the worker went to fifty, the manufacturer made nine hundred and fifty. Inflation made it impossible for him to buy the product he worked on. The Abdoller Brothers Fund, the Atomic Bank, the Abdoller Foundation, the Union of Unemployed and a hundred more such organizations swallow all the extra profits that rightfully belong to us, and turn it into propaganda for free enterprise, Bankers World Union, Oil International, the intelligence service, Millionaires World Economic Corporation, new deal, middle deal, fair deal, but always a very lousy deal for us."

A well-dressed woman and a child passed by. "Mother, what are these people standing here for?"

"These are the unemployed, darling."

"Why are they standing here?"

"They wait here until they are permitted inside the offices of the Union of Unemployed."

"Why should they want to get inside?"

"Because, darling, you see, in our country the unemployed are very well off. In this big, beautiful building is the Union of Unemployed. Some of the unemployed get work there, some get support for their families, some just money. . . ."

"Mother, please, let's go there too. Maybe they'll give us money. I want a dollar!"

Near the front of the line a group of the more desperate had convened.

"Now we're being chased from railroad stations, bus depots, and airports—even from the park benches! As soon as you get a little warm, 'out you go,' they say, 'out! out!' "

"Warm yourselves, yeh?" a second mocked.

"In my neighborhood, before you know it the police come and take you to the station.

"I got myself a basement for living quarters," one man boasted. "It's beautifully furnished with all the rubbish from the elegant upstairs apartments."

"Sounds comfortable."

"He can do it, he's a bachelor. On Monday we were evicted, and there I was, with my family, on the street. It was raining, too!"

"Lucky guys who got themselves located in the agricultural resettlements of the Union of Unemployed."

"Don't say that! You've never seen those settlements. My cousin sneaked back and he told us all about it. Hundreds and hundreds of cubicles. Outside maybe a few trees, inside stench, and beneath the walls thousands of people, as many as in this line or more, and all of them curse and pray. When Minister Small or any other of those benefactors for the U. of U. come with their sweet talk, the people chase them out. They can't stand them any longer. It's worse there, worse than any place;

those people will never again get jobs. They are settled out there for good, and it's just a miserable trap. How can they ever get back?"

"There must be a better life for us somewhere," a small elderly woman piped up.

"For us? Where? We couldn't get there. Who's going to pay our fare?"

Another woman confided to her neighbor. "When the misery started with us, the children cried. They were hungry and cold. Now there is just fear and hate in their eyes, and they never cry. They are quiet, terribly quiet . . . it's so unnatural!"

"And that Union of Unemployed wants to teach us joy, the joy of living!"

A third woman looked frantic. "But what will become of the children, for God's sake? Drugs?"

Nearby some men talked vehemently. "You tell me," said one, stamping his feet to stay warm. "A jaguar, a wolf, a hyena, or a man—if he is hungry, he looks for food. If he feels cold, he seeks warmth. If he can't find either, the stronger destroys the weaker."

"To hell with the Atomic Empire!"

"And the U. of U. preaches dignity, humility, to accept whatever God sends us. First let God just send us work. . . ."

The street was jammed now and the enormous throng of unemployed swayed back and forth, as they argued with one another. One unemployed woman was pushed out of line and screamed loudly. A man called for help from heaven. There was shouting, yelling, crying. A policeman tried to arrange the chaos of bodies. The crowd, taking an antagonistic attitude, pushed him out. The policeman hurried away quickly.

Voices in the crowd grew worried. "He'll bring down the special forces."

"So what good was doing that then?"

"Who started this?"

"The Police."

"The pigs!"

They quieted down. "Now, today," said a man, "when there is so much affluence, there ain't supposed to be anybody hungry."

"I'm not worried about hunger," another said. "There is plenty of food in the golden garbage cans on the upper East Side. Late at night or early in the morning is the best time to look for food. But I have nothing to wear. Clothes are hard to find in garbage cans."

"For food, I beg for a few cents. Then I hit the supermarkets when they open to get the day-old everything. It's a mad crush there every morning, too." A good-looking young man spoke while the rest listened. "I also go pigeon-hunting in the park. I find a tree where they are nesting. Then I hit the trunk with a stick, and when the young cry, I climb up and look at them as they sit in their nests—just like the big bosses in their plush private club, they are, with smug faces, bald heads, their bodies choking with fat. I don't throw them down, though. What do you think, people? What do you think I do? I take them down carefully, each on its back, and then with a stick I stab their bellies! They start screaming, the old ones fly around like mad and try to pick my head with their sharp bills. Then these little ones are hardly breathing, so I squeeze their necks between my fingers. They flare their eyelids several times, and—it's over! Then I try to find another nest. One isn't sufficient for a meal."

A woman was outraged. "Why should you torture birds, you bastard?"

"That's justice, lady. A tortured man likes to torture other creatures. He doesn't feel like a real man, he's just a creature. So we get embittered and we get even . . . later we'll do a better job, on the fat ones, when they leave their clubs at night."

Some people laughed, some argued. A stocky man spoke up. "The minister tells you, down from his pulpit, 'God's hand touched you. With love you can overcome God's anger.' What's God's anger? I worked like an ox, ate like a goat, now I've got to go to beg forgiveness. What is God, why is he angry at me? Is there not enough misery in my life to please him? So the minister suggests, be humble and all will turn for the better. How humble can we get? For God's sake, how stupid can we get!"

"Oh, sure, humble! My dogs should eat the flesh of all the goddamn national benefactors and the U. of U. dignitaries who preach at us. Crazy dogs!"

At the end of the line one unemployed man had attracted a small circle of onlookers and was gesturing as he spoke. "In circumstances like ours every delinquent and thief should be excused, as far as I'm concerned. Delinquency, thievery, is the principle of our system, the great system which created the Abdollers, the De Jagers, and their Union of Unemployed. Who can live just being a regular, honest human being?"

"Because," a second started; but the first continued. "Those religious maneaters, they say that some spirit, that white pigeon out of picture stories will save us. Our atomic world may go to the devil, may the earth open up and swallow it and the Union of Unemployed. Too bad for the people in Africa. Too bad for the ones with the hope. The system of unions of unemployed is doomed, but there isn't any hope anyhow."

"But they always claim that they work for the benefit of the nation, of humanity, and they call on us to serve, while all of them, with those patriotic smiles, stuff their pockets. I've served in my last war, that's for sure."

"Where the devil is all the gold we earned the country?"

The first man smiled sardonically. "You mean that yellow metallic element, the most precious of substances, with a peculiar luster? You're joking! Don't you know where it is?"

Suddenly all eyes turned to the right, toward the entrance of the Union of Unemployed. "Who is that guy who just came out?"

"An official, an official of the U. of U. He wants to talk."

A voice called, "Let him talk."

After a short silence, Cianfarra began. "We can enroll for work in the North Pole Atomic Corporation fifteen unemployed. Those fifteen must not have families. Others . . ."

Tumult started. The crowd became hostile. Screams, shouts, and the sound of broken glass rose into the air. "We want work! We have the right to live!"

"Don't push. Go away, mister, I'll hit you."

"Don't push! You'll suffocate me!"

"You goddamned phony!"

"Bastard!"

"Bastards, all of you!"

"Let's beat them!"

"Let's kill them!"

Now it was the women. "Christ had a great heart to permit them to live."

"Bloody bastards, may you all suffer as we . . ."

"To hell with them! Kill them!"

"Go on! go on!"

"Give it to them!"

Cianfarra was attacked. A symphony of sirens was soon replaced by the sounds of wood striking flesh. A loud popping noise followed by a stinging, burning sensation of the eyes spread panic through the crowd. City block after city block echoed with screams and shouts.

After an hour the street in front of the Union of Unemployed was cleared of people. Just blood and torn clothes remained on the wide sidewalk.

From the park and into the Union of Unemployed strolled two well-known figures occupied in very serious conversation.

"You see, my dear counselor," William S. De Jager explained to his friend Jack Small, "in such matters one really must not hurry. One can too easily make a mistake that will cost millions and millions of dollars. As far as solving our country's social problems goes, one must remember that it is of utmost importance to pioneer slowly and very carefully. Only then will it be possible to insure excellent and perfect results at a minimum cost."

"True indeed, Willie the Whistle, true indeed. Only the unemployed, you know . . . they will, they certainly will . . ."

"Well, Jack, the unemployed! If there is one thing the unemployed have, it is time, plenty of time. They can wait."

✠ Chapter 53

Supreme Court: Franklin Kapistrot, plaintiff, against The Coast to Coast Railroad Company, William S. De Jager and Bartholomew A. Leach, defendants.

Examination by the defendant, The Coast to Coast Railroad Company, of the plaintiff before trial took place at the offices of Rollon, Casevant, Small & Abdoller pursuant to oral stipulation. Gilbert L. Lasher appeared as attorney for plaintiff. Rollon, Casevant, Small & Abdoller were attorneys for defendant The Coast to Coast Railroad Company, represented by Carroll A. Layton, Esq., and Augustine S. Neely, Esq., of counsel.

The participants confirmed: It is hereby stipulated and

agreed by and between the attorneys for the respective parties hereto that filing of the within examination before trial be and the same is hereby waived, and the attorney for the plaintiff shall be furnished with a copy thereof without charge; it is further stipulated and agreed that the witness may be sworn at the taking of his examination before trial by any Notary Public of the State, and that the witness may read, sign and swear to this testimony when the same is transcribed before any Notary Public of the State; it is further stipulated and agreed that all objections, except as to the form of questions, be and the same are hereby reserved to the trial of the action.

Franklin Kapistrot, the plaintiff, after having first been duly sworn, was asked by Mr. Layton:

"May we have your full name, please."

"Franklin Kapistrot."

"Where do you live, Mr. Kapistrot?"

"Thirteen West Fourth Street, New York."

"What is your occupation, sir?"

"Researcher."

"Do you know the defendant, William S. De Jager?"

"Yes, I do."

"Could you tell us when you first met him?"

"On his train."

"Where did you first meet Bartholomew A. Leach?"

"In his office."

"In Philadelphia?"

"Yes."

"As I understand it, Mr. De Jager and Mr. Leach said to you that the railroad was interested in engaging you to write a book about Mr. De Jager and the CCRR?"

"Yes. Also in financing the book and me."

"Did you make a promise to them at that time that you would write the book?"

"Yes. I agreed to write the book, because Mr. De Jager,"

Mrs. De Jager and Mr. Leach solemnly promised me that if I would write a book acceptable to them, they would not only buy one hundred thousand copies, but also would put me on a salary for two years at two thousand dollars per month, grant me a white railroad pass plus all expenses, and make me a wealthy man."

"Mr. Layton," interrupted Gilbert Lasher, the short, pleasant-mannered attorney for the plaintiff, "I do not want to object to anything, but the contract, of course, speaks for itself."

"Naturally, but I thought we might identify it. Do you have the original contract, Mr. Lasher?"

"Yes, I have the original."

"You do not want to identify it today?"

"Do you wish it?"

"If you have it with you, why don't we?"

"All right." He passed the papers into Layton's well-manicured hands.

"Mr. Kapistrot, is this the contract that you and Mr. Leach and Mr. De Jager executed?"

"Yes, Mr. Layton."

"Mr. Kapistrot, did you deliver the outline and two chapters of the book *Willie the Whistle* personally to Mr. and Mrs. De Jager and to Mr. Leach?"

"Yes, I did."

"Can you tell us what then transpired?"

"Mr. Leach, as a vice-president of the CCRR Public Relations Department, sent this memo to Mr. De Jager and to the directors of the railroad: 'Today Mr. Kapistrot submitted two chapters and an outline for the book *Willie the Whistle*. This is a most magnificent piece of writing, and I think it will be a great book.'"

"When did you next submit any material of the book to the railroad, Mr. Kapistrot?"

"I think it was in December or January, because Mr. and

Mrs. De Jager and Bart Leach gave me a few other assignments besides the writing of *Willie the Whistle.*"

"What other assignments did they give you?"

"A number of social assignments—entertaining Mrs. De Jager and her daughter Tessa; mixing with important people and reporting to Mr. De Jager what they said about him; evaluating a novel, *Brothers in Stalingrad,* written by William Wattson, the fiancé of Tessa De Jager; and preparing stories and articles about Mr. De Jager for the American and Canadian press. Here is a note from Bart Leach: 'Dear Mr. Kapistrot, thank you very much for the piece about Willie the Whistle for the *Detroit Free Press.* Great! I have sent it along today.'"

Mr. Lasher held a cigar in his left hand and the paper in his right. "Do you want to see it?"

"Yes, if you please." Lasher handed the paper to Mr. Layton, who then asked Kapistrot, "Did Mr. De Jager or Mrs. De Jager ever express dissatisfaction to you with any of your work?"

"No. As a matter of fact, they praised me all the . . ."

"He did not ask you that," said Gilb Lasher. "Will you please, Franklin, answer the questions."

"All right."

"Answer the questions, Frank. I want to get out before seven o'clock tonight. No stories, please," Lasher repeated.

"Did you thereafter finish the book *Willie the Whistle,* Mr. Kapistrot?"

"Yes."

"Do you have the completed book with you?"

"The original is with the De Jagers, the two copies are with the publisher. I have only my handwritten draft."

"Mr. Kapistrot, can you tell us the role that Mrs. De Jager was going to play in this book?"

"The book was supposed to be about both Mr. and Mrs. De

Jager and about the railroad."

"Was she to play a major role or a minor role in the book?"

"She played the role of the president's wife, plus some extras . . . and she asked me to dedicate the book to her daughter Tessa."

"Did you ever discuss with the publisher the price at which your book was to be sold to the public?"

"Yes. Six dollars per copy."

"Did anyone besides Mr. De Jager, Mrs. De Jager and Mr. Leach on behalf of the railroad speak to you about purchasing copies of your book?"

"Yes, many people. Roach, Berryman, Colegrove, Mellon, Puppett, even Amelia Leach and four directors. They promised to buy about two hundred and fifty thousand copies more. And Mrs. De Jager said, 'We'll do everything possible to satisfy you.' "

"I do not think," interrupted Gilbert Lasher, "you ought to go into these personal things."

"What did these others say to you?" asked Carroll Layton, with shrewdness in his black eyes.

"They clearly intimated that if I wrote plenty of pages about them, they too would help to see that I was well off."

"Am I correct, Mr. Kapistrot, that all these promises you have stated were merely to buy copies of your book?"

"Two hundred and fifty thousand copies, augmented by a hundred thousand, would mean a tidy bundle of cash for me."

"I will object to the form of the question," said the attorney for the plaintiff, playing with a fresh cigar.

"Mr. Lasher, all objections are reserved for the trial."

"All right."

"Mr. Kapistrot, how much money did you earn last year?"

"It is not your business, Mr. Layton."

"All right, I will not pursue the question."

Mr. Layton conferred with his colleague, Augustine Neely,

and posed a new question. "Mr. Leach agreed that the CCRR was going to buy one hundred thousand copies of *Willie the Whistle* for his Public Relations Department? Is that what you want us to understand?"

"Can't you read?"

"Yes."

"Here's a letter from Mr. Leach."

"I see."

"Is it not true that in your publishing agreement your manuscript had to be satisfactory to the railroad too, as well?"

"Yes. It *was* satisfactory to the railroad and to the publisher. Here are two more letters."

"Ah. I see."

At that moment Augustine Neely, a fleshy man of about fifty-five broke into the questioning. "By the way, I do not think this contract between yourself and your publisher undertakes to specify the amount of your royalty. Am I correct in that?"

"Yes, the first page, Mr. Neely."

"Oh, yes."

"This has nothing to do with the CCRR and the De Jagers' commitments. This is in addition."

"I see. I will withdraw that question. I think you told us when you first met with Mr. Leach and he discussed the arrangements he would make with you, he told you that you would have to get a publisher, did he not?"

"Yes."

"You knew that the CCRR was not in the publishing business."

"Yes, the CCRR is connected with everything—banks, oil, steel, glass, and social work—but not the publishing business."

"Was it your understanding that there was an agreement between the CCRR and the publisher?"

"Yes."

260

"With respect to this book, *Willie the Whistle?*"

"Yes."

"All right, I do not think I have anything more to ask."

"All right," said his partner Carroll Layton. "Do you have anything further, Mr. Lasher?"

"No."

"Mr. Kapistrot," said Augustine, raising his two hundred and fifty pounds. "May I have a few words with you in private, off the record?"

"Yes, why not?"

"We can't have two books on the same subject, Mr. Kapistrot."

"What do you mean?"

"It is only fair, I think, to tell you that Mr. and Mrs. De Jager have given the assignment to Jack Small, Junior—as to why, I don't know that myself."

"Oh, that's the reason!"

"And you'll lose this case."

"Why?"

"Simple: they have money, plenty of money, over four billion dollars. They have power, tremendous power here in the city, in the capital, in the whole country."

"Mr. Neely, help me."

"I?"

"What can I do?"

"Nothing."

"But they cheated me!"

"Sir, they cheated you, they cheat their friends, they cheat the whole nation. They cheat their wives and husbands. They cheat even themselves."

"What can be done?"

"Nothing."

"Nothing?"

"They can afford to cheat."

"Why?"

"Because they're filthy rich. They're the builders of America, they say."

"Why don't you tell the country, the world, about their fraud?"

"Me?"

"Yes, you. You're an important member of their society and you have all the facts and figures about them."

"But also I have eight children. They'll put me and my children on the blacklist for life. We'd get no jobs above a clerk's position, and even that is questionable."

"Perhaps it's better to be a clerk."

"They'll assassinate me."

"Where's the police, the law of the country?"

"Sir, the police and the law are on the right side, their side."

✠ Chapter 54

Monday morning was traditionally a dull and sleepy time inside the great Abdoller Foundation Library. There were very few of the usual telephone calls asking ridiculous questions and even fewer readers. Those who managed to straggle in dozed over their books trying to catch up on sleep lost over the weekend. The librarians, adjusting themselves to the peaceful surroundings, moved at a snail's pace, weaving quietly in and out of the tables and chairs as if trying not to scare off any remaining energy from their clients. The only sound was that of steady rain beating monotonously against the windowpane.

On such a day I was certain that I, as the special library investigator, would have very little work to do. So I locked the door to my room on the second floor and set about solving the crossword puzzles in the Sunday papers. I looked forward impatiently to my lunch hour in the basement cafeteria, where I would hear all the gossip making the rounds of the Jewish and Slavonic departments from my friend working there.

Suddenly someone knocked loudly at the door. I was startled out of my blurred concentration on the puzzles, and as the nervous knocking became louder, I got up and with one long step was at the door fumbling with the lock. In a second I had the door open and Mr. Kennedy, the supervisor of the rare-book department, stood before me. Pale and shaken, he pushed me into the room, crying out hoarsely, "Mr. Toneskes, we have been robbed!"

I led him to a chair and offered him a drink of water. "What was taken?"

"Copernicus is stolen!" He gasped, gulped down some water, and explained. "The first edition of *De Revolutionibus Orbium Coelestium* is missing!"

"*De Revolutionibus!*" I exclaimed in horror. "Kennedy, are you sure?" I was aghast, as I envisioned a situation which, if not immediately set right, would be very sad not only for Mr. Kennedy but for me as well. I don't know why in that moment I recalled the story of how, when this precious book had been published, friends had brought the first printed copy from the city of Frombark to the deathbed of its author. But I knew that today there were only two copies of it in the whole world, and this one was the gift of the Abdoller oil clan.

I could see too that this Monday might well be the end of me as special investigator. Regaining my full faculties, I grabbed Mr. Kennedy by the arm and we left together for the scene of the crime, the rare-book department on the third floor. Mose Kennedy walked beside me wiping the perspiration from his shiny bald spot and looking imploringly at me as if I were his last hope. On the way I mulled the problem over quickly and could envision only two alternatives: either the book had been misplaced and would soon be found, or someone who knew the schedule and habits of all the librarians had taken it. That meant someone working in the library, because it would be difficult for a stranger to pass through the iron gates that barred the room with a book worth over one hundred thousand dollars. As we entered the rare-book department and I looked around, I wondered why Mr. Kennedy had not tried to reach me by phone, instead of coming down to my office. It was his duty to remain in the room and watch over those readers who had been in the room at the time when he observed that the book was missing.

But I kept my worries to myself and began to question the people in the room. After checking on their names in the registry book, I asked them to leave the department for some length of time. Locking the door, I and three librarians began a systematic search of all the shelves and closets. There was no point in going elsewhere until this place had been thoroughly searched from top to bottom.

We were all working intently, about half an hour later, when Mose Kennedy let out a joyous shout and came over to me triumphantly, holding a book in his hand. I opened the book with shaking fingers and discovered to my disappointment that it did not contain the date of the first edition, 1543. Mr. Kennedy noticed this too and apologized nervously, mumbling in his embarrassment, "It's the second edition—how could I make such a mistake?" So astounded was I by this positively foolish oversight of Mr. Kennedy that I immediately suspected him of some hanky-panky. I therefore spent the next forty-eight hours investigating his entire life. I was fortunate enough to be able to search the effects in his home, an easy task because he lived alone. But this tiresome business brought no results. So I returned the following day to pursue another avenue of research into this terrible crime. I took home the registration book containing the names of all the persons who had visited the rare-book department in the last year. I promised myself not to overlook the employees of the library. I inspected the twelve names listed for the last day in June and somehow was drawn to one illegibly written signature with an address downtown. Flipping back the pages, I noticed that this person had come regularly every day during the past month at exactly the same hour.

I found from Mr. Kennedy that this Franklin Don Kapistrot was a middle-aged man who was supposed to be a researcher in philosophy and history, and was famous for his peculiar habits. People recognized him because of his goatee and mustache, and above all by the strong smell of garlic which always surrounded him. Other readers in the library kept their distance and he was always left alone in one corner of the room.

Mr. Kennedy listened to the many complaints of the readers and tried again and again to convince the man not to come to the library reeking of garlic. But Kapistrot quietly and phlegmatically, with the air of a scientist in the Middle Ages, replied in the same way to all complaints, "I eat garlic to prolong my life, so that humanity may have the pleasure of reading my twelve-volume work on American civilization. If I do not have access to the library and just sit home eating garlic, I will not be able to finish my work. One way or the other it will be a loss to humanity." And he always concluded with the rhetorical question, "What does a little smell of garlic mean, compared to my historical work? Here intelligent people of the world will find the answers to the Americans' behavior—and even how they forced me to eat garlic."

This queer fellow interested me very much and I determined to call on Don Kapistrot first before I tackled any of the other names in the book. It didn't take me long to find the four-story old brownstone house on West Fourth Street. Franklin Don Kapistrot lived on the second floor. He opened the door himself and invited me in. Without even asking me to sit down, he climbed up on a stepladder placed against a huge bookcase and began to ask me questions without looking in my direction. "What have you come for? Who sent you? Do you want to buy a Greek vase, a Persian rug?"

I remember Mr. Kennedy had told me that for the past few years this eccentric man, while writing his great work on American civilization, had lived on the money he made selling antiques brought over from Europe. Noticing my hesitation, as I thought of something to say, he added, "Now, you are young and handsome and look to me like a typical American who has just divorced his second wife, and while looking for another is killing time by buying antiques. . . . Well, that is not a bad way to spend your money."

"Perhaps you guessed right," I answered cheerfully, "but I am only interested in buying rare first editions."

"Books!" He shouted in great alarm, as he jumped down from the ladder. He stood in front of me for a moment, stroking his goatee nervously; then he screamed at me, waving his long hands in the air, "I do not sell books! I buy them myself with my last penny. We have nothing further to discuss. Good night!"

"Oh well, in that case I will make an exception and buy a rug from you," I answered hastily, not wanting to offend him. "I need a rug for my library. Please show me something suitable."

" 'Suitable,' " Don Kapistrot repeated, regaining his composure. "Evidently you do not know anything about rugs when you ask for 'something suitable'? Probably you know nothing about books also, and are just collecting those that are suitable."

I smiled agreeably. He too smiled, showing his uneven

266

teeth, as he continued to stand before me, his back against the shelves filled with books bound in skin and clasped with copper. In a flash I thought to myself that if I was to find the lost copy of *De Revolutionibus* anywhere it would be right here in those bookcases. I became more and more convinced, as I watched him glance sideways at the shelves and move back a bit as if trying to obstruct my view. I felt sure those shelves held many priceless editions. I knew that I had no authority to force him to show me what was in the ancient bookcases, and if I dared tell him why I really came he might become violent and try to throw me out of the house. I had no proof and could not antagonize him—knowing I could not hope to return to this house again.

My words and moves had to be planned carefully to try to gain his confidence. I decided to pay him partly for a rug and return tomorrow to see my purchase in the daylight as an excuse for further investigation. But before I could utter another word a girl entered the room. She was tall and blonde with grayish blue eyes. She moved slowly and unobstrusively. The myopic Don Kapistrot became aware of her after a moment and not moving from his spot called out, "Oh, it is you, Tessa." Turning to me he remarked, "This is my daughter. And what is your name?"

Surprised to find a girl as lovely as she in these weird surroundings, I replied, "Toneskes, Tom Toneskes."

She acknowledged the introduction with a smile and was about to say something when her father remarked, "This gentleman wants to buy a rug. Take him into the other room and show him what we have. I must finish some very important research."

Turning again to me, he explained, "Tessa is not only my foundling daughter but my guardian and my secretary. You will be able to come to terms with her. Whatever price she decides upon I shall accept. I am too busy at the moment to help you, so please excuse me."

There wasn't much I could do after such a definite dismissal, so I followed the shapely figure of the girl into the next room. I knew now that I was trapped and would be forced to buy some old rug or other routine antique which would be quite useless in my present living quarters.

Tessa offered me a seat in the dining room in which Victorian furniture was arranged with exquisite taste, and closed the door behind us. Turning unexpectedly to me she said in a soft voice, "You do not look like a man who would walk around on rainy evenings looking for old rugs. Let's be honest with each other. What do you want here?"

Taken aback by this frank question, I merely sat there looking at this pretty girl before me. There was something sincere in her face and eyes and I decided to come to the point of my visit.

"I will be truthful with you. I am a special library investigator. A few days ago a rare copy of *De Revolutionibus Orbium Coelestium* disappeared from our library."

She turned pale and her slender fingers gripped her knees. She seemed to know what was coming next.

"Miss Kapistrot, do you . . ."

"Mrs. Wattson, very soon to be the former Mrs. Wattson."

"Well then, Mrs. Wattson, do you know anything about this?"

Her large blue eyes looked straight into mine, as she answered, "You probably suspect that my father is unbalanced in respect to collecting first editions."

I nodded an affirmative, beginning to feel that at last I was on the right track and that this woman would try to help me.

"Perhaps you also know that for some years my father has been writing a series of books on American civilization. Even though I am not a specialist on the subject, what he writes sounds logical to me. But what he does with the rest of his time never makes sense. He did try to build a normal life, but he always seemed to be a victim of horrendous misfortunes, terrible, stupid accidents. Now he spends many hours in antique shops, public auctions, and libraries, where he always hopes to find old first editions. . . . Sometimes I suspect that he even steals them. His only explanation is that he needs these books for his work. I have had a lot of trouble because of this and even have taken him to doctors, but no one can find any cure for his peculiar ways. 'He is normal,' they say."

Trying to ease the pain of this lovely, straightforward woman, I remarked hopefully, "Perhaps he did not take Copernicus. But there is only one way to find out, if you will help, and that is to search his library and all the most likely places which could hide such a priceless book. If you should find it, let me know immediately and I promise not to notify the police or cause any embarrassment for you or your father."

I knew I would have a hard job explaining such a future situation at the library, but I didn't care; there was something about this Mrs. Wattson that aroused my interest.

"I promise to do just as you suggest," she answered gratefully, her voice trembling with emotion.

I shook her hand, and on my way out told her, "I have a good friend who is a great American psychiatrist. His methods have proven to be very successful. Perhaps you would care to take your father to see him."

"Thank you, but it is useless to try any further. He is too intelligent for that, and too stubborn," she answered, turning her head away. "But if I do find the book I shall return it instantly, please believe me."

"Think over my proposition. I am sure my friend can help your father. I shall speak to him, and then if you like, you may call him up."

Mrs. Wattson shook her head, and I noticed that she was anxious to get me to leave before she burst into tears.

That night I tossed from side to side in my bed finding it impossible to go to sleep. I picked up one of my detective books and started to read. Usually this tactic would work and I would be sound asleep in a matter of minutes, but tonight it failed. I could not finish the story, not because I fell asleep, but because the whole Don Kapistrot incident kept appearing before my eyes. Rather I should say the face of Tessa prevented me from finding the words on the page. I saw her large expressive eyes filled with tears peering up at me. Everything about her, the way she walked and talked, gave me no peace.

Here I was, a man of thirty-four, acting like an adolescent, falling in love at first sight. Angry at my own behavior, I came to the conclusion that my silly conduct was the outcome of spending too much time as a special investigator and not enough at my studies of anthropology. I made up my mind that starting tomorrow I would get back to more serious study. I decided that after I cleared up the matter of Copernicus I would give up my job as a detective and with the money I had saved, continue my anthropological studies where I had left off. After that, in a year or two at the most, I could become an instructor at a first-class college. This was something I had dreamed about secretly for a long time. It seemed to me that I had my future perfectly mapped out as I lay there in bed.

The next day, punctually at nine, I was in my office arranging my strategy for dealing with Mose Kennedy and Copernicus. With the approval of the library heads, I would rather have given the whole affair over to the police, because suddenly I seemed to have lost all ambition to unravel clues, to search out people and their consciences. In one night my universe had been transformed, and my interest in the job of investigator had disappeared. I would rather have been a dishwasher, just so I would not have to look into someone's tearful or frightened eyes.

As I sat with these thoughts racing through my head, Tessa unexpectedly entered the room. Now in the daylight I really became aware of her proud beauty. She held her head high, her cheeks were flushed and her lips slightly parted like an innocent girl's. Trying to hide my surprise and pleasure, I asked her to be seated. She refused and began immediately to report in detail.

"I searched practically the whole night in every conceivable corner and shelf, but nowhere could I find the book. Finally around four o'clock in the morning, when I realized my search was hopeless, I awakened my father and told him the reason behind your visit. He swore on his life and everything sacred that he did not take the book. To him your library has been a paradise where he has been able to explore all the books which were needed to complete his monumental work. I know him well and I believe him. Even though, as he admits, he had been reading *De Revolutionibus* the day it was stolen, I know he did not take it."

"Well, then, where can it be?" I inquired, my tone changing to that of an investigator.

"That is your affair," she retorted, convinced of her father's innocence.

Perhaps my next move would have discouraged her completely had not the telephone interrupted with a piercing ring. Mose Kennedy was on the phone, yelling excitedly. "The book, the book in some mysterious way has been found on the shelf! Come and see for yourself!"

"Copernicus has been found!" I cried out, as I grasped Tessa's hands and wrung them, apologizing for my suspicions. She was as excited as I. Her blue eyes shone radiantly. My heart was floating on a cloud, but my thoughts were remorseful, because I had done her and her father a grave wrong. There were no words that I could utter which would erase the pain she had felt, so I took her in my arms and pressed her gently to me. She offered no objection to this way of handling library matters. In fact, I felt a measure of sincere response. At this moment I was happier at finding her than if I had found a thousand priceless books.

After checking on the find in the rare-book department, and seeing that everything was miraculously in order, I phoned in my report on the recovery of *De Revolutionibus* to the director. Then I called my friend Blum Brownell, the psychiatrist, to ask him about cures for a rare-book mania.

"In order for Mr. Kapistrot to become a normal person, he must be allowed to do certain things without interference. I am sure this will not cause any trouble for anyone."

"What's he saying?" Tessa clung eagerly to my elbow.

"You, Tom," Brownell said, "must find some library that has many rare first editions and permit Don Kapistrot to sit there from morning till night where no one will bother him about anything, including strange smells. There let him work until he can finish his volumes on American civilization."

"That won't be too difficult to arrange." I hung up the phone in relief.

We left the library, puzzling over how it was possible that a book lost for so many days could reappear suddenly in its regular place without any explanation. Tessa jokingly suggested, "Someone who hates my father or the smell of garlic hid the book, just to get rid of him. Is there a law that says people who eat garlic cannot attend a public library?"

"Of course not!" I laughed.

Ten minutes later we arrived at Tessa's home to tell her father the good news. At first the house was silent; then we heard a noise—a sharp, loud gasp. When Tessa opened the door and looked into the library she collapsed without a word. I leaped over her and cut the rope.